Knot What You Expected

HOLLY MONROE
REALITY TV OMEGAS

Copyright © 2026 by Holly Monroe

All rights reserved.

No part of this book was created by, or can be used to train AI.

No part of this publication may be reproduced, distributed, or transmitted in any form or by any means, including photocopying, recording, or other electronic or mechanical methods, without the publisher's prior written permission, except as permitted by U.S. copyright law. For permission requests, contact authorhollymonroe@gmail.com

The story, all names, characters, and incidents portrayed in this production are fictitious. No identification with actual persons (living or deceased), places, buildings, or products is intended or should be inferred.

Cover art by Mads @Linehouse.art

Headers and Page Break by Cat @bookishlymacabre

ISBN: 978-1-971820-01-9

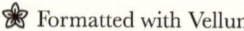 Formatted with Vellum

Contents

Onion and Sax: The Origin Story	vii
Introduction to the Omegaverse	ix
For Your Consideration	xiii
Chapter 1 *May, 2016*	1
The Daily Beta	9
Chapter 2 *Ten Years Later*	11
Chapter 3 *Three Months Later*	20
Knot What You Expected	29
Chapter 4	31
Chapter 5	38
Chapter 6	46
Audience Reactions	53
Knot What You Expected	55
Chapter 7	57
Chapter 8	63
Chapter 9	71
Chapter 10	77
Chapter 11	85
Chapter 12	94
Audience Reactions	103
Knot What You Expected	105
Chapter 13	106
Chapter 14	113
Chapter 15	119
Chapter 16	126
Chapter 17	132
Chapter 18	139
Audience Reactions	147
Knot What You Expected	149

Chapter 19	150
Chapter 20	158
Audience Reactions	167
Knot What You Expected	171
Chapter 21	173
Chapter 22	180
Chapter 23	187
Chapter 24	193
Audience Reactions	201
Knot What You Expected	203
Chapter 25	205
Chapter 26	209
Chapter 27	216
Chapter 28	222
Audience Reactions	229
Knot What You Expected	231
Chapter 29	232
Chapter 30	239
Chapter 31	241
Chapter 32	249
Audience Reactions	261
Knot What You Expected	263
Chapter 33	264
Chapter 34	269
Chapter 35	275
Chapter 36	281
Audience Reactions	289
Chapter 37	291
Chapter 38	300
Chapter 39	307
Chapter 40	313
Chapter 41	318
Chapter 42	323
Chapter 43	330
Chapter 44	335
Chapter 45	340
Knot What You Expected	351

Chapter 46	352
Epilogue	360
Acknowledgments	369
About the Author	371
Also by Holly Monroe	373

Onion and Sax: The Origin Story

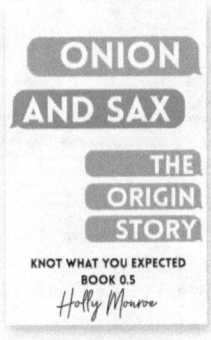

Scan below for a free download of *Onion and Sax: The Origin Story* for a peek into the past.

Introduction to the Omegaverse

Knot What You Expected is set within the Cirque de Mordu Omegaverse. If you read One for the Money and Two for the Show, you're familiar with these mechanics, but if you're a new Omegaverse reader or have only read my Lunarcrest novels, I highly recommend reading the below.

Omegaverse, also known as A/B/O, is a modern alternative universe that operates on principles commonly associated with wolf packs and shifters in the paranormal romance genre. The social structure includes Alphas, Betas, and Omegas, but none of the characters are shifters. The Reality TV Omegas series operates similarly to other A/B/O universes, but there are some slight differences.

Omegas are regarded as the most submissive designation and the rarest. They can receive an Alpha's knot or lock and undergo a heat cycle roughly four times a year, depending on suppressant use. An Omega's heat is a period when they are exceptionally fertile and have an increased sex drive. During heat, an Omega falls into a haze that impairs their ability to care for themselves, and they rely on their pack for assistance to meet their needs and remain healthy. An Omega is the only designation that can initiate a bonding bite. Other designations can choose to reject the bond, which can cause pain for both parties, with the potential for severe harm, hospitalization, or potentially death, for the Omega, but there is no way to trap anyone with a claiming bite.

Omegas scent match with Alphas and Betas, which is a mechanism by which their pheromones attract a particularly compatible partner for them. There is no "one true" scent match, and theories suggest that an Omega could have a large number of matches out there. Omegas are fine without scent matches, but once identified, the draw to one another is powerful, and they struggle to separate from their matches. Both Omegas and Alphas can find that their "hindbrain", the part of them ruled by instincts, can subconsciously mark another designation, indicating a desire to bond with them.

Omega Storm is a rare condition some Omegas can fall victim to, characterized by a fugue state an Omega can enter during pre-heat, often spurred by anger and fear. It can only be calmed by a scent matched Alpha, and has side effects that range from mild, in the form of panic attacks, to severe, in the form of psychosis.

Another health condition that can affect only Omegas is Foresaken Omega Syndrome. In this rare disease condition, an Omega who is not regularly exposed to compatible Alpha pheromones begins to waste away, eventually becoming hospitalized and dying. Omegas are at risk of this after prolonged suppressant use or isolation.

In all Cirque de Mordu Omegaverse books, reproduction does not follow human biological means.

All Omegas have uteruses, and male Omegas also produce sperm.

All Alphas produce sperm, and female Alphas do not have uteruses.

Male Betas produce sperm, and female Betas have uteruses.

Fertility is highest in Alpha-Omega and Beta-Beta pairings. Omega and Omega, Alpha and Beta, and Beta and Omega pairings are much less likely to reproduce, but it is possible.

Pregnancy will never be a storyline for the main characters of my books. Pregnancy or children may be mentioned, but only in the epilogues.

Alphas are considered the top of the food chain. They have possessive characteristics and strong personalities and are, on average, physically larger than the other designations. Male Alphas have a knot at the base of their penis, which inflates after sex to 'lock' the Alphas into their partner until it deflates. This aspect of anatomy is the main difference between an Alpha and a Beta. Female Alphas have a lock that can clamp down and trap a male Omega inside them. Alphas form packs around their Omegas, or through a familiarity with one another, similar to a fraternity. There is no magic or pheromone draw between Alphas. Their packs come together through necessity or chance. Packs serve as a means to share the responsibility of caring for an Omega. They have scents that are recognizable and attractive to all designations, a result of their pheromone composition, that can draw Omegas and Betas to them.

Some Alphas who are not bonded to an Omega begin to deteriorate physically. No one knows why this happens, and science believes it may be an inherited condition. The opposite of Omega Storm, which is aggressive and dangerous to others, Alpha Rot is only dangerous to the Alpha. The further it progresses, the weaker the Alpha becomes, eventually having so few pheromones that they can no longer scent match. This can be expedited by exposure to an Omega that lacks compatible pheromones. A scent match can stabilize the Rot, which may eventually reverse itself after enough time. However, research is unclear.

Betas are the 'normal people' of A/B/O universes. Betas have scents and can match with both Alphas and Omegas, but can only be bonded to an Alpha through an Omega.

For Your Consideration

Knot What You Expected is a high angst contemporary MMMF Omegaverse novel and the first book in the Reality TV Omegas series, set within the Cirque de Mordu Omegaverse.

Several of the elements below may be upsetting for some readers, so please review them carefully before proceeding. If you discover anything that needs to be added while reading this book, please email me at authorhollymonroe@gmail.com.

Your mental health matters.

- Death of a sibling
- Grief
- Agoraphobia
- Anxiety
- Discussion of death with dignity
- Explicit language and sexual content
- Medical trauma

If you ever had an online partner who said they were one thing and turned out to be another, this one is for you.

I, too, was the victim of several catfish because I am gullible and had unrestricted internet access.

Chapter One

MAY, 2016

MOVIES WOULD HAVE you believe brothers and sisters either don't get along or, if they do, that the sister still kind of hates her brother, because he is an asshole chasing off all of her romantic prospects.

That's never been the case for Calvin and me. He may be nine years older than me, but he's my best friend. Always has been, from the moment I was born. I know I can go to him with any problem, and he'll drop everything to be there for me, even if it means getting on a plane.

Which he did.

He got a plane and flew from Hollywood, California, to Hollywood, Florida, because Pops called him and told him I presented as an Omega.

I'm not being dramatic when I say that it was, without a doubt, the worst presentation ever. There is literally no way that anyone else had a worse presentation. It was so bad that I am still red-faced with mortification.

It's a good thing he got here as fast as he did, because my life is *over* with a capital O. I may as well change my name and move across the world.

"It can't have been that bad." Calvin strokes my hair from where it pokes out of the blue quilt I've buried myself in. "No one's presentation is perfect, and everything feels like the end of the world when you're sixteen."

"That's because it *is* the end of the world! Ugh, it's not just that it was imperfect, Calvin." Now I'm whining. Is that going to be a thing now that I'm an Omega? "I could handle imperfect. It was the fact that I presented in front of the entire school!"

His hand pauses mid-stroke. "The whole school?"

"Yes!" I moan, the memory of that day making me want to run away and join the circus. "It was during the sophomore debate."

"Debate…" he echoes.

"Yeah, I was arguing against that asshole William about Omega registration. He was for, I was against."

"Of course you were. Apt topic." My brother pulls back the corner of my quilt and crawls under with me. "I'm sure you were winning."

"Of course I was! I finished the debate and got the trophy. But let me paint you a picture. Me, on the stage. All eyes on me. Spotlights. I tried to rebut his stupid argument that registration is for Omegas' protection, which it isn't, and I started whining! Actual, honest-to-God whining, Calvin. My scent spiked, and *everyone* could smell me. It was mortifying. But the worst part is that I slicked through my pants!" I wail, burying my face in his chest. "My life is over. I can never go back."

Calvin's mint tea scent is muted, like it has been since his pack died, but still comforting in its familiarity as it surrounds me. "You can go back, and you will. There is nothing to be ashamed of about presenting as an Omega. Being one is a beautiful, wonderful thing."

"It doesn't feel wonderful. Feels sticky."

Chapter One

He chuckles, my head bouncing as his slim chest moves. "Of course, it doesn't seem great right now. But one day, when you meet your pack, you'll realize that it is the best thing that could ever have happened to you. There is nothing like the love a pack can give you, little Onion. There are people out there made for you. It's science and magic and *wonderful*. You have to hold strong until you find them. The wait will be worth it."

His voice cracks, and my heart does, too. Calvin's pack all died suddenly a few months ago in a helicopter accident on their way back from filming a movie. He's been holding on surprisingly well, all things considered. Sure, he's become a bit of a homebody, but grief can do that to a person.

"I'm not going back to school. I can never show my face there again. I'm going to do virtual school from now on."

"You'd hate virtual school." He pulls the blanket down and shifts so that we're both sitting up. "And you're not one to run and hide, Ariana Cooley. You're too tough to let something like a little slick get you down."

"It wasn't a little slick!" I gesture aggressively toward my laundry basket. "Check for yourself if you don't believe me. It looked like I pissed myself!"

He changes tactics. "At least you have a nice scent. Imagine if you smelled like... I don't know, licorice or something?"

"I hate licorice."

"Me too! See, luck is on your side, making you smell like oranges and cream." He makes a dramatic sniffing noise. "Mmm, like summertime popsicles."

"Ew! Don't sniff me, you weirdo!" I shove him the way I used to when we were kids. "Of course, you're going to say I smell good. You're my brother. You have to."

"Okay, so? I'm your brother. If anyone was going to tell you that you smelled like gym socks, it would be me. I would never let you live it down, honestly." He slides out from under me and rips the blanket off me with all the flair of a magician's assistant. "Now, come on, let's go get some food."

I sit up and swing my legs off the bed, allowing me to get my first good look at my brother since he got here. He came directly from the airport, and his disheveled appearance shows it, but the dark bags under his eyes seem too permanent to be from a single red-eye flight. His skin is sallow, and his usually impeccably manicured nails look brittle.

My brother looks sick. Like, really sick.

"Are you okay?" I ask him, pushing to my feet. "I've made this all about me. How are you holding up? You'd tell me if something was wrong, right?"

He waves me away. "I'm fine, Onion. I have good days and bad days, like anyone."

This doesn't seem like a bad day. Calvin wouldn't keep something this big from me, would he?

"You're not getting sick, are you?"

Omegas who meet their scent matches, then lose exposure to them, or have an adverse reaction to long-term heat suppressant use, are at risk of developing Foresaken Omega Syndrome, or FOS. We have a whole unit devoted to it in designation biology class. It's a devastating illness, but a lot of Omegas can heal from it. Most Omegas are fortunate to often have several scent matches available to aid pheromone treatment.

Scent matching is not a one-and-done type of deal, despite what some fairy tales may suggest. Everyone has multiple scent matches somewhere out there. It's all about whether you can find them. There are billions of people in the world. Of course, there isn't only one person out there for everyone. That would be a statistical improbability.

Scientists have been trying for decades to determine what causes scent matching and whether there is a way to predict or root out its cause, but they've come up short. Honestly, it's not a well-researched field from what I've been taught in school. There isn't much money to be made in the study of scent matches, so the government isn't funding it.

It's estimated that most Alphas have three or four matches out there, and Omegas can have up to ten. Which sounds like a lot, but there are billions of people in the world. Running into one is so rare that most don't wait to pack up.

But Calvin was lucky. He was scent matched to his whole pack—all five of them. It's one of the reasons, aside from their moderate fame, that the media loved them.

Of course, the downside of finding scent matches is that if you lose them, FOS becomes a major risk.

"I'm not getting sick," he insists, wrapping his elbow with mine. "I have a little cold. Nothing you need to worry about."

"Are you sure?" I let him lead me to the kitchen, where Dad is sitting down to breakfast. "You'd tell me, right?"

"You know I don't keep secrets from you." He ruffles my hair like I'm still a child. "Now, go eat. You have school."

"I am *not* going to school!" I stop dead in my tracks and try to flee back to my room. "I can't face everyone! Not yet!"

He puts his hands on my shoulders and shoves me into my seat. "If you don't go, you'll be showing them all that you're ashamed of your designation, and you're not going to do that. Female Omegas are so rare. You'll be so popular now. I know this feels like the end of the world, but it's not. All of the Alphas are going to want to talk to you, all of the unpresented girls are going to want to be you."

I scowl into my cereal. "No, they're not. No one wants to be an Omega."

Dad pushes a glass of orange juice to me. "Then they're stupid. Being an Omega is a blessing, not a curse."

"Both of you? Ugh!" I roll my eyes, fully embracing the petulant teenager stereotype. "Seriously. It's not that great. People think that you're incapable of complex thought when they find out you're an Omega."

My Omega father stares at me with a straight face. "Not capable of complex thought? I'm a mathematician, Ariana."

"Yeah, but you're different."

"It sounds like you have the prejudices against Omegas that you're trying to claim everyone else has." Calvin lowers himself beside me with a mug of creamy coffee. "Promise me you'll give it a real chance, little Onion. Don't let your fear keep you from living."

"I'm not," I insist, taking a bite of my cereal and talking with my mouth full. "I'm not afraid of being an Omega, I just don't *want* to be one."

Dad reaches out and pats my shoulder. "You'll think otherwise when you find your pack. And when you build your first nest."

My ears perk up a little bit at that. Building a nest does sound fun. I like to be cozy, and what's cozier than a pile of blankets and pillows that I can burrow in?

Calvin drains his cup of coffee and places the empty mug on the table. "How about this? Go to school, and when I pick you up, we can go nest shopping."

"You promise?" Excitement about my designation

blooms for the first time. Maybe it won't be all bad. There's got to be some good parts of being an Omega. My best friend Marlie presented two months ago and says she loves it.

"I promise." He leans and kisses my head before nuzzling against my cheek. "You'll see. Being an Omega is a blessing."

"You seriously believe that? Even though…"

"Even though I lost them?" Calvin takes my hands in his, pulling me to my feet. "Yes, even though I lost my Alphas, being their Omega for any amount of time was better than never knowing them. You'll understand one day, when you find the people for you. And I'll be right by your side, welcoming them to the family. After I make sure they're good enough for you, that is."

"You promise?" I repeat.

"I promise."

The Daily Beta

CALVIN DREVEN, SOCIALITE AND INFLUENCER, DEAD AT 25

NOVEMBER 12, 2016

THE FAMILY OF CALVIN DREVEN, SOCIAL MEDIA SENSATION AND OMEGA TO THE LATE PACK DREVEN, REPORTED THAT ON THE MORNING OF NOVEMBER 11TH, HE PASSED AWAY AT AGE 25 AFTER A SHORT BATTLE WITH FOS.

HE WAS PRECEDED IN DEATH BY HIS PACK, PACK DREVIN. THE PACK, CALLED "HOLLYWOOD ROYALTY," WAS RETURNING FROM FILMING THE CRITICALLY ACCLAIMED MOVIE "BROKEN AND BEAUTIFUL" WHEN THEY DIED IN A TRAGIC HELICOPTER ACCIDENT. PACK DREVEN FORMED WHEN THEY WERE TEENAGERS, HAVING GROWN UP IN THE BUSINESS TOGETHER. THEIR RELATIONSHIP WITH CALVIN WAS A STORYBOOK ONE THAT CAPTURED AMERICA'S ATTENTION AND HEARTS AFTER A CHANCE MEETING AT A MOVIE premiere, where he was conducting interviews on the red carpet.

Calvin said in multiple interviews that it was love at first sight.

Sources close to the pack claim that since the unexpected death of his Alphas, Calvin had been showing signs of Foresaken Omega Syndrome (FOS), the devastating illness with symptoms that range from discomfort to death.

Calvin is survived by his three Alpha fathers, his Alpha mother and Omega father, and his Omega sister. The family asks for privacy as they deal with their grief.

Chapter Two

TEN YEARS LATER

IT'S BEEN ten years since Calvin passed, and I still don't know how to live without him.

But I can do anything for thirty seconds, so I count in my head as I breathe in and out, before I loop back to one and start again.

Everyone says that grief isn't linear. I never expected it to be. However, I did think that it would lessen, if only a little.

I've been told that grief never shrinks. It bumps up against the sides of you, taking up every inch of space within your body and making itself known. Supposedly, I'll grow around the grief, so that it only hits my sides every once in a while, but it's still the largest part of me.

It's not that I should be over it by now, because I don't think anyone can get over this type of loss, but I should know how to live with it better. I shouldn't still be locked in my home, drowning in my grief.

But it's been so long now that I don't know if I can step outside my door into the real world.

Eight years.

It's been eight years since I left my house by more than a few steps.

Sax says I only need to take one step. I have to breathe deep, count to thirty, one step, then another, until I'm on the sidewalk. Once I get on the sidewalk, he says it'll be no big deal to take a few more steps until I get to the corner store.

And if I make it to the corner store, why not try for the coffee shop?

He hasn't said as much, but I know that if I ever want to meet him, I will have to leave my home. He deserves so much better than an Omega who hyperventilates at the idea of bumping into an Alpha on the sidewalk.

Sax and I met on a forum for the paranormal television show *Unexplainable and Bizarre,* which followed a team of paranormal researchers investigating reports of extraordinary activity. It was canceled after four seasons, almost nine years ago. I was sharing my theories of places I thought they'd visit in season three, when Sax jumped into my post to argue with me that it was all fake.

This was shortly after I presented as an Omega. Less than six months later, my brother Calvin died of Foresaken Omega Syndrome. In my grief, I basically lived on the forum as a way to escape reality, and Sax was right there, going toe to toe with me.

Eventually, Sax must have grown tired of our back-and-forth conversations, which were getting increasingly off-topic and public, because he messaged me privately, and that was all she wrote.

We're no longer teenagers sending messages back and forth whenever we could scrape time together. Now we're adults with cell phones who can make video calls.

I still don't know his name, and he doesn't know mine either. After spending so long calling each other by our

Chapter Two

screen names, our real names don't seem to hold any meaning anymore.

Part of me tells myself that if I don't have his real name, I won't have to tell him my very real feelings for him.

I'm in love with a man on a screen.

I think he may be one of the few people left who haven't given up on me. My family almost has. All that's left is Christmas, and after inviting me for years and me not showing up, they started coming here.

It's one of the only times my house feels alive.

What they don't understand is that just because I don't leave my house doesn't mean that I am without friends.

Sax doesn't count. He's more than a friend now. He's family. Even if he never feels the way about me that I do about him, he's in my life for good. He's made that more than clear.

My best friend, Marlie, visits me all the time. We met in middle school and have been close since. She tries to get me to go out, but she also accepts my no and doesn't push me. It would have been easy for her to cut me out of her life, but she never did.

I love her for that.

I also have my gaming buddies, Victor and Julie. Victor became a bit of a public figure earlier this year when he went on the reality TV show *Knot What You Expected* after posing as an Omega named Tif to get revenge on his high school tormentor.

Except he caught real feelings, and was terrified that Kit wouldn't forgive him for the duplicity.

Spoiler alert: he did.

Marlie came over every Tuesday and Thursday to watch the episodes as they aired, and damn, it was good TV.

Knot What You Expected is one of the most popular shows in the nation right now. The hosts, Bridgette and Bradley Wilcox, a married Beta couple, bring together people who chatted online but have never met in person and put them in a house together for a week to find out if the person on the other side of the screen is who they claimed to be.

While some cast members have been exactly who they say they are, most were keeping major secrets. Victor was lying about his gender, there was a contestant who was the best friend of the person they were talking to, and one where it was even the Alpha's own mother.

It's all very salacious.

I can't imagine finding out someone I thought I knew was lying to me and then being trapped in a house with them. It's a nightmare. But damn if it's not entertaining when it happens to someone else.

I have had brief thoughts about applying as a way to meet Sax, but there is no way I can do that. Going from a shut-in to being on national television? Absolutely the fuck not.

And I don't need a TV show to meet him. If I wanted to, I think he'd meet up with me in a heartbeat. He's stopped asking because he doesn't want me to feel bad about it, but I know he'd be happy if I came to visit.

Except I need to get out of my house and travel to him.

Besides, I've seen him. We talk on video calls at least once a week. We know what each other looks like, what we sound like. He's not hiding his identity from me. We're using nicknames for one another. It's sweet.

Calvin called me little Onion from birth. He said my head was shaped like one when I was a baby, and when I'd scream, I'd turn all purple like one. I hated it for the longest time, but I embraced it as I got older. Now that it's what Sax calls me, too, it feels as much like my name as Ariana is.

The doorbell rings, and I shoot Julie a message that I'm going to be away from my keyboard tonight, and I'll catch up with her tomorrow.

"Wake up, bitch!" Marlie slams my door open before I have a chance to answer it. She's had a key for years. I don't know why she bothers ringing the doorbell, since she never waits for me to open it. "I've brought tacos!"

I roll my eyes at her as I pull her into my arms. "Tacos on a Tuesday, what a revelation. You're a real trendsetter."

"Hey, if you don't want it, you can go pick up something else." She fists her hips and glares at me, trying to puff her chest out to look more intimidating. She couldn't scare me if she tried.

Marlie is an Omega, like me, but she's tiny. I'm not exactly tall, and I still tower over her slight frame. She's adorable, with sun-kissed skin and bleached-blonde hair, looking more like she belongs in Hollywood, California, than Hollywood, Florida.

"You know I'm just kidding. I love tacos." I grab a couple of beers from the fridge and two plates. "Let's eat. I'm starving."

"Oh my God, you wouldn't believe what happened today." She talks through a mouthful of carne asada. "That student I told you about, Robby? He presented at lunch and was mortified. Before I could get him out of there, he scent matched with Jackson."

Marlie loves telling me high school drama, but sometimes I think she embellishes it a little, because there is no way her school has that much going on. "Isn't Jackson the captain of the football team?" Memories of my own less-than-stellar presentation come to mind, but I shove them down.

"Yeah, and the one who has been teasing Robby mercilessly about how he was definitely going to be an Omega, so he shouldn't bother doing anything other than learning to be a homemaker."

"Ew." Backward attitudes toward Omegas still exist, but I was hoping they would be few and far between by this point. Except kids who are raised with prejudiced parents end up spewing those ideas themselves until they are shown that what they've always believed is wrong.

And sometimes they refuse to see it, even when the truth is right in front of them.

"What happened then?" I squeeze a lime over my carnitas taco before adding more cilantro. I don't care what anyone says, cilantro is the best thing in the world, and if someone thinks it tastes like soap, then their tongue must be broken.

"Well, Jackson immediately scooped him up and ran out of the cafeteria with Robby in his arms. We had to go after them, of course, because, like hell am I letting an Alpha run off with a newly presented Omega. I found Robby ripping Jackson a new one. I had to bite my tongue to keep from laughing at how heartbroken Jackson looked."

My best friend takes a long sip of her beer and burps so loudly I'm surprised my windows don't rattle. She may look cute and dainty, but she has five Alpha brothers and acts like it.

"So Robby rejected him?"

She waves her hand. "For now, yeah. You know it won't last, though. How fortunate for them to meet their scent matches at such a young age. They'll have their whole lives together."

The food sours on my tongue.

Marlie holds the romantic ideal that meeting her scent

match will be the greatest day of her life. She's been putting herself out there, attending speed-dating events and even signing up for a new service that stores Alpha pheromone samples for Omegas to smell, in hopes of finding her match.

She's been unsuccessful thus far.

As much as Marlie loves me, I know she doesn't understand why I am so against finding my matches. She couldn't possibly, since she has never lost someone to Foresaken Omega Syndrome.

She doesn't understand how serious it is. How bad things got for Calvin at the end.

"Look, Ariana." Her voice is soft as she touches the back of my hand. "I love you. You know that, right?"

Looks like it's time for our quarterly argument in which Marlie swears she's met the Alpha for me and tries to get me out of the house, I refuse, and we get into a fight that takes us a week to get over.

I brace myself for the 'but' that is sure to follow.

"But..."

Called it.

"You can't keep living like this."

She practically has a script at this point. I could stage my own intervention.

"The world is scary. I could get in a car wreck on the way home. You could get cancer. Everything could explode into dust. There is risk to everything. What is the point of being alive if you aren't really living?"

I bury my face in my hands, using my index fingers to rub my temples. "Marlie..."

"No, let me finish. Anything could happen. You're twenty-six. You have one life, and you're not living it. Your parents are worried. I'm worried. I feel like I've been enabling you." She gets up from her chair and grabs the legs of mine, wrenching me around and crouching in front of me. "You have to get out of this house."

Bile rises in my throat. "I... I can't, Marlie. I've tried. I just... It's safe here, okay?"

She hums and strokes my hair from my face, tucking one of the unruly brown strands behind my ear. "I know. I know it's hard. And I know you've tried, and you couldn't. I think you can, though, with the right motivation."

I narrow my eyes. "What does that mean?"

"It means you need a compelling reason to get out and stay out of this living tomb."

"Hey! My house isn't a tomb, thank you very much."

I love my house. It's cozy and lived in, with three bedrooms and a nesting suite. Not that I need it. I don't have a nest. I've had one nest in my life, and Calvin helped me shop for it.

I don't want another.

"Not yet it isn't!" She pushes to her feet and grabs her oversized purse from where she dropped it on the counter. She starts to dig through it. "You know, with everything being digital nowadays, it's hard to have dramatic reveals like there used to be. It's frustrating, honestly. Colleges email acceptances, they don't mail those massive envelopes like you see in movies anymore, you know?"

"I guess?"

She finds what she was looking for and holds a folded piece of paper up triumphantly. "It takes away a bit of the flair of the moment. The drama of it all. You know I live for those big reveal moments."

I stare at the paper in her hands, nerves on edge as I worry about what she's building up to. Marlie has always made a production of things, but this time feels much heavier than others.

"What have you got there, M?"

"I love you, Ariana. You know that, right? I would do anything for you. I want nothing more than for you to be happy." I try to snatch the papers from her, and she runs to the other side of the table out of my reach. "You have to remember that, okay? You have to remember how much I love you. Say it. Say you know I love you."

"What did you do?"

"Say it, Ariana."

"Fine. I know you love me. Now, what did you do?"

Her face flushes red, and she holds out the paper to me, ducking her head into her arm as she does so. "It's for your own good."

I take the page from her and unfold it, my eyes struggling to focus on what I'm seeing.

There is no way. Absolutely no way this says what I think it does.

I'm staring at the printed email, addressed to me, from an address I don't recognize, but my hands are shaking so much that the words are blurring.

"I didn't think they'd accept you," my traitorous best friend babbles. "I figured, if they did, it was a sign that it was meant to be, and you'd forgive me because of fate or whatever."

My heart is pounding so hard I'm surprised it hasn't ripped out of my chest.

"How… what?" I stutter, unable to make sense of the words in front of me.

She steps forward, and grabs my wrists with gentle hands. "I applied to *Knot What You Expected* as you. You're going to meet Sax, Ariana."

Chapter Three

THREE MONTHS LATER

IS it too early for another anxiety med?

How many can I take before I fall asleep where I stand?

I don't think that one was enough. It got me out of the house, but I'm not sure if I'll be able to climb into the town car that sits at the curb.

There's a line that separates my front path from the sidewalk, but it may as well be a chasm for how wide it feels.

Thirty seconds. Can I do it for thirty seconds?

What would Sax say?

I can do anything for thirty seconds. One foot after the other.

We haven't been able to talk since we signed the show's contract. I couldn't even tell him I was signing it. Not that he's tried to call. They had to have given him the same directive.

But it'll be worth it.

Just two more days. Or is it three? Doesn't matter. All

Chapter Three

that matters is that I have to take those fifteen steps to the curb.

I'm sure the driver is pissed at me because I can't seem to make my feet move, judging by the way he looks at his watch as he stands outside the passenger side door. I do feel bad that he's been holding open for five minutes. If I weren't "the talent", I bet he would've driven off by now.

But he's an Alpha.

I'm not even on the sidewalk, and I'm about to run into my first Alpha.

It's a nightmare. My actual nightmare.

Why would they send an Alpha to pick me up? I told them not to. They promised to keep me away from Alphas. They know that I can't do it. It's hard enough to leave, I can't also be around a bunch of Alphas.

But Sax is going to be there.

I say his name like a prayer, an encouragement that I sorely need.

I'm going to get to meet Sax.

"Ariana, you need to get in the car. You're expected on the plane soon." Drew's voice is kind through my phone. He's the production coordinator of *Knot What You Expected*, who has been assigned to me while I'm on the show.

He's also the one who sent the town car.

They chartered me a private flight to Georgia for filming, but that doesn't change the fact that I have to get in this car.

"The driver is an Alpha! I told you, I need a Beta driver."

I understand that I'm being difficult, I do, but this was one of my concessions to keep me from backing out of filming.

My first phone call with the *Expected* team was rough. I

explained to them that I had never applied and therefore could not do the show. They did not like hearing that.

Apparently, Marlie had given them all the information they needed to find Sax, and he had already agreed to meet me. I felt like I couldn't back out once they told me that.

He wanted to meet me.

Over the years, my relationship with Sax has evolved, and no matter what's been happening in our lives, we've always made time for one another. Except when we were nineteen, he went quiet, responding to texts with a few one-word answers and promises to catch up soon. I assumed it was because he started college, joined a fraternity, and was outgrowing his internet friend.

He came back to me a few months later, all apologies for pulling back.

I forgave him, because, of course, I did.

He's Sax.

He's been there with me through everything, supported me with every step I made.

And they've been so hard to take sometimes.

After Calvin's death, my relationship with my mother was strained because he looked just like her. How could I look into her eyes when all I saw was his, dim and glassy when they disconnected his life support?

We used to be so close, and now she feels like a stranger.

Or maybe I'm the stranger.

I don't know who I am in a world without Calvin.

"I understand, but not all requests can be accommodated. We've done our best to reduce the number of Alphas on set, but our hands are tied. We've got contracts and unions we're dealing with, here. But Paul has a bonded Omega. It's why we chose him."

I understand what he's saying. Logically, it makes sense.

Chapter Three

But anxiety isn't logical. It doesn't care about sense. It cares that my home is safe, and that the car is not. My home has no Alphas, and that car will.

I can't do this.

I can't.

Sax will understand, won't he?

What would he say if I could call him right now?

Baby, sometimes a step can feel like a mile, and it's okay if it takes you some time to take them.

I take one step closer to Paul.

"What if I scent match him?" My voice is so low that it's a shock Drew can hear me.

"If, on the very slim chance you scent match with Paul, we'll figure out what we can do to keep you safe and healthy, Ariana. I know you don't know me from Adam, but I promise I have your best interests at heart here."

"You have the show's best interests at heart." I'm pissed, but I take another step forward.

Walking into a world where my brother isn't breathing anymore feels like peeling off a layer of my skin.

I'll survive, but at what cost?

"You need to be here, Ariana. I cannot tell you anything more than that, just that I know you need to do the show."

Drew has said something like that a few times, implying that it's important for me to come on *Knot What You Expected*, and I don't get the vibe that it's about ratings.

I take another step forward.

Sax used to get so disappointed when I didn't go out. Maybe disappointed in the wrong word. He wanted more for me than a life behind doors. He told me that the world deserved to see my sunlight.

I told him I was a storm cloud the world didn't ask for.

One day, he stopped asking me whether I was going

out that day. After a while, even the Omega-only hours at coffee shops and grocery stores were too much.

But why would I need to leave my house?

The internet is incredible; I can have everything I need delivered and still attend my therapy appointments with Dr. Frank on video call.

Of course, he also says I need to leave my house, but what does he know?

Okay, so he knows a lot. But that doesn't mean he's right. Maybe if I were truly unable and afraid to go outside, he would be, but that's not it.

I'm not afraid. I know the world isn't out to get me. It's just anxiety. I could leave if I wanted to.

But I don't want to.

Because I know that if I go outside, I could run into an Alpha.

And that Alpha could be my scent match.

And then if something happens to that Alpha, I could get Foresaken Omega Syndrome.

And I'd die.

And my parents would lose their only living child.

Really, I've been locking myself up in my home for my parents' sake.

It's easier to stay inside where it's safe, where I don't have to worry about the potential of death just because my biology is wired to need an Alpha.

So it's not that I'm afraid to leave my house. The situation is far more nuanced than that, and Dr. Frank understands.

Most of the time.

I take another step.

I haven't been this far away from my front door in three years, when I had a delivery driver leave my groceries at the end of my driveway instead of on the stoop. It was shitty, and it took me two hours to get them, but I managed.

It's how I know I can leave my house if I want to.

Baby, sometimes a step can feel like a mile, and it's okay if it takes you some time to take them.

Sax's words are a mantra, running through my mind every time I lift my foot.

I want to do this, don't I?

I want to meet Sax.

I don't want to be a prisoner in my home, my body, my mind.

Okay.

One more step.

One.

More.

Step.

"Could you... Can I close my own door?" I ask Paul, still several feet from the door.

Paul nods, the expression on his face morphing from frustrated to kind, as he circles the car and slides into the driver's seat.

"There we go," Drew's gentle voice fills my ear. *"You're doing so great. You've got this, Ariana."*

"And when I get there, only Betas?" I confirm, my hand on the car door. "You promise?"

"Several of the light and sound crew are Alphas, but Bridgette and Bradley are Betas, so are your hair and makeup artists for the introduction interview. We're doing our best, but you did sign a contract that we could not be held liable for exposure to Alpha pheromones."

That contract was non-negotiable for them. I had a lawyer look it over, and they said it was enforceable, but that it was only going to be used if I came after the network for emotional distress or medical bills, should I unfortunately develop FOS from Alpha exposure.

I didn't feel great putting my signature on that line, but I did. Almost like I was signing away my life.

It's worth it, though, because I'm going to see Sax.

I'm going to see Sax.

I slide onto the bench seat in the back of the car, and it takes me another minute of deep breaths and Drew encouraging me in my ear before I can pull the door closed. As if worried I'm going to leap out of the car at any moment, Paul doesn't wait for me to put on my seatbelt before driving me away from safety.

"THIS IS where you'll be staying until you move into the *Expected* house." Drew scans a keycard and opens the door to a boring and basic room that looks like it's from a mid-level chain hotel, with its mass-produced art and a chair in a corner that may or may not be for cuckolding.

The room is plain, with a bathroom, a sitting area, and a bed all shoved into a small space like a studio apartment, but I'm not concerned. I'll only be here for two days before I move into the house.

The flight here was atrocious. Paul sat in the farthest seat away from me, and I spent most of it with headphones on, blaring music through noise-cancelling headphones, a hoodie pulled over my head, and my face in my e-reader. Anything to try to help me forget that I was in the air and not on my comfortable couch.

Now that I'm here, having taken three anxiety meds

right at the recommended time between doses, I'm going to try my best to make the most of this.

Even if I flinch every time someone walks beside me.

This will be worth it.

I'm going to meet Sax.

It will be worth it. It has to be.

The *Expected* house is the focal piece of the compound Paul drove me to once we arrived. Several small buildings have been built around it, including this one. The crew lives in a lot of them because they film four seasons in a six-month period, which means they have one to air every quarter. Once filming starts, the property goes on lockdown.

Everyone comes onto *Expected* knowing they will have to stay an entire week in the house, and a few days before it for filming extras and interviews. America loves a peek into the beginning of a relationship, and into the difficulties the couple faces as they uncover the lies they've both told.

Knowing I have to be away from my home, from my room, for over a week, makes my skin itch. One benefit of having a crew around is that I don't want to make a fool of myself by having a meltdown in front of the cameras, so I'm fighting to keep myself together.

I think it's working.

Mostly.

There have been some tears.

Okay, there have been a lot of tears. But I have managed not to scream. That's a win, right?

"You did great today, Ariana. We're going to do our best to make sure this is a good experience for you. Now, get some rest. Hair and makeup will arrive at six tomorrow morning to get you ready for your entrance interview." Drew backs out of the door slowly as he talks.

The Beta is handsome, in his early fifties, with greys

running through his black hair at the temples. I liked him the moment I heard his voice, and being around him has done a lot to calm me. I was surprised to find out his scent was soft, almost like baby powder. He's short and slim, and meeting him for the first time helped relax a lot of the tension I had from the trip out here.

The door closes behind him with a click. I'm alone. I'm by myself in a strange place. A place that I am not supposed to be.

Alarms are blaring in my head, demanding I open the door and run out.

I can't be here.

I can't do this.

I'm going to meet Sax.

I'm going to meet Sax.

Baby, sometimes a step can feel like a mile, and it's okay if it takes you some time to take them.

I flop onto the bed and lie back, staring at the ceiling. It is not my ceiling.

I'm not in my home.

This is not my room.

I'm not in my home.

But I'm alive.

I made it.

I did it.

And soon, I will get to meet Sax.

Knot What You Expected

EPISODE ONE

BRIDGETTE: I HOPE YOU'RE READY FOR THIS SEASON, AMERICA, BECAUSE I PROMISE YOU, THIS WILL BE ONE FOR THE BOOKS.

BRADLEY: IT SURE WILL. I DON'T THINK OUR TITLE HAS EVER BEEN MORE ACCURATE THAN IT IS WHEN IT COMES TO SAX AND ONION. IT FEELS LIKE THE SHOW WAS MADE FOR THEM, DOESN'T IT?

BRIDGETTE: I HAVE TO ADMIT, I AM A BIT NERVOUS ABOUT HOW THIS WILL WORK OUT. WE ARE GOING TO HAVE OUR WORK CUT OUT FOR US AS WE TRY TO GET THEM THEIR HAPPY ENDING.

BRADLEY: NOW, NOW, BRIDGETTE. DON'T SCARE OUR VIEWERS LIKE THAT!

BRIDGETTE: FINE, FINE. BUT THE SENTIMENT STILL STANDS. I WANT TO INTRODUCE YOU TO ARIANA COOLEY, ALSO known as Onion. I had the pleasure of sitting down with her before this all started...

Chapter Four

THE BRIGHT LIGHTS, which Bridgette swears I will get used to, are nearly blinding as I adjust in the uncomfortably firm chair.

Not my chair.

Not my house.

This is not my house.

I can't do this.

I need to leave.

"We're just about to start." Drew adjusts one of my curls to lie more naturally on my shoulder. They put a glaze on my hair as they styled it this morning to make my normally mousy brown hair more 'TV-ready,' whatever that means. I don't hate it. It helps me pretend that Onion isn't Ariana. Onion isn't afraid. Onion just wants to meet Sax.

"Just pretend like no one else is here."

I struggle not to roll my eyes at the Beta. Like I'll be able to forget that I've got cameras trained on me from all angles.

"Alright, roll camera." The assistant director calls to

start filming. Bridgette adjusts in her, pasting on a beautiful smile.

She's stunning, precisely the type of woman you'd expect to see on television. Her hair is deep chestnut brown, and it is so shiny, so smooth, that it looks like she's a living photo from a magazine cover. Her pale brown eyes are wide and expressive, taking up a large portion of her face. She has a small, upturned nose and plush, full lips. Her long, beautifully bronzed legs are on display in a tight red dress, and even though the room is full of people, I can still pick out her sugared berry scent. She must be wearing scent-enhancing perfume because it's strong for a Beta.

Next to her, I'm self-conscious in my black jeans and sapphire blue blouse. They told me I was supposed to look casual, as if I just arrived on set, so even though I spent two hours in hair and makeup this morning, I have a casual, girl-next-door look.

Whatever that means. Any girl can live next door.

I'm wearing enough makeup to avoid washing me out, but it should still look natural and soft on camera. The type of makeup that men mean when they say "I don't like a girl who wears a lot of makeup."

"Well, Ariana, welcome to *Knot What You Expected!* I gotta know…" She leans over like she's telling me a secret, and I angle my body closer to hers. "Is this what you expected?"

It's the same line at the start of every first interview, every season.

I'm supposed to play everything up for the camera. Drew and I had a long conversation about how the most important thing I can be is the three f's: friendly, funny, and fuckable. That's what makes for good reality television.

How do I appear fuckable when I'm a virgin?

Chapter Four

How can I be funny when I'm scared that bumping into the wrong person is going to be a death sentence?

I guess I have to shoot for friendly.

"I don't know what I expected, honestly." I'm hoping my smile isn't a grimace, but the way her eyes tighten at the corners isn't promising.

"That's a valid reaction. This is a new experience for you in more ways than one, right?" I nod, and she doesn't give me a chance to answer verbally. "I know this is your first time out of your home in a long time. Are you comfortable talking about that with us?"

No, I'm not comfortable with that. What makes her think I would be? Is it the way I cried when I got on the plane? Perhaps how my makeup artist had to reapply my makeup three times because I wiped it off and hid in the shower to scream?

But I don't have a choice. This was another of the network's non-negotiables. I have to talk about it.

Why did I agree to do this? Why didn't I call Sax and ask to meet?

Fucking Marlie.

They want me to lay my trauma out like a TV dinner, and I'm going to do it.

All to meet Sax. It'll be worth it.

"Sure, Bridgette. It's a bit of a long story. My brother, Calvin..."

Bridgette interrupts me. "That's former socialite and influencer Calvin Drevin, right?"

"Right. I sometimes forget that's how everyone saw him. But he wasn't any of those things to me. He was my big brother and my best friend. When he died, I didn't handle it well."

That's an understatement.

"I don't think anyone would. How old were you?"

"I was sixteen. It was only six months after I presented as an Omega myself. When it happened, he was right there, holding my hand, talking me through the whole process. I didn't want to be an Omega. I honestly expected to present as an Alpha, like my mother. But both of us got the Omega gene from our dad, I guess. Calvin was everything to me. He died of Foresaken Omega Syndrome." I can already feel my voice growing thick, but I promised myself I wouldn't cry. I dig my nails into my palms, knowing that, if I were to unfurl them, crescent moons would greet me.

"It's a devastating illness. No one deserves to go that way." Either Bridgette is being sincere, or she's a great actress.

"I was there with him in the end." My voice is barely above a whisper, but I'm mic'd up, so it shouldn't be an issue being heard on cameras. "I held his hand as he passed. It was not a peaceful death, Bridgette."

Don't think about it.

I can't think about it.

"I promised myself, then and there, that I would never allow myself to be put in that situation. I was never going to find a scent match. I was never, under any circumstance, going to have an Alpha."

"Which is why you've not left your home in years," she concludes. "This must be stressful for you."

My laugh is watery. "Sure, we'll go with stressful. It's been eight years since I've gone farther than my driveway, and here I am, hours from home, trying to keep it together in front of you all, when all I want is to hide under my covers."

Another understatement. Right now, I'd rather die than be here.

"That's understandable. Now, I have to point something out to our viewers at home." Bridgette turns toward the camera. "Ariana is not on heat suppressants, despite production recommending that she get a prescription for them. We can't require it, of course, but it is standard practice in television for Omegas to go on low-level suppressants before filming begins. Would you like to talk about your reasoning behind avoiding them?"

Can I blame my red cheeks on the heat from the stage lighting? Talking about my suppressant use is just the tip of the iceberg of the personal information they're going to find out about me through this process. Still, it doesn't make the conversation any easier.

"I know it was hard for production to understand, but there is a risk to developing FOS when suppressants are used too often, for too long. Will going on them once cause it? Probably not. But I do whatever I can to mitigate the risk, since I have a family history of severe presentation of the disease."

"Now everything is starting to make sense. You've stayed home to avoid exposure to Alphas."

"I thought that was obvious?" She giggles girlishly at my response, and I fight a frustrated eye roll. I'm glad my trauma is amusing. "If I don't meet an Alpha, I can't scent match, I can't get FOS."

"But meeting Sax was worth that risk?" she asks, pivoting the conversation back to the real reason we're here. "Because while we have tried to limit your exposure to Alphas, it's unavoidable. We have several Alphas on our crew."

I met a few of them earlier, and they tried their best to keep their distance. I was still able to detect their scent, which means I was exposed to their pheromones. I held my breath until I realized none of them was my scent match, but every time I realized what was happening, I felt like I was going to be sick.

"Yeah, it is. Sax has been my closest friend since I was sixteen. He was there with me when my brother died. He's been such a major figure in my life, and he's so important to me, that I could not turn down this opportunity. Getting accepted to the show was the kick in the pants I needed to finally take this leap."

"So you've never tried to meet up before? He never came to visit?"

"We don't know where the other lives. We never even exchanged names. But it doesn't change how I feel about him. How I've felt about him for so long. We may not have met in person, but we have videochatted for years. He's gorgeous, frankly, but that's not what pulls me toward him. He's smart and clever, funny and flirty, sensitive and kind. He's the whole package. Everything I've always dreamed about having in a partner."

I get quiet when I realize they might play this clip for Sax. I've never said anything like this to him before, and now I am spilling my guts to the world before I do to him.

I'm going to consider it a practice run for when I say this to his face. I need to get the words right.

"He sounds dreamy." Bridgette rests her elbow on her knee and her chin on her hand. "So you expect him to be exactly who he says he is?"

"I do. You can't know someone this long and not know who they are at their core. I know Sax. I'm excited to finally get the opportunity to hug him. To feel his heartbeat beneath my ear. It's cheesy, I know. But Sax is a part of me. He's… fuck." Bridgette winces at my swear, and I slap my hand to my mouth. "Sorry. I can't say that, can I? I was just going to say that he's everything. I love him. And as terrifying as it is, it's also liberating to know that I'm finally

Chapter Four

going to get to tell him that. Wait." I lean forward and touch the back of Bridgette's hand. "You're not going to play this for him, are you? I want him to hear it from me first. Not through a recording."

She smiles indulgently. "Of course not. This is just between our viewers at home and us. I don't think anyone wants to take that moment from you two. I know he's anxiously awaiting seeing you, as well. What do you think was his motivation for agreeing to come on the show? Have you two talked about it since you were accepted?"

I shake my head and cross one leg over the other to keep myself from bouncing my knee. Do I have to pee, or is it just anxiety? "No, production required that we cut off communication once we both accepted our invitations here. I hate it. It's been months. I miss my friend."

Bridgette claps and turns toward the camera. "Well, Ariana is not going to have to miss him for much longer! Tomorrow, she'll head into the house and meet the man behind the screen." She turns to me with a dazzling white smile on her face. "Are you ready, Onion?"

Hearing my screen name from her makes my stomach do a flip.

If I needed any proof that this is real, that's it.

Sax is here.

He's somewhere on this compound, waiting for me.

"I'm ready."

Chapter Five

TODAY IS THE DAY.

I'm going to meet Sax.

I'm going to be sick.

After puking up my guts, hair and makeup fixed me back up, and Drew came to collect me and take me to the house. He's quiet, almost somber, as he climbs into the golf cart to take me to the other side of the complex.

He pulls us into a spot in front of the house. "This is a good thing. I promise. It'll all be worth it."

I wrinkle my nose. "Why are you talking like I'm going to the gallows, Drew?"

"I'm not. I know you're scared, and I want you to know that things will be fine. It's going to work out between you and Sax."

"Have you met him?"

Drew ducks his head and rubs the back of his neck. He doesn't make eye contact with me. "I sat in on the interview with Bradley."

I want to grab him by the front of his stuffy polo and

demand that he tell me everything, but I don't. I'll find out for myself in just a few moments.

The *Expected* house is incredible, but I knew it would be. From the outside, it is unassuming, but inside, it's pure luxury. It has all the latest gadgets, some not yet released, is impeccably decorated, and is outfitted with cameras everywhere except the bathrooms. Drew shows me how I can turn off the bedroom cameras as he walks me through the house.

"But if you do, or if production thinks that something juicy happened off camera, there will be a mandatory interview the next morning to go over what happened while they were off. It's better to leave them on, if at all possible. The mics on them are sensitive, and there are more hidden around the house, so you won't need to be mic'd. Just remember, the crew has seen it all before. You don't need to worry about what they see. They'll edit out or censor the most salacious bits."

"I think I'll take the interview, thanks."

Not that I think Sax and I are going to fall right into bed with one another, but if the mood arises, I wouldn't say no.

Bridgette comes gliding into the living room with Bradley, her husband and cohost, beside her. This is the first time I've met him, since he was the one who interviewed Sax. He's just as beautiful as his wife, but his is manufactured, while hers feels natural. With his unnaturally tanned skin and bleached blond hair, he looks like every other reality television host.

"Are you excited, Ariana?" He adjusts his tie and beams at me. "This is the moment that will change your life."

"No pressure, then."

Bradley laughs heartily, clearly playing it up for the

cameras. They are always rolling in the house, and there is no telling what footage will make it into our episodes.

"In a few moments, we'll leave the house and send Sax in. After that, the doors will lock, and we'll be communicating with you via the televisions." Bradley points to a small camera mounted above the television. The TV is on, and the show's logo fills the screen. "Expect us to pop up every so often to update you on anything that you need to know over the week."

It's not enough that Sax and I will be getting to know each other in person, but the producers make a game of it. Over the next week, they will give us daily challenges tailored to our relationship.

I've seen everything from team-building exercises to trivia games. One time, they even hooked one party up to a lie detector when the other didn't believe a word they were saying.

We will get incentives for passing their challenges. Some of them don't seem like rewards to me, but we had to fill out a lot of forms about what we liked and disliked before filming, so they can make sure it's something we would want.

I have no idea where they come up with the challenge ideas, but I keep telling myself it's worth it to get to spend some time with Sax.

Bridgette gently touches my shoulder. "Ariana." Her smooth, kind voice interrupts my thoughts. "This is going to be a good thing, I just know it. Keep an open mind, okay?"

Why does everyone keep telling me it's going to be a good thing? Why would they assume I'd think it's not? Despite how difficult it was to leave my home and put myself at risk, finally meeting Sax is worth all the discomfort.

Chapter Five

I can do this.

I've done this.

I'm here.

I'm chewing on her words, trying to decide how I'm supposed to react to them, when Bradley angles his body toward a camera mounted on the front of the refrigerator. Odd place for a camera, but what do I know?

"We've got Ariana all settled here in the *Expected* house. Doesn't she look beautiful? Sax is going to be blown away." He winks dramatically at me before facing the fridge again. "And now, my beautiful wife and I are going to send in Sax. Ariana, I hope this is everything that you expected."

My heart beats loudly in my chest as I watch them leave out the front door. The sound it makes as it closes is deafening in the tense silence.

That door is where he's going to come in. That plain wooden door with the golden knob. It's going to open up, and he's going to cross the threshold, and my life is going to change forever.

Do I wait here and watch him walk in? Is that weird?

Maybe I should sit on the couch and pose myself beautifully, with this uncomfortable dress spread out around me. Or go into the bedroom, recline on the bed all sexy like, and have him find me.

Should I make a drink to offer him when he comes in? Have it in my hand like a vintage housewife?

No, Sax wouldn't want that. He knows who I am. He won't want me to pretend I'm anything I'm not.

I run my hands down the front of my dress, a knee-length A-line copper satin number that wardrobe shoved me into this morning. Apparently, the outfit I packed for this moment wasn't "dramatic" enough. It tucks in my waist and pushes my breasts up, giving an enviable silhouette.

I still look like myself, don't I? What if I don't? What if, God forbid, we get intimate, and he hates the way my body looks outside of this dress?

What if he isn't as attracted to me as I am to him?

He has to be at least a little attracted to me. All the sensuous phone calls during my heat couldn't have been faked.

I'm still standing in the middle of the room like an idiot when the front door opens. The sun momentarily blinds me, but when my vision adjusts, he's standing right there.

Sax is standing in front of me, haloed by the sunlight, every bit the person I expected him to be.

He's just as gorgeous as he was on my tiny phone screen. Tall, with a trim waist and broad shoulders. Classically handsome, with a strong nose and shy smile. He's the type of man people salivate over.

And I hope he wants me the way I want him.

He's taller than me, with blond hair that is neatly styled, longer on top and faded on the sides in a trendy, fresh cut, and slate grey eyes shimmer behind his glasses. They dressed him in an uncomfortable-looking pair of slacks and left the top two buttons of his collar undone, highlighting sand-colored skin that I just know is soft. An unreadable expression flashes across his face as he stares at me from the doorway.

"Onion." It sounds like a prayer on his lips, and my throat immediately tightens. I didn't realize how much I needed this. How much I love him. "Hi."

"Hi." I don't know what else to say. I'm afraid that if I try, I'll devolve into relieved, desperate sobs at finally standing in front of him and scare him away.

We stare at each other for a moment in a heavy silence. My heart is skipping in my chest, and I want to run to him,

Chapter Five

but I can't seem to make my legs move. They're heavy with the weight of this moment.

He takes a few steps forward, and several things happen at once.

The mouthwateringly sweet scent of fresh-baked pecan pie swirls around me, causing a whine to build in my throat and my panties to grow slick.

Oh, fuck.

No no no no no no no no.

This can't be happening.

This can't be happening.

Sax is my scent match.

My scent match.

I know that as surely as I know my own name.

And that isn't the scent of a Beta. It's too intense, the reaction it produces in me too primal.

He's an Alpha.

Sax is an Alpha.

And he lied to me this whole time.

Ten years down the drain. Ten years of lies and deception.

I take several steps back, tears threatening to spill down my cheeks, and his face falls.

"Onion, wait." I try to tune out his pleading tone as he takes another step toward me. "You have to let me explain." His pupils are blown wide, and I know my scent is having the same effect on him as his on me, even though it is no doubt sour with distress.

I can't think about that right now.

All I can think about is the fact that my worst fear has come to light.

The thing I have spent my adult life afraid of has happened, and it's all his fault.

The man I love, the one person who was always there for me, has ruined everything.

"You lied to me." It's a whimper that I once would have been embarrassed about. Not this time. "For ten years. You lied to me the entire time."

"I know, and I'm sorry but-"

I bite back a whine, choosing to turn my distress into fury. "But nothing! You agreed to this, knowing how scared I was of this exact situation happening." I turn to face one of the nearby cameras, a sneer on my face. "For the viewers at home, not only has Sax been lying to me about his designation, hiding the fact that he's an Alpha, which I guess you already know based on his interview, but he's my scent match. Which means without exposure to his pheromones for the *rest of my life*, I could die, just like my brother did."

He tries to say something, taking another step closer to me, but I don't let him. "I've cried to you about this more times than I can count. No one knows me as well as you do. Did you come here to embarrass me on national tv? Is this funny to you?"

"Of course it's not funny!" The distress in his voice does absolutely nothing to me. It does not make me want to curl up in his arms until he feels better. Not even a little bit. "But you have to understand, Onion."

I flinch back as if slapped.

How could this happen to me? I have hidden away for years to make sure this never happened, and the person I love most is the one who doomed me. My voice is high-pitched, veering on hysterical.

"You've ruined my life, Sax."

His face falls. Shoulders slump. His rich scent turns burnt and bitter.

Before he can say anything, the door behind him

Chapter Five

opens, and I breathe a sigh of relief. Bridgette and Bradley must be coming back to take me out of this living nightmare, even though my contract says they're not liable if I scent match someone during production of the show.

They knew he was an Alpha. They knew this could happen. And they let me do it for the ratings.

I'm a joke. Everyone is laughing at me.

I shouldn't have left my house. My fears were legitimate. Validated. I was right to be afraid of this, because the first time I leave my house in eight whole years, I scent match with an Alpha.

I don't have time to be smug in my validation, because when the door opens, it's not the beautiful Beta hosts.

Two gorgeous men file in and stand on either side of Sax.

An Alpha and a Beta, both of them with scents that make me feel lightheaded. Something floral, something spicy.

What is happening? Oh God, how could this happen?

Sax speaks as if he is afraid to spook me. "Onion. This is my pack. And… we're all Sax."

My vision darkens at the edges, and I get a glimpse of Sax, the first Sax, lunging for me before everything goes black.

Chapter Six

"IF YOU'RE a fan of the show, you know this is not a situation we've run into before." Bradley's voice is somber as he looks at the camera. "A pack masquerading as a single person. It's almost unbelievable."

Since I am the original Sax, the face of Onion's deception, I'm sitting in the middle of the couch, directly in front of the host, and my packmates are on either side of me. Grant sits on my left, his hand on my thigh reassuringly, and Ivan on my right.

"It hasn't always been this way." I know that, no matter what I say, some people will hate me. Hate us. Not that I blame them.

We will be villains in everyone's stories, including hers.

I have to hope that we can have a killer redemption arc.

"Onion and I met when we were teenagers, and I presented as an Alpha shortly after her brother died. I initially believed I would remain a Beta. My presentation was late. It was never my intention to deceive her, but my feelings were already so strong for her. She was terrified of

Alphas, and I panicked. I didn't want her to cut me out of her life, so I never told her when I presented."

Bradley crosses his arms over his chest. "And you never considered telling her the truth? That was only the first in a line of many deceptions."

"Of course, I considered it. I didn't enjoy lying to her. But every time I tried to broach the subject with her, she'd say something that reminded me that if she knew I was an Alpha, I wouldn't be in her life. She'd never forgive me for lying to her. And I... I couldn't lose her, Bradley. I know that sounds like a cop out, but it's the truth."

I'd sooner lose a limb than her.

He turns his attention to the guys. "Tell me how you two got involved."

"I met them at a party." Ivan flashes a dazzling smile at Bradley. "He and Grant stumbled into an Anything But Clothes party my fraternity was throwing, and the rest is history." My packmate leans forward, like he's confiding in Bradley. "Grant turned a beer box into a pair of boxers."

Bradley blinks a few times, clearly unsure how to respond to Ivan's revelation. After a moment, he presses on with the interview. "Most packs form around an Omega. But you three found one another and decided that you're going to be a pack, regardless of Omega input?"

"Our pack didn't need an Omega to form around, because they have me." Grant crosses his legs and rests his hands on his knees with a playful, flirty smile on his face.

Grant's a Beta and my partner. We're scent matches, something that's not common between an Alpha and a Beta, but not unheard of. He's also scent matched to Ivan, but his relationship with both of us is different.

I've been in love with Grant since the first time I saw him. My heart stopped, my knees went weak, and I was all in. He's the most beautiful man I've ever seen, and I need him in my life.

I don't know if he and Ivan will ever fall in love, but they're affectionate and close, and they are happy to share a bed. The three of us work. It's been natural and easy from the beginning.

"Is that so?" Bradley leans forward, as if he doesn't know all of this information from the massive questionnaire we answered when we signed up for the show. "What do you mean?"

"I'm scent matched to both of them. Lucky me, right? I mean, look at them. Pretty wild odds that we were all at the same college at the same time, but fate was obviously shining down on me." He rests his head on my shoulder. "We knew that the three of us were meant to be a pack."

"How did you go from being a scent matched pack to all of you being involved with Onion?"

"Derrick talked about her nonstop." Ivan nudges me and waggles his eyebrows. He's in a pair of tight jeans with a sweater vest over his bare chest. His arms are well-defined, and his stomach is soft. A dad bod without having to have kids. He's handsome as hell, with a killer beard, and the hair and makeup crew had a field day over how nice his skin is. "He'd show us pictures, we'd overhear them having calls, and I felt the pull to her. I know Grant did, too. She felt important. Inevitable."

They wanted me to introduce them to her. But how could I explain my connection to them when she thought I was a Beta?

"So you decided, as a pack, to pretend to be one person?" Bradley does not seem nearly as friendly as he did at the beginning of this conversation. Not that I blame him. "I must say, this is one of the most devastating lies we've seen on our show. Onion has shared her story and her fears with us, and you are her actual nightmare. A pack of Alphas-"

"I'm a Beta."

Bradley glares at Grant for interrupting. "Two Alphas and a Beta who have been lying to her for what, seven years? Eight? That's not counting the two years that you hid your designation, before the others came along, Derrick. And now she is going to walk into a house and have all of the fears she's struggled with realized."

"Then why invite us here at all? You knew exactly who we were when you flew us out here! We were honest and clear during our interviews." I stand, angry at him for hitting my insecurity about this decision on the head. "Do not act so high and mighty when you're using Onion's fears for profit."

I expect the director to call "cut." I expect the crew to escort us out.

That doesn't happen.

Bradley takes several deep breaths before settling back in his chair.

"We invited you here because, despite everything, you all seem to truly care for her. Onion deserves to know the truth so she can decide how she is going to live the rest of her life."

Onion left her house for the first time in years to meet us. I know how hard that must have been for her, and she will hate me for what I've done, but I cannot bring myself to regret agreeing to this. The only way I'm going to get her to listen to me is by locking her in a house with me.

I've thought about meeting her so many times over the years, but I knew, once she did, she'd run. And I'd never see her again. I have to hope the time in the *Expected* house will be enough to get her to forgive me.

My pack was pulled together for a reason, and I know,

in my gut, that she is it. If I tried to explain it, I'd sound like I'd lost my mind, knowing that she was my scent match through a computer screen, but I do.

There's no other explanation for the way she makes me feel.

Which makes what I'm doing that much worse.

I haven't shared that with the guys because if it's not true, I think they would be devastated. They love her just as much as I do, and it doesn't matter if she's not a scent match. Onion is it for us. We've never even looked at another Omega.

"I do wish you four luck," Bradley says genuinely. "I want this to work out for all of you."

Me too, Bradley.

Me too.

"BREATHE, ALPHA." Grant takes my face in his hands, gently stroking my cheekbones. His soft, floral scent does little to calm my heart, which feels as if it's going to beat out of my chest. "Onion's on the other side of that door, waiting for you. It's here. It's real. We're going to get to hold her. To tell her how we feel."

A decade under her influence.

Onion is in that house, talking to Bradley and Bridgette right now.

I am seconds away from finally meeting the Omega of my dreams.

The sound of a door closing precedes Bradley and Bridgette coming around the corner, the latter looking at us with soft eyes.

Chapter Six

"She is waiting for you, boys. Derrick, you go in first. We'll hold these two back for a minute to not overwhelm her with three people at once."

Even if they hadn't said that, I would've requested it. It's selfish, I know, but I want one moment with her where she doesn't hate my guts for the lies I've told her.

One perfect moment where she wants me like I want her.

Ivan grips my shoulder, nerves rendering him silent, and Grant gives me a soft kiss before patting me on the ass. "Go get our girl."

The journey to the door feels like a mile. I can't help but worry that I am walking into my execution.

When my eyes adjust to the lighting inside the *Expected* house, and Onion comes into view, I'm pretty sure my heart stops. Video calls did not do her justice.

She's wearing a pretty copper dress, and I have never seen her in one like this before. Maybe production put her in it because it shows off her mouth-watering body. I feel like I've been struck stupid staring at her, and I can't make my mouth work.

"Hi."

Her voice is a chorus of angels.

I've only said two words to her when all of my dreams come true.

A mouthwatering blend of fresh orange and sweet cream washes over me. It's perfect. She's perfect. The zing of citrus tempers the richness of the cream, and it makes me want to lick up the line of her throat to see if she tastes as good as she smells.

Mine hits her at the same time, and that's it.

My one moment, where I got to see just how much I mean to her in her gorgeous eyes, is over.

She's pissed, and she has every right to be, ranting at the cameras and yelling at me. I sit there and take it.

I deserve this and more.

"You've ruined my life, Sax."

I have, haven't I?

Selfish, selfish, selfish.

I don't have the time to apologize because the door opens behind me, and the guys file in. I can see the moment she realizes who all of us are to her, her pupils wide and her mouth a little slack.

"Onion. This is my pack. And… we're all Sax."

I wasn't expecting her to faint, but I should have been. I dive for her, catching her before she hits the ground and cradling her to my chest.

The first time I am holding Onion in my arms, and she's out cold.

"That went well." Ivan's voice is sarcastic and teasing as he crosses the room and flops onto the couch. "But damn, she is even prettier in person." He gazes at her longingly, like he wants to pull her from my arms. "And please tell me I'm not the only one who… she's mine, guys. Ours, right?"

"She is. She's our scent match." Even though she's pissed at us, and I know this is going to be an uphill battle, my heart is lighter than it has ever been.

Because I have Onion in my arms, and she's mine.

I was right.

Audience Reactions

EPISODE ONE

forbidden.fruit.princess > *Knot What You Expected*

OH MY GOD WHAT? THREE PEOPLE? I'm sorry, I can't. I'm obsessed. How could they talk for ten years and she not know??

tinyboats24 > *Knot What You Expected*

I would also pass out if three guys THAT hot came into my house ngl. Holy SHIT. 😳

stilllifewaiting > *Knot What You Expected*

Am I the only one pissed on Ariana's behalf? Like, this is her actual worst nightmare, and these guys just… set her up? They say they love her, but if you love someone, how can you do this to them? Why not just have the conversation with her? They had to do this on tv for everyone to see? ▶▶▶

grottocustombooks > *Knot What You Expected*

God, I remember when Calvin died. I loved his makeup tutorials. That was so, so sad. I've lost someone to FOS, so I totally understand why Onion has been so afraid, but maybe this will be good for her. These guys are her scent matches. She probably just needs a little push.

Knot What You Expected

EPISODE TWO

BRADLEY: WELCOME BACK TO *KNOT WHAT YOU EXPECTED*! WE LOVED SEEING THE CHATTER ON SOCIAL MEDIA ABOUT THE FIRST EPISODE. WE TOLD YOU THIS SEASON WOULD BE SOMETHING SPECIAL, DIDN'T WE?

BRIDGETTE: I DON'T KNOW ABOUT YOU, BRADLEY, BUT WHEN I FOUND OUT THAT SAX WAS THREE GUYS, EVEN *I* ALMOST PASSED OUT. I CANNOT IMAGINE HOW ARIANA FEELS.

BRADLEY: I BET IT FEELS A LOT LIKE BETRAYAL.

BRIDGETTE: I DON'T SEE IT BEING ANYTHING ELSE. AMERICA, WE LOVED READING YOUR REACTIONS TO THE FIRST EPISODE, SO KEEP THEM COMING. WE'LL BE READING SOME OF YOUR POSTS TO ONION AND ... PACK SAX? IS THAT WHAT WE SHOULD CALL THEM?

BRADLEY: PACK SAX. I LIKE IT.

BRIDGETTE: We'll be reading your reactions to them during the reunion episode at the end of the season, so don't forget to share your thoughts on tonight's episode, Onion, and Pack Sax using the hashtag "Knot What You Expected"!

BRADLEY: Now, let's see what's happening inside the *Expected* house.

Chapter Seven

β Grant
orchids

MY ALPHAS ARE SLACK-JAWED, staring at the beautiful Omega we have fantasized about for years. It is so surreal to think that not only is she here, in front of us, but she's our scent match.

Our beautiful, orange-scented Omega with silky hair and creamy, ivory skin.

She's perfect. Better than my dreams of her.

That has to be why all of us felt so drawn to her from the moment we "met" her, right?

She was always ours.

The television alerts with an aggressive chime, startling the shit out of me. Bradley's face fills the screen.

"We're sending medical in." He sounds pissed.

"No." I can count on one hand the times I've heard Derrick bark. It doesn't have much of an effect on Bradley through the cameras, but I wince. "She's not hurt, she's overwhelmed. The last thing she needs is more people in here."

Bradley does not look convinced. "She needs to be checked out."

"Look." Ivan's gaze is darting between the multiple visible cameras, as if he's trying to figure out how to look Bradley in the eye but can't decide which one to focus on. "She was overwhelmed by all of our scents at once. This isn't an illness, this is an Omega who needs her Alphas."

And her Beta, but sure.

I don't think either of them thinks I am any less than because I'm a Beta, but honestly, it's a little annoying sometimes to know that there are things I will not be able to do for Onion because I am a Beta and not an Alpha. The "not having a knot" thing doesn't bother me as much as not being able to purr for her, which neither of these dumb assholes is doing.

"Hey, Alphas. Why not try purring for your Omega?" I can't keep the smugness at the idea being mine out of my voice.

What would they do without me?

Derrick blinks at me with wide eyes before clearing his throat and forcing out a stuttering purr. It's a sound I've never heard from him before, and it's a little awkward, but he's making it work. Ivan's usually jovial face looks stricken dumb, but he reaches out a hand to touch her while the sweet sound spills out of him.

"Hey, Onion." I move around Derrick so I can sit by her head and stroke her hair from her face. "I know this is a lot. This isn't what you expected or what you wanted from this experience. I know that. But give us a chance, okay? You know us, even if right now we seem like strangers."

After a few minutes of purring, the video feed on the television shuts off, Bradley and the producers deciding that what we're doing right now is better TV than sending in some medics.

I may not be able to purr for her, but there is something only I can do right now. "She's not going to like waking up in your arms. We should take her to one of the bedrooms."

Derrick looks at me like I've slapped him. "I don't want to leave her alone!"

"She won't be alone. I'll stay with her."

"Why would you stay with her? She's going to be mad at you, too."

Alphas. So handsome, yet so dumb.

"Because I'm a Beta. She came here planning to meet Sax, whom she thought was a Beta. I am a third of Sax and a Beta." I stand and hold my arms out, making grabby hands toward the Omega. "I'll warm her up to the idea of you two. I'll be your fluffer. Come on, it makes the most sense. Give her here."

Ivan finally throws himself into the conversation. "That's actually a good idea. I feel like waking up surrounded by us will knock her right back out."

"Correct you are, Left Alpha. I guess even a broken clock is right twice a day."

Ivan rolls his chocolate brown eyes at the nickname. He became Left Alpha, Left, LA, about a year after we met, named so because he's never right.

God, I'm funny.

"Come on. I'll take her, you guys get our stuff put away, and start on lunch." I gently lift our Omega from Derrick's arms and turn to leave. Before I get too far, I glance at the two of them over my shoulder. "Actually, maybe make it brunch. With mimosas. I feel like we're all going to need a little liquid courage to get through the next conversation."

Onion fits perfectly in my arms. I've seen pictures, but I was never able to video chat with her, for obvious reasons, and still photos did not do her justice. She's a shade or two too pale, which is to be expected for someone who doesn't go outside, and her skin is so soft I want to rub myself against it like a cat. Her milky, sweet orange scent is mouthwatering.

She is perfection made flesh.

If she bonds me, how will her scent change mine? Like most Betas, my scent is muted—not as strong as that of an Alpha or an Omega—but I have never gotten a complaint about it. Derrick says I smell like an orchid, which, until I met him, I didn't even know had a scent. He was the first person to say anything more specific than, "sweet and floral."

Maybe that's how I knew he was mine.

When an Omega chooses to bond with an Alpha or Beta, their scent will adjust their bonded mate's slightly, a way of telling the world that this person is taken. It's a biological claim.

I set Onion on the bed before closing the door behind me, careful not to make too much noise and startle her awake. I sink onto the edge with a sigh. I knew this wasn't going to be easy. It was unrealistic to expect her to be thrilled about the revelation and jump into our arms.

But I didn't expect her to pass out from overwhelm.

I can hear my Alphas banging around in the kitchen as I adjust myself to stretch out beside our Omega, and wait for her to open her eyes, so I can see for myself just how green they are.

I'M A CREEP.

A big ol, grade-A, certified weirdo.

Chapter Seven

But I'm sure no one could blame me for holding my Omega's wrist up to my nose for going on an hour now. She smells so good. Like the one thing I wanted more than anything in this world has finally come to pass.

It's then, with my eyes closed in rapture at her sweet scent, my nose pressed tightly against her skin, that I hear my Omega's voice for the first time in person.

"What are you doing?"

My back goes rigid, and I drag my eyes to hers, her arm still firmly clutched between my fingers. Her eyes are tired, a little glassy, but the prettiest, pale green that I've ever seen.

She's beautiful.

"I'm Grant."

"Hi, Grant. What are you doing?"

"Uh. Smelling you?"

That sounds even creepier out loud than it did in my head.

"Can I have my arm back?"

I drop her wrist, and that movement seems to break the spell we were under, because she shuffles as far away from me as she can on the bed, her chest heaving. I can practically see the anxiety coming off of her in waves.

"Tell me that was a dream. Tell me that it's not true. Tell me you're not Sax. That all three of you aren't Sax."

She sounds desperate, her voice pleading as she begs me to lie to her.

For a brief moment, I consider having this conversation with everyone around. Opening the door and calling to my Alphas to come in here so we can work this all out right now. But I don't. I'm making the executive decision that this needs to come from me, and she needs to be able to process it on her own, without two anxious Alphas breathing down her neck.

"I'm sorry. We are Sax. And it was wrong to lie to you."

"You're a Beta." Her nose twitches, like she's registering my scent for the first time. I hope she likes it. "You're my scent match."

"I am. Both of those things. How does that make you feel?"

"I don't know. This is a lot. You're my scent match."

I'm letting her process things out loud, stating the obvious as she tries to make sense of what is happening around her, because I know she sometimes needs to ruminate before things start to click.

I know that because I know her. I've watched as grey bubble after grey bubble popped up on my screen as she typed out everything that she was thinking, trying to help her make sense of her racing thoughts.

I've listened to hours of voice memos as she repeats herself, going in circles, rambling, and asking for advice before settling on the correct answer on her own.

I know all of this, and I don't know her name.

I know all of this, and she just learned mine.

It's starting to hit me how awful this situation is for all of us. Lying to Onion hurt her, but we're not getting out unscathed.

I'm in love with a woman who didn't know I existed. She doesn't know that I'm the one to whom she sent those late-night texts when she worried she was unlovable.

She doesn't know that it was me who cried with her when she watched a movie where the dog died.

She doesn't know that any of it was me.

She didn't even know I existed until I walked through that door.

I didn't realize how much it would hurt to love someone, to know someone, and yet be a stranger to them.

Chapter Eight

GRANT.

I don't even know the name of the man I knew as Sax, but I know the name of this Beta who had his nose buried on my wrist when I woke up.

Grant.

He's gorgeous. Ethereal. His hair is long, a blend of silver and lavender that waves around his face, perfectly highlighting his pinkish-ivory skin, and is immaculately styled in a blowout that brushes his collarbones. Somehow, I know that hair and makeup didn't style it like this. I bet he looks like this all the time. His outfit is like nothing I've ever seen on a man before, with billowing fabric draped across his frame in a way that enhances his trim figure but doesn't swallow it.

His honey-colored eyes are smudged with dark liner, and they're lined with tears.

Tears?

It's an unconscious decision for me to grab his hand, squeezing it in my own. "Are you okay?"

His face creases in a sad smile. "I should be asking you that. You're the one who passed out."

As soon as the words leave his pouty lips, my head throbs with my pulse. "Shit, I did pass out."

I look around my room for a bottle of water.

Wait. My room?

Looking at the room I'm in with a critical eye, I can see how the production crew has attempted to turn this bedroom into a replica of my own. Marlie must have sent them photos, because they got pretty damn close, even if it is missing my near-permanent clutter.

Is this their way of making sure I felt less unsettled? Because they knew who was going to walk through that door?

They knew.

Bradley and Bridgette knew.

Drew knew.

All those comments about how this was going to be a good thing suddenly make sense.

Fucking reality TV. Everyone knew, and they let me face the three of them without any preparation.

I know I'm not at home, but the familiar texture of the bedspread and the soft grey walls do more than I would've anticipated to calm me down. I can almost trick myself into believing that I'm home.

That I'm safe.

When my eyes land on Grant, the breath leaves my lungs.

He looks devastated.

His eyes are watery, but his makeup isn't running. He must have invested in the good waterproof stuff.

"I'm sorry." His voice is barely above a whisper as he fights to maintain his composure. "I'm sorry. This isn't about me and my feelings."

That gives me pause. "What do you mean?"

"We lied to you. We're the ones who deceived you. You're the only one allowed to be upset." He rubs his sternum over his billowy yellow shirt. "Ignore me."

I wish I could, but he's my scent match. I'm hard-wired to want to love and protect him.

The idea of a Beta scent match isn't as daunting as the two Alphas that wait for me on the other side of the door. I could never see Grant again without having to worry about getting FOS.

Except that the idea of not seeing him again is already making my stomach cramp.

"Maybe if you tell me what's bothering you, it'll help me process this whole situation better?"

"I don't deserve your kindness. You're the victim, here. My feelings don't matter right now. You're too fucking sweet, Onion."

"Ariana." My name leaves my mouth in a rush. "I don't want any of you to call me *that* anymore."

He winces, my words a harsh reminder of the situation. "I understand."

Hearing my nickname from his lips, lips I've never seen, in a voice I've never heard, felt wrong—wrong wrong wrong. I could almost have convinced myself that he was just a random Beta before then. Could nearly bury what is happening right now in the sand and hope I forget where I put it.

But when he calls me Onion, it reminds me of why he knows that name.

They deceived me.

I can't believe I fell for the lies, and now all of America is going to see what a fool I am on television.

"I just realized how much it hurts that you don't know who I am." His voice is delicate, like he's afraid that it may shatter. "I know you, Ariana. I know you drink your coffee with one too many sugars and heavy cream instead of half-and-half. I know that what really scares you about the dark is that you think spiders are going to crawl into your mouth while you sleep, and how you, for some reason I'll never understand, sleep with one sock on. I know your heat lasts around four days, and that you hate pineapple on pizza. Which Ivan will tell you is the wrong opinion, by the way." He tilts his head back, staring at the ceiling, as if it is too hard to look at me right now.

"I know that you're probably compartmentalizing everything right now, and that if I weren't a Beta, you'd be hyperventilating. I know that, so that's why I am the one who volunteered to bring you in here. To give you space from them. I knew that you'd be most likely to talk to me, since I'm not Derrick and I'm not an Alpha."

"Which one is Derrick?"

"He's Sax. The… first Sax. The one you video called with."

"Ah."

I don't know how to respond to that. How to respond to anything he said.

Because he does know me. Everything he said is true. Sax knows all of that, which means they all had to be a part of talking to me, if he knows all those things about me.

He knows all of my secrets. Everything I told Sax, I was actually telling three men. All of my secrets, desires, and fears were not for two ears but six.

It finally catches up to me, the realization of what happened, and my heart stutters in my chest. I clutch at the front of my dress, pulling at it.

I can't breathe.

Chapter Eight

My chest is tight, and my head is spinning, and I can't breathe.

This isn't my room.

It looks like my room, but it's wrong, wrong, wrong.

I'm not at my house.

I'm not home, and I scent matched two Alphas.

Two Alphas and a Beta who were just supposed to be one Beta. One Beta that I've been talking to for a decade. Who has lied to me for a *decade*.

Grant is Sax, but he isn't. Not really.

Wrong, wrong, wrong.

I can't breathe.

I can't do this.

I'm in love with Sax. I was going to tell him. I was going to confess my love, and we'd be happy together.

But I can't.

But who am I in love with?

I don't know who Sax is. How am I in love with someone who doesn't exist?

I tear at the neckline of my dress, tears running down my face as I try and fail to get it off, to give myself the chance to breathe because I can't.

Sax isn't real, and I'm not at my house, and this dress is too tight, and I can't fucking breathe.

I can't do this.

I can't be here.

I should never have left my house.

"I need to go home. I need to go home." I stand, turning to one of the cameras Drew pointed out to me this morning. "Please, please, I need to go home. Bridgette. Bridgette, I know you're listening. Please, let me out. I can't do this. I can't be here. I need to be home. I need to be home."

The TV that sits across from the bed flickers on with a soft chime, and Bridgette's beautiful face fills it.

"Ariana, dear, we're going to send the medics in, okay?"

"I don't need a fucking medic! I need to go home!" I continue to pull at my dress as I stare at the television. I know Grant has backed up against the wall, unsure what to do, but I can't look at him. I can't look at him and be reminded of the fact that I'm in love with someone who doesn't exist.

Sax isn't real.

This was all a game to them.

"I need to go home. I can't be here with them. I thought I could do this, but I can't. I need to go home. It's too much. I never should have come here. It's not safe. I knew it wasn't and I came anyway. I need to go home. Please, Bridgette. Please. I just want to go home."

Drew pushes into the frame beside the host. His eyes are soft, fatherly, as he looks at me.

Is he even looking at me? He's not, not really. He's staring at a camera, knowing I'm seeing him.

"Ariana, I'm so sorry. You can't go home. You signed a contract."

"Fuck the contract!"

"It has a damages clause. You backing out now will cost the production company a shit ton of money. If you back out, you'll owe them millions."

His words hit me square in the chest, and I stumble back and sink onto the bed.

I'm stuck. Trapped here.

I can't afford to buy out this contract.

"I want to go home." It's a whimper, a plea that I know won't be answered. "Please. Don't make me do this. I need to go home."

Chapter Eight

Unfamiliar hands clutch at my shoulders, and though I shouldn't, I melt into the touch.

"Ariana." Grant's voice is wobbly with emotion that he is borrowing from me.

What does he have to be upset about? He got what he wanted, right? A joke on the silly Omega. The foolish, terrified Omega, who couldn't leave her house, is now having a panic attack in front of the cameras.

"Don't. Don't touch me. I can't be here. I can't do this."

"You can." His grip is gentle but sturdy, and he moves into my field of vision. "I know you can. You've always been stronger than you think you are. Remember when your groceries were left on the curb? You went out, and you got them. You were terrified, but you pushed past your fears and did it. Do you remember what I told you?"

I stare at him, mouth gaping like a fish. I remember that happening, of course, but having the memory attached to Grant, someone I don't know, is off-putting.

"I told you that sometimes a step can feel like a mile, and it's okay if it takes you some time to take them."

"That… that was you?"

The mantra I repeated to myself to get here was his?

Hurt flickers in his eyes before he looks away from me. "Yeah, that was me." After a moment, he kneels in front of me, hands slipping off my arms. "You took so many steps to get here, baby. It's okay to be worn out, it's okay to be scared. But you have already come this far. Look how strong you are. How brave. Don't turn around, or all those steps were for nothing."

My heavy, panicked breaths are the only sound in the room.

I can't do this.

I can't.

"Where are your anxiety meds? Are they in your bag?"

"Yeah, front pocket."

I watch as Grant rustles around in my duffel bag. I know nothing about him, and yet he feels familiar. He called me 'baby,' like he's done a hundred times before, and he knows me well enough to find my meds for me.

Who is he?

He is Sax, but he isn't.

Those late-night texts where I felt like the center of the universe. The three words we danced around for years but never said.

Were they his?

"Do you love me?"

My question shocks him so much that he drops the pill bottle.

"What?"

"Do you love me, Grant? You say you know me, and you say all these things that I recognize but sound so strange coming from your mouth. You know all of these things about me, but I know nothing about you. Nothing but your name and your scent. So tell me this one thing about you. Do you love me?"

He takes a few steps closer to me, gently grabbing my face with his soft hands. His slim chest is heaving, his eyes are shiny, and he looks at me like I am the answer to all of his problems. "Yes, Ariana. I love you. So fucking much."

Then he presses his lips to mine.

Chapter Nine

I SHOULD PULL AWAY.

I should put my hands on his chest and shove him to the floor for his impropriety.

Except.

I don't.

I should, but I don't.

I have fantasized about my first kiss for a long time. I always assumed it would be with Sax. I couldn't picture myself meeting anyone else and wanting to be intimate with them.

But Sax?

Yeah, I've had that daydream a time or two hundred.

It was the man Grant told me is actually named Derrick that I pictured, not him, but still.

My first kiss is Sax, even if he's not what I expected.

I'm kissing Sax.

Or, a part of him. A piece of the man I have loved since before I knew what love was. I don't know yet what piece Grant is of the Sax I have fallen for, but he is Sax.

His tongue strokes the seam of my lips, and I part them

hesitantly, tripping over the movements in my inexperience. He gently probes into my mouth, his tongue sweetly stroking mine as I gasp at the sensation.

After a painfully short kiss that still manages to weaken my knees, Grant pulls his soft lips from mine and swears under his breath.

"Derrick is going to kill me."

It takes a moment for my brain to come back online. Kissing Sax was nothing like I dreamed it would be, and yet it was everything I could have hoped for.

Until this moment.

Until I see the regret that paints over Grant's delicate, elven features.

"Why would he kill you?" My voice is small, but at least it escapes past the lump in my throat.

"He wanted your first kiss. He's going to be so pissed I stole it from him."

His words crash down around me, ruining every good feeling that kiss provoked.

"Stole it from him? As if it was his to give, and not mine?"

Grant realizes his mistake, and he starts to stumble over his words. "That's not what I meant. It's just because you have known him the longest, and he's the face you know, so it made the most sense…" His words trail off once he locks eyes with me.

"You all made a plan. And you deviated from it."

"When you say it like that, it sounds kind of gross." He ruffles the hair on the back of his head.

"It is gross. So tell me. What else is on this plan? Who is on deck to take my virginity? Just so that I don't ruin it more than I already have."

I'm more hurt than angry. They came onto this show, knowing they lied to me about so many things, knowing

Chapter Nine

how much I didn't want to be around Alphas, and yet they made plans about who would kiss me first?

Like it was a foregone conclusion that I was going to forgive them?

When a few moments have passed, and Grant hasn't answered me, I deflate. My hurt and anger have given way to resignation.

"Just leave, Grant. Go."

He shakes his head and his soft, floral scent, bitter from my rejection, almost slaps me in the face.

"No."

"I'm not going to argue with you. Leave me alone."

"And then what? What happens after I leave?"

"I get a moment to myself to grieve!" As soon as the words leave my lips, my chest starts to ache. I was barely holding back before, but now that I've said it, my heartbreak has flooded to the forefront. "Give me some time to fall apart. To mourn the relationship I came here expecting to find. My life has changed forever. Not only is my best friend, the man I was in love with, three men, but they're my scent matches. I will have to be around your pack for the *rest of my life*."

I dash the tears off my cheeks with my hands. "So, you'll have to forgive me for wanting to fall apart on my own. The Ariana I was before I walked into this house has died, and she deserves a funeral."

Grant's face is stricken as he processes what I've said, and I don't give him time to respond. I close myself in the en-suite bathroom, knowing that here I am free from the all-seeing eye of the producers.

I slide to the floor, my back against the door, and cry.

I cry for sixteen-year-old Ariana, who has just lost her brother.

I cry for eighteen-year-old Ariana, who realized she was in love with her best friend and never told him.

I cry for twenty-year-old Ariana, who couldn't leave her home without extreme panic attacks.

And I cry for twenty-six-year-old Ariana, who shoved her fears down to put herself out there and meet her best friend, and found three men in his place.

I want to talk to Marlie. I wish I could tell her what has happened, curse her out for putting me on this show to begin with.

If I had my computer, I'd be searching up Forsaken Omega Syndrome, as if I haven't read every research paper on the subject already, trying to figure out how long I have.

Until the sickness kicks in.

Until my choices are taken from me.

Can a brief exposure be enough to trigger the disease if it isn't repeated? Could I leave now and be okay without seeing them again?

There was a small study done on people who presented with symptoms of FOS who, to their knowledge, had never met their scent matches. All of them had been on heavy suppressants for a while, though, so that was more than likely the cause of their suffering.

It's not that FOS is always a death sentence, but it's hard to see it as anything but after what happened to Calvin. It can be treated with pheromone infusions from scent-matched Alphas, if they're available. While that may sound like an impossible task for someone who has never met their scent match or lost them, there is a pheromone donation system, similar to blood donation, that can help with some milder cases, provided they are compatible enough.

Not that they helped Calvin.

Chapter Nine

We tried everything—even experimental research trials.

None of it worked.

I never told my mom this, but he didn't want to live anymore. He lost his entire pack. The men he loved. Why would he want to continue living without them?

He gave up on his body, so it gave up on him.

Maybe I could get the guys to regularly donate pheromones so I could get infusions without having to see them. That's the best-case scenario at this point.

Of course, my hindbrain is reeling, telling me that they're my Alphas, and I should give them a chance. That I already love Sax, so it would be easy to love them, too.

And maybe, if they had told me the truth over video call, I could have given them a chance. I could have at least heard them out.

But they knew my biggest fear, my deepest hurt, the event that shaped my entire life, and decided that it would be a good idea to have me face it on television. In front of however many people are on the *Expected* crew supervising, and the entire fucking country when this episode airs.

How can I ever forgive them for that?

There is no moving past this.

Sax knows me. Or should know me. It couldn't be a shock to them that this has broken me. I was holding onto the fact that I would be in Sax's arms right now as a way of ignoring that I was being exposed to Alphas on set, that I was away from my home, from my things, my comfort, and now I don't even get that.

I can't let Sax hold me, because how can I be held by someone who doesn't exist? By three men who lied to me?

How can I let myself be vulnerable to people who have heard my darkest secrets while concealing everything about themselves?

No, there is no moving past this.

I can't afford to break the contract, so I'll stay here for the week. I'll stay as far away from them as I can, then we'll go our separate ways.

And I won't get sick.

I won't.

I'll reduce my contact with them so much that there will hardly be any Alpha pheromones for my body to cling to.

I'll be okay.

I'll be okay.

I can do this.

This won't be the biggest mistake of my life. This won't ruin my life.

One week won't kill me.

Chapter Ten

α Ivan
pumpkin bread

"GET AWAY FROM THERE, you idiot. What if she opens the door and you're creeping on her? What would she think?" Derrick grabs me by the collar of my shirt and hauls me away from the door that's separating me from my Omega.

"She's crying!" I try, and fail, to wiggle from his grip. "And yelling."

He pushes me onto the couch and frowns at me. "Do you trust our Beta to take care of her or not?"

"Of course I do! But that doesn't mean she won't need us. I want to be the one in there smoothing her hair and wiping her tears."

Smoke starts to fill the space, and Derrick swears, running back to the stove. He's on his third batch of eggs, each one more burnt than the last.

He's a hopeless cook, always has been, but he's trying. Normally, I'm the chef of the pack, but he wanted to do this. I know he wants to impress Onion, especially since we got off on the wrong foot - eh, feet, and all.

"This is a delicate situation. We knew that going into

this. We knew that she'd be hurt, scared, and feel betrayed." He tosses the eggs into the garbage can and starts rifling through the fridge.

"Which is why I said we shouldn't do this. I said we should tell her over a video call so she could have a bit of time to come to terms with all of this."

"And we agreed that she'd never speak to us again if we told her like that. There would be nothing stopping her from blocking our number and forgetting we ever existed. We didn't even know her name. How would we have tracked her down if that happened? This was the best option to get her to give us a chance to explain." Derrick has always been the most level-headed of the three of us, and it's no surprise that he's not rising to my challenge.

When we received the producers' message saying Onion had applied and wanted to meet with us, it was a shock. We knew she watched the show, but the fact that she was willing to leave her home for this?

We couldn't give up this opportunity when she had gathered the courage put herself out there.

Before Derrick can snark something else, Grant appears in the doorway of the bedroom, looking worn out and devastated. His shoulders are slumped forward as he curls around himself.

"Alphas." His voice is cracked and bleeding, and emotion seeps from every letter he speaks. "I messed up."

Derrick has Grant in his arms faster than I can blink, whisking him to the living room and squeezing him onto the couch between us. I rub my hand down his arm to soothe his frayed nerves.

"What happened?" I don't think I want to know, but I can't stop myself from asking.

"What didn't happen? She begged to end the show, she

told me we've ruined her life, I kissed her, she locked herself in the bathroom…"

"Hold on." Derrick cuts our Beta off. "You kissed her?"

"She asked me if I loved her! I wasn't going to tell her yes and not kiss her." Grant crosses his arms over his chest and stares at Derrick, daring him to say something. "And don't think about getting on my case about it. She handed me my ass already."

Sometimes it's easy to forget that Derrick and Grant haven't been together for their entire lives. They fight like an old married couple sometimes.

Being scent matched to a Beta isn't what I thought it would be. I assumed I'd fall in love with my scent matches, but it's not like that between Grant and me. Not that we haven't tried. We've both left our hearts open to more, just in case. Currently, our relationship is more like close friends with benefits. We'll hook up when we're in the mood, and sometimes Derrick will join, sometimes he won't.

Honestly, it's one of the easiest relationships I've ever had in my life. Grant just gets me. He always has.

"She's in the bathroom, crying. I couldn't listen to it anymore. It was too painful." Grant weaves his fingers through mine and Derrick's. "We fucked up, guys. This was not the way to do this."

"Well, we can't take it back." Derrick jostles Grant a bit, shuffling our Beta halfway onto his lap before continuing. "We have to convince her to get to know us as individuals. So she can see that we're not strangers. She knows things about each of us. She needs to be able to attach memories of Sax to us as individuals."

"You act like it's one of those charts from grade school, where you draw a line to the associated object. What are those things called?" I wrack my brain, but come up empty.

"Not important. It's not as simple as matching up traits to our faces. She's gonna feel vulnerable because we know so much about her, and she doesn't know shit all about us."

I know that it's me who got into a car wreck and don't like driving anymore, but she doesn't know that. She knows that happened to Sax, but she's going to have a hard time connecting the things she learned about Sax to each of us.

The idea hits me all at once. "What if we start over?"

"Start over?" Derrick's confusion is reflected on Grant's face.

"Yeah. Let's not try to remind her of all the things she knows about *Sax*, because Sax is gone. The Sax she knew doesn't exist anymore, now that she knows he's not one dude or a Beta. And everything she knows about Sax isn't just you, Derrick. It's all of us. So rather than trying to convince her that she knows us, let's date her. Court her. Let her get to know us without the pressure of Sax and Onion weighing on us."

Derrick clicks his tongue as he thinks. Grant has calmed down after contact with both of us and has wiggled off the couch. He heads to the kitchen and grabs several beers from the fridge. When our packmate questions his choice with a raised eyebrow, our Beta shrugs and cracks open his can.

"We're locked in a house for a week. I don't think the time I start drinking matters, especially since I'm not getting my mimosa brunch."

"So, what, we ask her on a date?" Derrick stares at the room where Onion has locked herself away. "Just go knock on the door, say 'Let's start over'?"

I shrug. "Why not? She's literally in a bathroom, crying. It can't get much worse."

Before they can stop me, I slip out of the living room and into the one where Onion is. The sheets on the bed are slightly rumpled, but it's the soft, hiccuping cries from the closed door on the left side of the room that catch my attention.

I rap on the door softly with my knuckle.

"Hi." I slide to the floor and press my back against the door. "I'm Ivan. I was wondering if you'd be willing to let me take you on a date?"

Silence answers me, but I suppose it's better than the crying.

"I know we don't know each other, not really. And all of this isn't what you expected when deciding to come on this show. I guess that's why the show is called that, huh? I bet this season is going to have great ratings, being as this is going to be the biggest reveal ever on it." I'm rambling, I know, but I struggle with the need to fill dead air constantly. Especially considering she's not yelling at me to leave or asking me to shut up.

I'll talk until she asks me to stop.

"Anyway, I'm Ivan. I'm twenty-eight, and an Alpha, but you knew that already, and you hate it. Sorry about that. If it makes you feel any better, I'm not too keen on being an Alpha myself. It's a hassle on the best of days. Not to be all TMI with you, but holy shit, do you know how annoying going into a rut is? I guess you do, heat isn't much different, but like you don't want to murder people when you're in heat, do you? I mean, not that I'd blame you, that shit seems like it *hurts*."

A soft chuckle rewards my rambling, and I'm going to be insufferable about it.

I got her to *laugh*. She's crying on the bathroom floor, and I, Ivan Miller, got her to laugh.

Yeah, I'm going to be riding this high for a long time.

"I once beat the shit out of Derrick while in a rut. I don't know if you know that's his name. He's the other

Alpha. I don't even remember what triggered the rut, but I felt so bad when I came to. I mean, not too bad, because the dude can be a bit of a dick if I'm honest. It's not that he's an asshole or anything by nature, but he's 'pragmatic', which on the surface seems like a good thing, but sometimes you need someone to listen to you, not to solve shit, you know?"

"Yeah." Her voice is soft and shaky, and if I weren't on the floor, I'd have hit my knees at that single syllable. "Solutions are good, but there are times when it's just nice to be heard."

"Exactly! You get it. You know, I'm a great listener. Heard it my entire life." I raise my voice in an imitation of my mother's, knowing she's going to want to slap me upside the head when she watches this episode. "'He was such a sweet, observant child, my Ivan.' I was always a pleasure to have in class because I did everything my teachers told me to do. So uh. Is there anything you'd like me to listen to? We've just established that I'm excellent at it. May as well put me to good use."

It takes a few minutes, but eventually, I see a shadow shift under the door. I picture her turning to her side, leaning her shoulder against the wood. I mirror the pose to feel closer to her.

"I didn't sign up for this show. Marlie did it on my behalf." Marlie. Her best friend from school. I've seen pictures of them together. She's a pretty Omega, but does not hold a candle to mine. "I didn't want to do it. I almost backed out so many times. But Sax accepted, and I let myself get excited about finally meeting him. It was fucking terrifying getting here. I hated it. I still hate it. This place is all wrong, and I feel like a ticking time bomb now. And I don't know what to do, Ivan. I love Sax. Loved? I have no idea if I should talk about him in the present or past tense, because the Sax I know doesn't exist. Not in the way I thought he did."

"I can see how that would get confusing. I would say past tense? Since the Sax you knew is never coming back?"

Oops, I offered a solution. I wasn't supposed to do that. She doesn't seem to mind.

"Yeah, that makes sense. I loved him. I never told him that. I didn't want to hold him back from finding his forever by putting the weight of my feelings on him, especially since we could never be together. I'm not that selfish. But I figured since he wanted to meet me, maybe he felt the same way. Sax was the only person I would do this for. I don't even go to my parents' house anymore, did you know that?"

I did, but I don't interrupt her to say that.

"So I did this big, massive thing that has me feeling like the world is falling out from under my feet. I told myself that it would be worth it because I'd have Sax. And now I don't. I did this scary thing that has me feeling unsettled and terrified, like I'm going to crawl out of my skin, and I don't even have my best friend to talk to about it. He's gone, and he's never coming back."

Her voice cracks, and I know she's crying again, but this is the kind of thing she needs to get out. She can't bottle these emotions up and expect everything to be okay.

"Want to know the stupidest thing, Ivan?" It's a rhetorical question that she doesn't give me time to answer. She barely takes a breath between words. "I want to call Sax. I want to call him, tell him everything, and ask for his advice on how to handle this, but I can't. I can't. Because he's the one who did this to me. I don't know what to do. I'm so fucking scared. I have spent my entire adult life worried I'd meet my scent match, and it happened, and I want to call Sax and ask for advice, but I can't."

"Why can't you?"

My stupid question flies out of my mouth before I can stop it.

"Are… what? You know why I can't."

"But what if you could? One last time? What if you talked to Sax one last time, got his advice, and told him goodbye? If you did that, if you got that closure, do you think you could maybe, possibly, want to meet my pack and me?"

She's quiet for an excruciatingly long amount of time. I'm trying to figure out how, if she wants to do this, I'm going to pull it off. Whatever I need to do, I will, because she deserves closure. She deserves the ability to say goodbye to Sax for real and start anew with us.

"Can I? Do you think I really could talk to him one last time?"

I push my fingers under the crack in the door, gently brushing hers. She snatches her hand back, but that's okay.

"Yeah, sweetie. I'll figure it out. I promise."

Chapter Eleven

I MIGRATE from the bathroom to the bedroom that looks eerily like mine after I'm sure Ivan is gone.

I'm getting hungry, but I don't want to go out there yet. Facing the three of them will make this real, and I want to give Ivan a chance to help me say goodbye to Sax, like he said he would. I don't know if it will help, but I don't think it could hurt.

The TV, which had been idle on a screen with the show's logo, pings and then flashes on about an hour after the Alpha leaves. Bridgette's face fills it.

"Hi, Ariana."

"Hey."

She smiles kindly while holding her hand to her chest. "This has been a wild day, to say the least. How are you holding up?"

"Uh, I'm not. I cried on the floor of the bathroom for like three hours."

"About that." Her eyes dart to the left, like she's looking at something off camera. "The producers have asked that you have any heart-to-heart conversations as you and Ivan did earlier outside of the bathroom. Because you were at the door, the mics were able to pick up most of what you said, but obviously, it's not going to be an ideal experience for our viewers at home. We may have to double-check with you before airing to ensure that the subtitles are correct."

"Oh, yes, cannot forget the viewing experience when my life is falling apart, and I am in actual, physical danger of dying from the same illness that took my brother. My bad, producers. I forgot that your bottom dollar is the most important thing. Gotta crank these numbers up."

"Ariana, that's not fair." Bridgette is right, of course. She's been nothing but kind to me, and I'm taking out my anger on her when she's not the one who lied to me for years. "We are concerned about your safety. We've already consulted with a physician who specializes in Forsaken Omega Syndrome. I know you signed the waiver that we're not liable in this situation, but we wanted to find out exactly what kind of risk we're looking at here."

I hate to admit it, but that's incredibly thoughtful of them. They knew what I was walking into, meeting with Alphas, and though they're legally in the clear, they still care enough to do what they can to make me comfortable.

"What did they say?"

She twirls her dark hair around her finger. "A lot of things. They're still doing some research, but the gist is that there's no hard-and-fast exposure threshold for triggering FOS. And just because Calvin died from it doesn't mean you'll develop it at all, much less such a severe case."

"But there is a genetic component to it. I did the research."

"We'll let you know when they get back to us with more information." She clears her throat and sits a little straighter. She flips her hair off her shoulders and plasters a broad smile on her face.

Oh.

They're not going to air any of that conversation. She just put on her TV face.

"Ariana, I have a phone call for you."

I blink slowly, the conversational switch giving me a bit of whiplash.

"I didn't think we could take calls from home?"

"The call is, as they say, coming from inside the house." She titters girlishly as I roll my eyes. "We have arranged for you to have a call with Sax, as you and Ivan discussed. Are you ready?"

Ready? Hell no, I'm not ready. But I can understand why this is happening so fast.

They want me out of this room. They need me to interact more with the guys. The first episode of *Expected* is always the interviews with the participants, the backstory, and it ends as soon as that door opens. So I'm living in episode two right now, and reality television won't work if I'm on the other side of the door.

"I suppose I have to be," I answer after a beat. "Video?"

I'm momentarily self-conscious about what I must look like after so much crying. It's not that I care what America is seeing, but I don't want Sax to see me so upset.

Especially not when he's the cause.

"Audio only, actually. I'll patch the call in now. Bye, Ariana. I hope you get the answers you need."

The TV flickers to an image of a phone, a sound wave hovering over it.

Then that familiar voice I love so much fills the room.

"Hi, Onion."

"Sax." Saying his name feels like a weight has been

lifted off my chest. I know, logically, that this voice is the man who first walked through that door and is just feet away, but still.

Something about being here, in this room that looks so much like mine, hearing his voice, is helping.

"Are you doing okay, honey? You sound stressed out."

His voice is a little strained, but that's okay. It's a strange situation.

"I am. I... we're not going to be able to talk anymore."

There's a quiet beat before he answers me. *"I know. I hate it. I'm sorry."* He sounds devastated, and the emotion choking his voice has tears running down my cheeks.

"I don't know what I'm going to do without you."

"You're incredible, Onion. There will be a learning curve to what comes next, but you've always been brilliant. You don't need me."

"I do. I do need you, Sax. I haven't been the same since I lost Calvin. Who am I going to be once you're gone, too?"

"Hey. Hey. You are more than your relationships, okay? You are not defined by the people around you. You were a whole person before you met me, and you'll still be one when I'm gone."

I brush the tears off my cheeks as I lie back on the bed, staring at the ceiling. "Yeah, sure. I'm so whole I cannot leave my house without devolving into panic."

"Where are you right now?"

"I'm in a room that looks surprisingly like mine."

"So, you're not at home."

"No, I mean-"

"And you're not hysterical. You're not a puddle of anxious Omega goo on the floor. You're upset, for sure, but you are not falling apart."

"My worst fear came to life, Sax. I scent matched a pack. Going back home isn't going to unring that bell, as much as I wish it would. I want to be home more than

Chapter Eleven

anything right now, but it's because I want to be home a week ago. I want to have never come on this show."

Sax doesn't say anything. The line is still, no sound bars moving with his breath or anything. When his voice comes back, it startles me a little in the quiet of the room.

"That sucks, Onion. I know that's your biggest fear. I'm sorry that you've been put in this position. I wish I could tell you what to do. I wish I could tell you to give the pack a chance, but I can't. This is your life. You get to make the decisions here, and anyone who takes those from you is an asshole."

I've never been great at making decisions. I would always bend over backward for what everyone else wanted, ignoring my own needs. I was born a people pleaser.

"Can I ask one thing, honey?"

I nod, forgetting that he can't see me. "Yeah."

"What would Calvin want you to do?"

I inhale sharply, clutching my gut like I was punched. "I don't…"

"I know. I know you don't want to think about that. But maybe it's time to open the letter?"

The letter.

The letter from Calvin's estate attorney that I received at the will reading.

The letter I have carried with me since I was sixteen.

It's beat up and crumbled from the years of handling, but I've never opened it. I've never been strong enough to read the last words I will ever have from my brother.

Once I read them, that's it. There will be nothing new from Calvin.

My brother will officially be gone.

"I can't."

"You can."

"Can you stay on the phone with me?"

He sighs, and I know what he's going to say. *"I don't*

think I can, Onion. I need you to know that I love you, okay? I should've told you sooner. I've meant every word I've said to you over the years. You have fundamentally changed me, and I will always love you, no matter what."

This is goodbye. I know it is.

It's not just goodbye to Sax, though. It's goodbye to the girl I used to be. To all of the plans I had to keep myself safe, and my heart intact.

"I love you too, Sax. Always."

The line goes dead.

A dreadful, pained sob escapes me, and I collapse into myself.

He's gone.

Sax is gone.

It takes a while before my sobbing calms enough to sit up. My body aches like I ran a marathon, but I know it's not over.

If I don't do this now, I never will.

Every step to my bag is harder than the one before it, my legs weighed down with the realization of what I have to do. I stare at the front pocket of the bag where I tucked Calvin's letter.

This is it.

This is the moment where the last new thing he will ever say to me is gone.

Everything from here on out will be in the past tense. Until now, I have clung to this letter as a way to keep him in the present and the future. Calvin still had things to say to me.

My hands are shaking as I smooth it onto the bedspread in front of me.

A sob bursts from my throat as I see the familiar handwriting.

My sweet Onion,

This fucking sucks.

I mean, I didn't think dying would be pleasant, but this is worse than I thought it would be. Maybe it wouldn't be so terrible if I had them by my side, but if I did, I wouldn't be in this situation, would I?

The hardest part is seeing how much this hurts you. Mom and the dads, too, of course, but you're so young. You have so much life left, and I'm not going to be there to see you live it. And that blows.

If I know you, and I do, because you're the other half of my soul, you're no longer sixteen. If I had to guess, I'd say you're nineteen? Twenty? I'm sure it took you some time to heal enough to be able to handle a letter from me. I hope you're reading this before it's too late. Before you miss your shot at happiness.

Meeting my pack was the best thing that ever happened to me. And I can say that, because I'm about to die, and nothing else is going to happen to me, so the votes have been tallied. I had a few incredible years with them. They loved me so much, so fiercely, that I forgot I ever once felt rejected.

All of those moments where I felt like I wasn't enough went away the first time we kissed. I knew. I knew when I saw them across the room that they were mine. I didn't have to catch their scent to tell me. My heart recognized theirs.

It wasn't easy. Even true love has its struggles. The Beast may have turned into a man, but he still doesn't have table manners. Even though we got into stupid arguments sometimes, and we had our struggles, there was honestly nothing that we couldn't work through when we were in each other's arms.

I know you think being an Omega sucks. I know that you're probably going to resent it, and maybe even me, because if I weren't an Omega, I'd still be alive right now. And you're not wrong to be upset. I'm sure seeing me like this has tainted your view of our designation. But I don't want your fear and anger to force you to forget all of the wonderful, beautiful things that have happened to me over my life because of my designation.

Look. I'm not going to tell you what to do, because there's no way I'll know, anyway. But if you could indulge me one more time and let me impart some brotherly wisdom to you, I'd appreciate it. Call it a dying man's last wish. (Did you laugh at that? Has enough time passed?)

Do not run away from love because of me. The idea that you'd give up on such a beautiful, fundamental joy of being human because of what is happening to me hurts. I don't want to be the reason why you don't take risks. I don't want to be your excuse for hiding. I don't want to be the ghost that haunts your footsteps.

I want to be the reason why you take a chance on something. I want to be the reason why you follow your heart. I want to be the reason why you trust yourself enough to fall in love.

Please? Don't let this be my legacy. Don't let my dying be the most memorable thing about me. Remember me as the man who loved his Alphas so much that he would, and did, follow them into another life.

I love you, Ariana. I will always be with you.

Calvin

PS. Please forgive me.

Chapter Twelve

THE TV HAS GONE IDLE, the screen taken up only by the show's logo.

That call was ... intense.

Grant is squeezing my hand so hard it hurts, and Ivan has buried his face in his hands.

I don't think Onion was the only one who needed this. I think we all did. Like it or not, all of our relationships, with her and each other, are going to change.

Gone are the days of us crowding on the couch and texting her together, coming up with responses as a group. Sure, we all had times where it was just us and Onion, but for some of the tougher things, we all weighed in.

Kind of like how we do when we need to come up with a solution to something that affects the pack. She just didn't know she was already a part of ours.

"Do you think that was the right thing to do?" Ivan's voice is filled with an unusual amount of hesitation. This phone call was his idea. I was surprised the producers went for it.

"It was a good idea." Grant rests his head on Ivan's

shoulder, his silvery hair falling into his face. My packmate looks down at our Beta with a fond smile that crinkles the corners of his rich brown eyes. "I'm glad you suggested it. Hopefully, it'll allow us to start over."

"Do you think she'll finally read the letter?"

When Onion told me about the letter, I encouraged her to read it immediately. She wasn't ready, so I dropped it, but every year, on the anniversary of her brother's death, we reminded her she had it and suggested she open it up.

I knew she was afraid to. The last words her brother will ever 'say' to her carry a weight that may be hard to adjust to once it's gone.

I hope she opened it up.

I hope she read it, and that whatever it said helped her in this moment. Maybe it eased some of her fears, or propped her up as she felt herself falling.

Ivan's stomach roars, and he clutches in typical Ivan dramatic fashion, sniffling away his emotions in an attempt to be funny. "I'm wasting away over here. What kind of food do they have in the fridge?"

"There's stuff for sandwiches." I wave toward the kitchen. "Why don't you make one for Onion, too? Even if she doesn't come out, we can set it by the door for when she's ready."

He bounds over the back of the couch like a child, crashing into the kitchen. I'm sure America is going to wonder if he's playing up for the camera, but he's not. He's clumsy, overexcited, and affectionate, like a puppy.

A big, handsome puppy.

I didn't think about it before now, but what if she's not attracted to us?

I don't know why I'm worrying about that, because it

doesn't matter if she's attracted to us if she never wants to see us again.

Grant cards his fingers through my hair, and I hum happily at the contact. "I love you."

His fingers stop moving, and he pecks me on the cheek. "I love you, too."

"I don't want you to feel… replaced. Or like how I feel about you is any less with Onion here."

"Ariana. She wants us to call her Ariana." He slips onto my lap, straddling me, and captures my cheeks with his hands. "Why would I ever think that? I love her just as much as you do. I know I'm not being replaced."

I rest my forehead on his, luxuriating in his sweet orchid scent. "I read online that some Betas feel neglected when an Omega enters the picture, especially during heats. I don't want you to feel that way. I want you to know that my feelings for you won't change. You are my Beta, and I need you."

He kisses me with a soft, delicate sweetness, the way he's done a thousand times before. "Alpha. I know that. I've known from the moment I met you that I wasn't the only person you loved. And I've always been okay with that. Are *you* okay with sharing her affections? Is it going to upset you if Ariana wants to be romantic with Ivan or me?"

"Of course not. You both love her as much as I do."

"See? Why would you assume that I'll feel slighted?"

"I don't know. I'm just…" I hold his hips, pulling him closer to me and resting my face on his slim chest. "I'm afraid that everything is going to fall apart. That there is no way I'm going to have everything, everyone. I'm owed some negative karma after lying to her for so long."

"Ah, I see. You're feeling guilty, and you're assuming the rest of us see you the way you see yourself."

Chapter Twelve

As always, Grant immediately latches onto the core of the issue.

I don't want to look in the mirror right now, because I know I won't like what I see. Ariana has been locked in a room for hours, and it's my fault.

Sure, Grant and Ivan helped me keep up the lie, but there were two years before they came into the picture, when it was only Onion and me.

I'm the one who decided to lie to her about my designation.

If I had told her I was an Alpha the moment I presented, would we be here? Would she have cut me out as soon as the words left my lips? Or would she have determined then that I was worth the risk?

I'll never know, but it doesn't stop me from ruminating on the what-ifs.

"Dinner is ready!" The clanking of dishes on a table and Ivan's words have Grant hopping off my lap and running toward our packmate. "I made sandwiches for all of us. Couldn't just feed myself and our girl."

Our girl.

I have to hold onto hope, no matter how blind it is, that she will be our girl one day.

The three of us spread out, like we've done hundreds of times before, and tuck into our sandwiches. We're joking around, chattering away about bullshit, when a soft voice interrupts us.

"Uh. Hi."

She's behind me.

Holy shit, she's behind me.

I stop breathing, and my body goes rigid. I don't know what to do or say, and my packmates seem to be similarly frozen.

"Guys? I'm not a dinosaur. I know you're there even if you're not moving."

Ivan is the first to recover. He jumps to his feet, holding out his hand like he's welcoming her to a business luncheon.

"I'm Ivan Miller. We talked through the door."

I peek over my shoulder and see a pretty flush stain on her cheeks.

"Ariana Cooley."

Oh, and it is a beautiful name. I roll it around on my tongue, speaking it silently, getting used to the way it feels. Hearing it from her is way different than hearing it from Grant.

"Are you hungry, sweetie? I'm not a chef or anything, but I make a mean turkey sandwich." Ivan gestures at the plate next to me, the one I have been studiously avoiding looking at. "The secret is two different kinds of mustard—plain yellow *and* dijon. Don't tell anyone, though."

Her eyes land on a camera in the corner of the room. "I think the secret's out, Ivan."

He blows a raspberry over his shoulder in the direction of the camera. "Well, maybe they'll edit it out to protect my trade secrets. Who knows how much of this they'll air?"

The chair beside me squeaks a little as she pulls it out. "Can I sit here?" I nod, speechless, as she lowers herself stiffly onto it and folds her hands on her lap.

I may have heard her voice just a little bit ago through the television, but here, beside me? It's the sweetest music in the world.

"I'm Derrick." I force myself to make eye contact with her, to watch the way her face transforms and flickers with her thoughts as she stares at me.

"Derrick." She says my name slowly, carefully. "It's nice to meet you."

She picks up her sandwich and takes a bite, and the silence around us is thick and uncomfortable. After a few moments, she clears her throat.

"Do you have the card?"

"What card?" Grant asks as he leans onto his elbows.

"Today's challenge. Did they send it in with you?"

Oh.

That card.

Amid the chaos, I forgot that we have actual challenges to complete while we're in here. One for each day, if their pattern holds up.

"Yeah, I have it." It's a bit crumpled from being shoved in my pocket, so I have to smooth it out on the table as I pull it from the envelope.

"Wait, that's it?" She's leaning around me, her shoulder nearly brushing mine, and my heart beats a desperate rhythm in my chest. She smells like summertime, like sweet treats and ice cream trucks. I want to touch her. I want to pull her close and bury my face in her neck.

But I don't.

I can't. Not yet. I can't scare her off by revealing how obsessed I am with her so soon.

"Looks like it. We just have to survive."

That's all it says.

"Survive?" Ivan snatches the paper from me. "Huh. It really does say we just have to survive. I guess they didn't expect this to go well."

"Well, they were right, weren't they?" Ariana's nose scrunches at Grant as she looks at him. He holds up his hands in defense. "You passed out. That's not exactly a smooth introduction, is it?"

Ivan huffs a small laugh. "I suppose not. But survive makes this sound dangerous and ominous."

"It is dangerous." Ariana's harsh words make my chest ache. "Maybe not for you three, but it is for me."

"We could Rot, you know?" I'm not arguing with her, per se. It's more of me challenging her. "Alphas without their Omegas can and do get the Rot all the time."

Alpha Rot is a chronic condition that Alphas can get without a bonded Omega. For some, it comes after their Omegas die, but for others, it sets in before they even meet their Omegas. Like Forsaken Omega Syndrome, it's not usually fatal, but it is a severe health condition that requires a lifetime of treatment. Eventually, an Alpha can lose the ability to produce pheromones, meaning they will not be able to scent match.

And if they can't scent match, they can't find their Omega, who can help their Rot go into remission.

"Except you won't die from Rot, will you?" Her words are bitter. "Not to downplay the seriousness of Rot, because I understand it's painful and can reduce an Alpha's lifespan, but it's not nearly as common as FOS, and it can go into remission. If FOS isn't caught early enough and treated…"

"Then the Omega dies," I finish for her.

"Then the Omega dies."

She pushes her plate across the table, the sandwich only half finished. It's impossible to miss the way her hands shake as she stands.

She looks so small. I never realized how short she is. We didn't share heights. It never felt relevant, but she's at least six inches shorter than I am. She's still wearing the copper dress production put her in, and though she looks gorgeous, I know she has to be uncomfortable.

"I'm going to go to bed."

Chapter Twelve

It's what I expected her to say. This has been a long day.

"Would you like turn down service?" Ivan jokes, standing and folding his arm like a butler holding a towel. "Or perhaps to schedule a wake-up call?"

Exhaustion draws her features down, and she doesn't seem to be able to muster up a smile.

"No thanks."

The door shutting behind her sounds like a gunshot in the quiet, and I can't help but wonder if it's a killing blow.

Audience Reactions

EPISODE TWO

Roz > *Knot What You Expected*

Okay, I cannot be the only one sobbing right now? 💔 The phone call saying goodbye? Oh my god. 🥲 That was so sweet. It's so obvious that they really do love her. I wish we knew what was in that letter, but I can understand why the show would keep that private.

…ladyjanemua… > *Knot What You Expected*

That dinner was SOOOOOO awkward. 😬 They need to have a proper date. Candles, low music, the whole nine yards. Let them take her on a date as if they met her at an Omega social!! Ariana deserves it!!!

slothieereads > *Knot What You Expected*

Yeah, they lied, but like. Think about the groveling they're going to have to do 😊 I love a man on his knees (in more ways than one)

lzleavemebehind > *Knot What You Expected*

Uh, is anyone else #teamIvan? Funny and sexy? If she doesn't want him, I'LL TAKE HIM. Gimmie that big boy.

Knot What You Expected

EPISODE THREE

BRADLEY: WHAT *WAS* IN THAT LETTER FROM CALVIN?

BRIDGETTE: WE DIDN'T EVEN ASK. ARIANA HELD ONTO THAT LETTER FOR TEN YEARS, AND IT WOULDN'T BE RIGHT TO SHARE IT WITH ALL OF OUR VIEWERS. ALL I KNOW IS THAT IT WAS PRECISELY WHAT SHE NEEDED.

BRADLEY: IT MUST HAVE BEEN, IF SHE JOINED THEM FOR DINNER. THOUGH I HAVE TO ADMIT, IT FELT A LOT MORE LIKE THE LAST SUPPER THAN THE FIRST.

BRIDGETTE: IT CERTAINLY WAS UNCOMFORTABLE. BUT THEY COMPLETED THEIR FIRST TASK. THEY SURVIVED THE DAY. LET'S SEE WHAT THE NEXT HAS IN STORE FOR THEM.

Chapter Thirteen

β Grant
orchids

I NEVER SLEEP WELL in a new location. Vacations are a special kind of hell for me, because it takes me three days to adjust to sleeping somewhere new, and then the vacation is over, and I have run myself ragged for a week.

Which is probably what's going to happen here.

I shared a bed with Derrick last night, hoping his familiar presence would help me sleep, but it didn't. He tossed and turned all night, making my night even worse than I anticipated. I can only hope Ivan and Ariana got some good sleep, otherwise we may end up at each other's throats today.

The television pings, switching to a live video stream. Bradley's face fills the screen, his almost too-white teeth flashing.

"Grant! Good morning! Where are the others?"

I glance at the clock on the top of the stove. "Uh. Sleeping? It's not even seven yet."

"Yes, well, the early bird catches the worm! Or, should I say, the early Beta?"

Why are the jokes TV hosts tell so bad? Do people

respond positively to them? I can't imagine they do. I don't think anyone is going on social media gushing about how funny Bradley is. Unfortunately, I have to smile and chuckle like he's the most clever man in the world.

"There is a delivery outside the door. Since you're the only one here, you can decide how to use it. Enjoy!"

His image fades as fast as it came.

I knew they'd bring us things throughout our stay here, but I wasn't expecting it at ass-o'clock in the morning. The door swings open easily, revealing a large, brown box. It's surprisingly heavy as I tote it inside and drop it on the table.

Part of me feels like I should wake everyone before I open it, but Bradley said I get to decide how we use it. Do I want to give up that opportunity?

No way.

I pull open the flaps and peek inside.

Spa supplies. Bath bombs and salts, massage oils, hair and face masks, and four fluffy white robes. On top of all of it is a small note from production.

READ THIS OUT LOUD:

"GOOD MORNING, PACK SAX AND ONION!

TODAY, WE CHALLENGE YOU TO RELAX. YESTERDAY WAS STRESSFUL FOR YOU ALL, SO WE THOUGHT YOU DESERVED A BREAK. TAKE SOME TIME TO BREATHE AND GET TO KNOW ONE ANOTHER. IF YOU COMPLETE THIS TASK AND USE ALL OF THE SUPPLIES OFFERED TO YOU, YOU'LL RECIEVE A REWARD THIS EVENING. AND TRUST US - YOU WANT THIS ONE.

There is a pack suite in the back of the apartment. I think you'll find the bed is perfectly sized for four.

Have a relaxing and restorative day!
   Bradley and Bridgette"

DO NOT READ OUT LOUD:
   There are no cameras in the bathroom, so try to limit your time in that room. All pack members who enter the bathroom must give an interview about what happened, per our off-camera rules.

A spa day? We have to convince Ariana to have a spa day with us?

No. No way.

That seems almost insensitive of the production crew to ask of us. I will look like nothing but a creep if I ask her to let me rub her down with this oil right now.

Unless…

Would she want to watch me massage Derrick or Ivan? Because I could do that. I do that all the time.

No. No. That's no better.

Is this what Bradley meant, that I get to decide? I could hide this from everyone and not give them the choice. Or I could suggest it, and we can decide as a group whether to make use of this stuff.

And how we would do that.

The door to Ariana's room opens before I can make up my mind, so I panic and shove the letter in the pocket of my joggers.

She seems surprised to see me here. Her brown hair is

sleep-rumpled and sticking up around her face, and she's wearing a cute pair of round, black glasses.

I didn't know she wore glasses. Did Derrick know that? They used to video call a lot at night, so he must have. How come he never told me how cute she looks in them?

My breath catches when I see the low-slung PJ pants she's wearing, showcasing the soft curve of her belly. She's wearing the tiniest tank top, which seems to have ridden up while she slept, and I cannot take my eyes off of her.

Or her one single sock.

"Holy shit!" She stumbles when she catches sight of me. "Oh my God, I forgot where I was."

"That's good, right? I mean, it's better than freaking out about not being at home?"

I don't know how she's going to feel about me bringing up something that Sax would know about her, but not Grant.

Maybe it's just because she's tired, but she doesn't seem to mind.

"They made the room look eerily similar to my bedroom. I guess it's helping, but it's still a little off-putting." She shuffles past me into the kitchen and starts making coffee.

One sugar too many, with heavy cream.

"Do you want yours with cream?" Her question is innocuous. She has no way of knowing that it's a bit of a kick to the chest.

"Ah, I'm lactose intolerant."

Her spoon clatters on the counter. When I turn, her knuckles are white from how she grips the edge of it. Her head hangs heavily, her shoulders slumped, and she keeps her back to me.

"Oh. Right. I thought-"

"Yeah. Derrick likes cream in his coffee."

How many times is this going to happen? Ivan had this grand idea that we start from scratch, but how is that possible when I know that she sleeps with a teddy bear that her brother gave her when she was nine, but she doesn't know that I'm the one who spent the entirety of ninth grade with half of my head buzzed because I thought it made me look edgy?

"How do you take your coffee, then?"

"I add a teaspoon of sugar and a pinch of cinnamon."

She rifles through the cabinets and comes out victorious, a glass jar clutched in her hand. "I can do that." After a few minutes, she hands me my mug and leans against the counter. "So Derrick likes his coffee with cream. How about Ivan?"

"Ivan drinks Turkish coffee." I take a sip from the warm mug and sigh happily. It's perfect.

Though I wouldn't tell her if it wasn't.

"I've never had that before."

"Don't let him hear you say that. He'll force you to drink so much of it that you'll be buzzing around the kitchen."

For a few minutes, it's easy to forget the pressure that hangs between us. She's my scent match. One in a billion. The perfect Omega for me. Most people, upon meeting their scent matches, fall into bed almost immediately. It's a primal draw, one that's hard to deny.

Except that can't be us. Not with the way things have gone for us thus far.

But I am fighting the urge to grab her by the hips and pull her flush against me. I know I shouldn't, so I won't, but her scent is going to my head. I want to grind my cock into her, sip from her lips, feel the way her body melts as I bring her to the brink over and over.

I want to worship her with my tongue. I want to kneel

Chapter Thirteen

at her altar and do my penance over and over until she is a sweaty, slick mess.

I want to give her all the things she fantasized about in the quiet of her room.

Oh, wonderful, I got myself all worked up. I've got to figure out a way to hide this raging hard-on from her before she writes me off as a gross pervert. The guy who sniffs her wrist and gets hard over coffee.

"What's in the box?" She moves out of the kitchen into the dining room, peering into it. "Spa stuff?"

Now's the time to decide. Should I tell her that having a spa day together is the day's challenge? Or do I let her believe it's just a gift, something for us to have? I don't want her to feel pressured to do something so intimate with us.

"Yeah, I guess production thought we'd want to have something relaxing after everything that happened yesterday."

Wait.

Wait.

Wait.

That's a lie.

I'm lying to her.

Again.

If she finds out, even if it's not until the show airs, it'll ruin everything that I'm trying to do. She will never trust me if she believes everything that comes out of my mouth is a lie.

"They said it's today's challenge. We have to use all of it, as a group, to get a reward." I take the letter from my pocket and hand it to her. "But I don't expect you to want to do something so intimate with us. I think it's shitty that the producers are asking that of us." I look up into the camera in the corner, scowling. "You hear me? You're asking her to put herself into a vulnerable position with us when she's not ready. Not cool."

She rests her hand on my shoulder. "Defending my honor?"

I place my hand over hers, squeezing it softly. "Always, baby."

Chapter Fourteen

THE PRODUCERS of *Knot What You Expected* spared no expense when setting up this house. This bed is a cloud—an absolute dream.

By the time I'm up and showered, it's nearly nine. Everyone else is in the living room, awkwardly silent. Ariana is curled up in the chair with her e-reader, her hair wet, but not dripping on the soft black sweater she's wearing.

Grant and Derrick are cuddled up on the couch, discussing the photoshoot Grant had to cancel to be on the show. I can tell Ariana is trying not to listen, but she keeps peeking out of the corner of her eye at the two of them.

We haven't discussed the fact that Grant is scent matched to us, have we?

Shit, we've not discussed anything. We need to do that. That's first date stuff, right?

I wonder why they're not trying to get to know her? Right now, there is a divide in the room, us versus her, Sax versus Onion. Someone needs to bridge the gap. How are we supposed to win her over if the guys won't even talk to her?

Must I do everything for this pack? I guess it's up to me to get this conversation rolling.

I'll get right on that as soon as I make some coffee.

The producers asked us for a list of things we needed for the week, and they supplied me with a cezve to make my coffee in. I was prepared to bring my own, but I'm glad I didn't have to. It was my grandmother's, and thinking about flying with it makes me a little nervous.

I'm stirring the coffee and sugar into the water as it boils over the stove when I feel a presence behind me.

"Is this how you make Turkish coffee?"

I need to play it cool. Not too giddy, or I'll scare her away. But the fact that she's showing interest in something so important to me is making it hard to keep my excitement under wraps.

"Yeah! You add the sugar in with the grounds and serve it unfiltered. It's a symbol of friendship and community, a way to come together. My grandmother used to say that there was nothing that couldn't be fixed over a cup of coffee." I glance over my shoulder with a soft smile. "Can I make you a cup?"

She sets her empty mug beside me on the counter. "I'd love to try it."

They have espresso cups on a rack on the counter, so I grab a few. "Guys?" I call over my shoulder. "Let's all have some coffee, yeah?"

Every time we need to discuss something as a pack, like when we decided to come on this show, I make us coffee, and we sit around the table to talk. There is something about the whole thing that encourages open communication and community, and it's precisely what we need right now.

Chapter Fourteen

I try not to watch like a creep while Ariana takes a sip of her coffee. I tried to make it a bit sweeter than I do for myself, because I know she doctors her coffee to the point where it is almost unrecognizable. She doesn't screw her face up, so I'm going to consider that a win.

"Ariana, did you know Grant is a model?" I gotta get the conversation rolling if we're going to get anywhere, and I'm assuming my packmates didn't give her any background.

"You make it sound more exciting than it is," Grant mutters. "It's not a big deal."

"How is telling her what you do making your job more exciting? It's a factual statement."

He turns his body toward Ariana. He's all done up today, his lavender hair perfectly framing his glowing face. He even put on a little mascara.

I see you, Grant. Trying to appeal to her feminine wiles. Well played.

"A local designer asked me to model his clothes. He's up-and-coming and trying to get into a few of the larger fashion shows. It's not like I'm in magazines or anything."

"Yet." He glares at me, and I wink at him over my cup.

"That's really cool. What do you do when you're not modeling?" She's got her body angled towards him, a clear sign of interest, even if she's not doing it purposefully.

I watched a lot of those body language videos online. Guess it's paying off.

"I'm a pharmaceutical sales rep. I don't love it, but the money is good, and I'm always meeting new people."

I shove my hand in the air, like I'm asking for permission to speak. "I am a very expensive pencil pusher for a cell phone company. Not the dream job, but I get to work from home, so it's awesome. And Derrick is a physical therapist, but you knew that already."

She winces a little. *What did I say?*

"Ah, I was wondering which of you…" Her words trail off, and she takes a small sip of coffee. "Anyway, I'm assuming that's how you met Derrick, at work?"

Grant shakes his head as he clutches his cup. "No, we met in college. We had a few of the same courses, and once we found out we were scent matches…"

Her cup clatters to the table. "Scent matches?"

Maybe we should have started with that.

"Yeah, uh. All of us? I mean, not Derrick and Ivan, obviously, but I'm scent matched to both of them." Grant rubs the back of his neck.

What if she's not okay with sharing her Alphas? It wasn't something she ever talked about, because she would never entertain the idea of being with an Alpha.

Is this going to be over before it starts? Asking Derrick and Grant to choose between her and one another would be not only cruel but also impossible. Not that I'm keen to give up Grant, either.

"So you're all together?"

Grant's voice is cautious. "Ivan and I aren't romantically together, but we're still… together together." *Polite way to avoid saying we fuck when we want to.* "I'm in love with Derrick. We've been in a relationship since we met."

She swings her head toward Derrick. "That's when you stopped texting, right? Freshman year of college." *I guess it's impossible to pretend like we have no history together, especially not the two of them. He had Onion to himself for two years before he met Grant, and they had her for a year before I came into the picture.*

Seven years.

I've known her for seven years, and she just learned my name.

Their relationship is going to be the hardest to repair,

Chapter Fourteen

because not only is he the face of our deception, but he's the one she fell in love with first. I fully believe she will realize she loves Grant and me, but it may take her a little longer.

"It felt wrong to continue talking to you like we were, when I was with Grant. Dishonest. But I missed you too much, and he encouraged me to get back in touch with you."

"Dishonest." The word echoes around us. "Right. Dishonest. Because you care *so* much about honesty." She pushes her coffee cup away and stands. "I'm glad you respect him more than you respect me."

"Wait. That's not-"

But she's gone before he can justify himself.

He slams his fist on the table. "Fuck! Fucking fuck." His face is lined with frustration and disappointment. This won't be our only setback, I know that, and what he needs right now is to know that all hope isn't lost.

"We're going to trip up. We have to keep being honest with her. It's all we can do."

Grant places his hand on Derrick's arm to settle him. "She's not wrong, though. You were honest with me, and had the chance to do the same with her, and didn't take it. You're not the only one at fault. We all agreed to do it and fed into the lie. But she's right to be upset about it. In a way, it makes the lie she was told worse. I bet it makes her feel like she's not on the same level as me. Like you care about me more."

"That's ridiculous. It's different, but no less."

"Don't tell me that!" Grant points at the room Ariana disappeared into. "Go tell her. I'm not the one you need to convince."

I clap my packmate on the back. "He's right, man. I think you two need to clear the air before we move forward. I thought we could start over, but I don't think that's gonna work, at least not with you two. There is too much history and hurt there." I clear everyone's cups before grabbing a bottle of water from the fridge. "Bring her this. Clear the air."

Chapter Fifteen

α Derrick
pecan pie

I WAS seventeen when I fell in love for the first time.

It wasn't "teenage love", even though we were teenagers.

And even if it were just teenage love, is there anything wrong with that?

The media tries to downplay the way teenagers feel for one another, as if the kind of hurt that results from it doesn't matter. At that age, emotions are cranked up to eleven, so when it falls apart, it feels like your life is ruined.

I was seventeen when I fell in love with words on a screen. Onion. I knew her as a screen name. Someone I argued with on public forums until we brought it to private messages, where the arguing gave way to meaningful conversation.

Which then became texting.

Phone calls.

Video calls.

Every piece of Onion I got made me crave her even more. There was no limit to my affection for her.

I presented as an Alpha a few months after her brother

died. She was still deep in her grief, and I truly believed that her fear and anger toward Alphas would lessen as time went on. It felt, at the time, that it was the right call to lie to her about it.

It wasn't supposed to be forever, just until she had healed enough for the truth of my designation not to sting as much.

I didn't want her to cut me out of her life. I loved her, and she needed me. She couldn't talk to her parents. They were grieving as well, and she refused to burden them.

Sometimes, it's easier to spill your guts out onto a keyboard than it is to hold someone's hand and flay yourself open. And when you're already held together with tape, it feels impossible to allow yourself that sort of vulnerability.

I wanted nothing more than to hold her every time she cried.

But I couldn't.

Her fear of Alphas worsened by the day. She attended virtual school after Calvin died to avoid Alpha exposure. When she opted out of attending college in person and chose to take only online classes, I worried I'd never have the chance to tell her the truth.

Then I met Grant.

How was I supposed to tell her I met my scent match? Betas don't match with other Betas, and so my options were to tell her I matched with an Omega, which would break her heart, or that I matched with an Alpha, and she'd leave me.

I'd never get the chance with her, because being with me meant proximity to an Alpha.

So I pulled away.

I thought I was doing right by both of us, but I wasn't. I

was miserable. Grant convinced me to start talking to her again, and he quickly became enamoured with her. He'd sit at my feet while I video called her, hanging onto her every word.

I was nineteen when I fell in love for the second time. With a beautiful Beta with soft skin and kind eyes, who wanted me to have the Omega of my dreams. Who wanted her just as much as I did, even though he had never spoken to her.

I don't think I could've fallen for him if I thought he wouldn't accept Onion. The first time I heard her voice, I knew she was mine.

And now I'm faced with the possibility that I have ruined everything.

I won't force her to be with me, Foresaken Omega Syndrome be damned. I will undergo a pheromone extraction every day for her if it means she can choose for herself.

I won't let her body force her into a decision she doesn't want to make.

The bottle of water sweats in my hands, making them clammy. I knock on the bedroom door several times, but only silence greets me.

"Ariana." I press my shoulder against the door. "It's Derrick. I know you hate me. I know I'm the last person you want to see and talk to right now. But please, let me in. Please. Please. Yell at me. Throw things at me. Scream. I will gladly take whatever you need to do to feel comfortable around me, but please let me in."

She's right here, on the other side of a panel of wood, and yet this is the farthest I've ever felt for her.

The door flies open, making me stumble and struggle to regain my balance.

My Omega stands before me with red cheeks and

furious eyes. "You want me to yell? You want me to throw things?"

"I don't *want* that. But I deserve it. I'll accept it."

"Oh, how noble of you."

I don't exactly force myself in, but now that the door is open, I'm not going to be on the other side of it, so I follow her as she strides away.

"I don't hate you, Derrick. Don't you get that? If I hated you, this would be easy. We'd stay here for a week and go our separate ways, and this nightmare would be over. But I don't hate you. How can I? How can I hate you when it's your face that I've pictured every night as I've fallen asleep for as long as I can remember?"

I close the door behind me, pressing my back against it as she paces around the space. I don't interrupt her. I couldn't, even if I wanted to. She's talking so fast that it's all I can do to keep up with her.

"I'm in love with you. Y'all? I don't know. That's what's frustrating! Who the fuck was I talking to? Was it mostly you, but sometimes them? Was it equal? Grant doesn't take cream in his coffee. That's you. Are you the one who is allergic to kiwi, or is that Ivan? Who was it that helped me prepare for job interviews? Who did I tell my secrets to? Who knows my fantasies?"

She collapses onto the bed and buries her face in her hands. I wish I could block her from the cameras. I wish we didn't have to have this conversation in front of an audience.

I should've told her the truth a long time ago.

I let this go on too long, and she's hurting all the more for it.

"I'm embarrassed, Derrick. Mortified. The whole world is about to know that I am a sucker. That I was terrified to leave my home for *years*. And I knew that in coming

Chapter Fifteen

here, my fears and faults would be made public, but it would be worth it if I finally got to meet you. You were going to be worth it. All of the risk, all of the fear, all the tears. It didn't matter because you were at the end of that road. Do you know how many Alphas I came in contact with before you walked through that door?"

She wipes tears away from her face. No one is a pretty crier, but Ariana looks breathtaking.

"Do you want to know what the worst part is? If you had told me the truth, that you're an Alpha, I probably still would have risked it for you. Instead, I've learned the intimacy we shared was a lie. That everything I ever told you became a topic of conversation at the dinner table!"

Her scent is sour with distress, and I am fighting my instincts not to gather her in my arms, bury her face in my neck, and purr for her.

But I can't. I know that. That is not a privilege I have earned. My arms ache to hold her, but I may never get that chance.

I lower myself onto the bed beside her. Not right next to her, but within touching distance. Close enough that I can whisper, in an attempt to keep microphones on the cameras from picking up what we say. I always thought that on shows like this, the people had to wear microphones, but we were told that they're hidden inconspicuously around the house, and the ones on the cameras are super sensitive.

This may not stay between us, but I'm praying it will.

"You were never idle gossip, Onion. You were our obsession. Our greatest desire. You were what drove us to do better, to be better. It got out of hand. I never should have let it go on so long. I should've told you the moment I met Grant and introduced you to him so you could fall in love with him the way I did. When Ivan came along, I should have let him video call you so you could see his smile, the way his eyes lit up when he heard you laugh."

It's killing me not to touch her. I want to hold her hand, to stroke the sensitive skin of her inner wrist. She's shifted toward me, almost closing the distance, and I worry that a wrong move will have her flying across the room.

"But I didn't share all of you. How could I, when you were whispering your darkest desires to me with your hand between your thighs? I was the one who talked you through it. Every. Fucking. Time. I would never have deceived you about that."

There were several times when she was in heat, Onion would call me while out of her mind with desire. I'd tell her everything I'd do to her if I were there. I'd listen to her fuck herself. I'd sit there with my cock about to rip through my pants, my knot sore and aching, and imagine what she tasted like. I'd lock myself in my room, unwilling to break her trust by involving the other two, and listen to her come over, and over, and over, until she passed out in a haze of heat.

She would always wake up mortified that she called me, and we'd pretend like it never happened. We'd go back to business as usual, as if I didn't know what she sounded like when she came. Ignoring how much we wanted each other.

Her chest hitches at my words, making her voice breathy. "That doesn't mean they don't know."

Deciding to risk her rejection and her anger, I gently kiss her shoulder, teasing my nose along the curve of her neck.

"You're right. They do know some of it. It wasn't always me you were texting. But they don't know what you sound like when you come. I do."

Her hand grips the front of my t-shirt, and I think she's

Chapter Fifteen

going to use it to shove me away, but instead she pulls me closer and crashes her lips to mine.

Kissing her is like coming home.

Every dream I had, every fantasy, pales in comparison to this.

To the unequitable rightness of this moment.

She's aggressive, nipping my lips and refusing to let me take control. It's a punishment of a kiss, and I will take my lashes every time if it means I get to feel her body pressed against mine.

"I never shared the photos," I whisper against her lips when she lets me up for air. "Those were only for me."

"You didn't have a knot." She grips me over my pants, right on top of my knot. "Was that Grant's cock?"

"All me, honey. Just with some clever angles, clothes, and hand placement." I chase her mouth with mine, savoring her gasp as I buck my hips into her hand.

Vaguely, in the back of my mind, I realize this is too fast. That she may hate me more than she already does if this goes further. That even if she doesn't, this won't fix the problems I caused.

But then she shoves me onto my back, swings a leg over my hips, and I lose all reasonable thought. My world begins and ends with the taste of her lips.

Chapter Sixteen

I'M KISSING SAX.

Holy shit, I'm kissing Sax.

Derrick.

I'm kissing Derrick.

His hands are on my hips. Large, strong hands that I've fantasized about for years, and I can feel the rapid rise and fall of his chest beneath my palms.

He thrusts up, grinding his cock against me, and I can feel the ridge of his knot. He's not supposed to have one, but he does, and I can't deny that it would feel incredible. I moan with desperate abandon into his mouth, needing him more than I can say.

I burn for him, ache for him, and I cannot wait any longer to have him. The need is too strong, the pull between us impossible to deny.

Did I imagine that our first time together would be in front of cameras, for the world to see? No, of course not. But I cannot find it in me to care now that I am in his arms.

Chapter Sixteen

Derrick grabs my face, angling me perfectly for his tongue to fuck into my mouth, and I melt against him.

My body burns for him. I can feel him everywhere.

He slips his hands down my neck, gently drags them over my breasts. I ache for him.

But the kiss feels like it's over just as it's beginning, and he pulls away. He looks up at me with wild eyes, swollen lips, and a heaving chest.

"We can't do this."

It takes a moment for the words to settle inside me, and once they do, I nearly fall to the ground in my haste to get off of him.

"Wait!" His voice is strained as he rolls off the bed onto the floor, kneeling in front of me as he grabs me by the hand. "Stop, honey. Wait."

I cannot speak. Words won't come when I try. I want him. I want him with every part of me, and he doesn't feel the same way.

What the hell was I thinking?

Of course, he doesn't want the stupid little Omega who couldn't get her groceries off the curb without help.

"Honey." The pet name makes my stomach cramp. How many times has he called me that over the years?

"Don't." Tears run down my face as the gravity of the situation hits me.

I met my scent match.

I met the man I have loved for a decade.

And he doesn't want me.

"Ariana, stop!"

The power of Derrick's bark washes over me, and I freeze in place A whine claws its way out of my throat.

He grabs my chin and forces me to look him in the eye. "I'm not rejecting you." Just the word makes me cry out, gasping an embarrassing sob. "I'm *not* rejecting you. You're burning up. I think you're having a heat spike, and I'm not going to take advantage of you."

There's no way. My heat isn't due for another two months. Filming was scheduled around it. They didn't want to start as soon as my heat was over, just in case I had some breakthrough spikes, but I'm in the clear. I'm regular. My heats have always been regular.

There's no way I'm having a heat spike.

"Your body temperature is elevated. Your scent is thicker, richer. You're needy. I bet you're cramping, too. You wouldn't want me if you weren't in a spike. I know you're not ready for that."

"Who are you to tell me what I'm ready for?" I yank out of his grasp, stumbling backward. "I shouldn't be surprised. You've already proven you'll make decisions for me. What's one more, right? This is just another situation where you think you know better than I do."

He swears under his breath and rubs his hands over his face. "No, Ariana. I'm trying to be a gentleman here. Do you not understand how hard this is for me? I'm in love with you. I have loved you for years. You're my scent match, and you're standing in front of me, slick and begging for me, and I have to push you away. I'm trying to be a good guy, because if I give you what you're asking for right now, if I fuck you right now, you will never forgive me. I want your bite. I want to be yours. That will never happen if you come out of this heat spike on my knot."

"You're not supposed to have a knot!" Tears run down my heated cheeks. I don't bother dashing them away.

Let him see the effects of what he did. Let him know how much he hurt me. I won't hide it from him.

"Too fucking bad, Ariana! I do. I have a knot, and I'm your scent match, and I'm Sax, and I lied to you, and it's all too fucking bad because this is our life now. You and I

Chapter Sixteen

have always been destined to be together, and no amount of hiding away is going to change that. You're scared, and you have every right to be. And you're mad, and I will never try to tell you you shouldn't be. But I'm trying here. I'm trying not to take advantage of you. I'm trying to make decisions that we can both live with when your base instincts no longer control you. I won't ruin this."

His sweet pecan scent is drowning me as his Alpha pheromones fill the space. I ache for him, my body screaming for a touch, a taste. But my mind is processing his words. I'm warring within myself, fighting against the parts of me that don't value logical thinking over instincts.

The door slams open as Ivan and Grant pile into the room.

Just what I need, more delicious scents going to my head. Grant's sweet, soft floral scent is nearly overpowered by the cozy, spicy aroma of pumpkin bread.

"What is - holy fuck." Grant's voice is pained as he stumbles toward me. "Baby, you smell like heaven."

So do they. I want to rip my clothes off and rub myself against them, covering them in my pheromones. I want to kiss Grant again, this time in a way I can appreciate more. I want to suck on his tongue, kiss down his throat, nibble his ears, and lick a stripe up the bottom of his cock.

I want to feel the chest hair that is poking out of the V of Ivan's shirt rub against my breasts and tickle my nipples as we fuck.

I want Derrick to impale me on his knot.

I'm starting not to care about the lies or the deception. Maybe I can forgive them if they fuck this pain away.

"She's having a heat spike." Derrick grabs his Beta and pulls him close, out of my reach. "She's upset. We need to find a way to bring her out of this."

He's talking about me like I'm not here.

Like I'm unreasonable.

Like I'm out of control.

Am I? I don't think I am.

Is wanting to be with my scent matches out of control? Isn't this how we're told it's supposed to be when we meet our scent matches?

"Why are you acting like I'm out of my mind with heat? I'm fine!"

Ivan clears his throat and chews on his lower lip. "Uh. Well. You're whining when you're not talking. And you look like you're in pain. Plus, you smell so good, I'm pretty sure I'm about to have a permanent imprint of my zipper on my dick. I don't think you're fine."

Now that Ivan has drawn attention to it, it's impossible to ignore.

He's right. Derrick is right.

I'm out of my mind.

I'm embarrassing myself. Once again, I am making a fool of myself for the world to see.

"I fucking hate it here." I push past them and crawl onto the bed and under the covers. "I hate this, I hate this. Because, of course, I needed more obstacles to overcome! More ways for America to watch and laugh at me. The pathetic, scared Omega goes into heat on TV."

"I'm going to go run you a bath." Grant reaches under the blanket and strokes my hair, sticky with sweat, off my forehead. "We've got all that spa stuff. Maybe that'll help."

I lean into his touch like a cat, purring with pleasure. It was a light graze, but it feels like heaven, and I chase the sensation. "Don't go. Don't leave me. Please."

He coos above me. "Okay, baby, I won't. Derrick and Ivan can draw you a bath. I'll wait here with you until it's ready. How does that sound?"

Grant was part of the conspiracy to deceive me, and

Chapter Sixteen

yet he feels safer than the others. I lean into his hand, the gentle pressure of it soothing my heated flesh.

Every part of me aches. I cannot remember a heat spike ever feeling like this.

The men are arguing. It doesn't sound like Derrick or Ivan wants to leave me, but Grant is insisting they both do. After several moments of back and forth, I hear their footfalls as they go.

I have so many questions I need answered, but right now, while my body is wracked with cramps and my thighs are slick with my need, they seem unimportant.

Chapter Seventeen

β Grant
orchids

IT DIDN'T TAKE LONG for Derrick and Ivan to set up the bath for Ariana. It took longer for me to coax her from the bed and to the bathroom of the pack suite.

"Let me help," I plead from outside the door. "I'll close my eyes. I'll be a consummate gentleman. No funny business."

Ivan scoffs at my words. "I make no promises."

I hear the sounds of her continued struggle to get out of her clothes, which are stuck to her sweat-drenched body. Every so often, she has to pause because of a painful cramp, and the whine that escapes her has me wincing.

This feels more intense than a run-of-the-mill heat spike, but I won't be saying that outloud.

"She's not going to let you. You know how stubborn she is." Frustration laces Derrick's tone as he leans against the wall of the suite.

"Go away!" Her voice is muffled, as if her face is covered by fabric. It probably is. "You guys did this to me!"

"Technically, biology did this to you. Exposure to your

scent matches can trigger a heat spike, especially when in close proximity for extended periods of time."

Derrick glares at Ivan and makes a 'cut it out' motion with his hand. "Do you think that's going to help?"

He shrugs with one shoulder. "Nah, probably not."

"Then why say it?"

Ariana throws open the bathroom door, panting, wearing only her bra and panties. Her chest is heaving and splotchy red, her eyes fixed on Ivan, face twisted into a glare.

"I would not be at the whims of my biology if you weren't here, Ivan."

He waggles his eyebrows at Derrick and stage whispers, "That's why." He takes a step closer to the furious Omega. "Since we're all together now, let us help you."

"I'm not going to fuck you." The way she crosses her arms pushes her breasts up, and Jesus Christ, I'm going to faint from how fast all my blood rushes to my dick.

"Never say never, sweetie, but that's not what I was suggesting." He reaches behind his head and pulls his shirt off. My Alpha is sexy, with dark hair covering his torso and a soft, cozy belly. If the deepening scent of vanilla and oranges is any indication, Ariana thinks so, too.

"Let us join you in the bath. No expectations. We'll hold you, massage your feet, whatever you want. If you won't let us ease you, at least let us comfort you."

She stares at Ivan, mouth slightly open, but I don't think she heard a word he said. He's clearly aware of the attention his body is getting, because his smile is wicked. As Ariana rubs at her neck and her scent thickens, Derrick swears under his breath.

She's getting harder and harder to resist.

After a long, pregnant pause, my Omega dips her head and scampers back into the bathroom. She doesn't close the door behind her, which is apparently all the invitation Ivan needs.

I'm right on his heels as he strips the rest of his clothes off and climbs into the tub with his underwear still on. She's already under the water, her bra and panties scattered on the floor, teasing me with images of what her wet, naked body will look like.

Fuck.

I turn my back to them and attempt to adjust myself, but I know it's going to be pointless.

"Just take your pants off and get in there quickly, Grant. It's only going to get worse, so don't bother trying to hide your reaction." Derrick's lips are so close to my ear that chills run down my spine with his words.

I think I'm going to die in that tub.

All of my blood has rushed to my aching cock, and I will surely slip beneath the water, drowning as I'm surrounded by the three sexiest people in the world.

It seems unfair that Derrick and Ivan aren't into each other. Shouldn't they also have to deal with being wet and nearly naked with three people they want to fuck? Instead, both of them only have to battle with attraction to the two of us, but let's face it, neither of them is going to be paying me much attention.

Not that I mind. They've seen it all before. We've waited so long for Ariana, and she deserves to be the center of attention.

Ariana squawks in surprise as Ivan pulls her to his lap. She struggles for a moment, but he bands an arm around her chest and pins her against him.

"Damn, quit fighting and let us help you, Omega." His words precede a rumbling purr, and I watch as she melts against him, her head falling back onto his shoulder.

I can imagine plenty of scenarios where Ariana would

Chapter Seventeen

be held to Ivan like that, and nearly all of them make my stomach clench with desire. Derrick must sense it because he pulls me against him, mirroring their position, and rests one of his hands right over the waistband of my briefs.

Our Omega's eyes widen as she watches his arm move beneath the water as he strokes across my belly. "I…" Her throat bobs as she swallows her words.

Ivan places a soft kiss on the curve of her neck. "Aren't they beautiful together?"

"Yes." Her voice is breathy and desperate.

"You know, I bet watching them together could help you. The pheromone exposure may ease the spike a little." Ivan's voice is thick and syrupy like honey as he fills Ariana's head with ideas. "Would you like that? Like to watch them together?"

Derrick's fingers dip beneath my waistband and brush the top of my straining cock, and I choke on my breath. I want to thrust into his hand, but I don't. I hold my body stock still, as if moving will break whatever spell she is under.

"Grant is so pretty when he comes. His cheeks turn red on the apples, he throws his head back and makes delicious, whimpering sounds." Ariana squirms on Ivan's lap, and the tops of her breasts slip above the milky water. Ivan bites his lip, stifling a groan. "I bet it wouldn't even take them long. You've got them both so riled up. Do you want to make a bet on how long it would take?"

Her shiny green eyes lock on mine, and there is a question simmering there. It's almost as if she's asking me for permission to answer his questions, to play along with Ivan's teasing words.

I dip my chin and mouth, "I'm into it." She doesn't know that I'm an exhibitionist, but it looks like she's about to learn.

A pretty pink flush dances across her cheeks. "I... I don't know how long."

"Well, Derrick, why don't you show us?" Ivan's teasing voice has dropped to a seductive rasp as he grabs Ariana's chin and holds her gaze on me.

Derrick's chest rumbles softly against my back with a groan as his hand finally, blessedly, wraps around my shaft. My relieved moan is answered with a desperate whimper from Ariana.

"You ready to put on a show, Grant?" Derrick brushes his lips against my neck. "Maybe, if you're really good for me, she'll want to give you a reward."

He slowly pumps my cock, and the way the water moves around his arm is almost as obscene as the sounds leaving my mouth. It splashes against my chest as he picks up the pace.

Ariana hasn't looked away, eyes trained on my waist, trying to see something other than the shadowed outline through the water.

I'm regretting telling the guys to add all of the bath bombs that have clouded the tub.

I want her eyes on me.

Before I can think better of it, I stand, the water running off my body as Derrick's hand stays tightly wrapped around my dick.

Ariana makes a surprised, squeaking noise as she attempts to scramble farther away from me. She succeeds only in pressing herself tighter against Ivan, who makes a pained sound.

"Sweetie, keep moving against me like that, and I'll be the one giving you a show."

"Say no, Ariana." My voice is quiet, but she is so keyed in on me that she hears me all the same. "Say no, and I'll step out, grab a towel, and leave you to your relaxation."

Chapter Seventeen

Derrick slips around my body, both of his hands going to my hips. "Say yes, and I'll show you exactly how our Beta likes to be pleased." His voice is thick with want, and my dick weeps at the sound of it. "I still don't want to take advantage of you while you're going through a heat spike. But I can do this."

Her tongue wets her bottom lip, and I want nothing more than to suck it into my mouth. One kiss with her was not enough.

There will never be enough.

"Please. Please. He... he needs you." Her whine goes to my head.

I look down at my Alpha on his knees in the water and grab his cheek, rubbing my thumb over the bone. "I do, Alpha. I do need you."

Derrick kisses up the sides of my shaft before wrapping around my head. His hot mouth has me panting and feeding my fingers through his hair. It takes every bit of my self-control not to fuck his throat. I cannot remember ever feeling this desperate for release.

I can smell Ariana's creamy orange scent over the bath additives as Derrick bobs up and down my length. Ivan makes a strangled sound, drawing my eyes to him.

Ariana has her hand underwater, and though I can't see it, I have a guess at what it may be doing, because Ivan isn't paying attention to me at all. His gaze is trained on where her forearm disappears below the water.

When Derrick takes me into his throat, I push on the back of his head, holding him there as I thrust shallowly. My panting moans and desperate groans are nothing compared to the labored breathing coming from the beautiful Omega across the tub from me. My Alpha swallows around me, and I know I cannot hold back much longer.

I struggle to bite back my moans enough to speak.

"Baby. Are you going to come with me?" She sucks her bottom lip between her teeth, worrying it in embarrassment, before nodding her agreement. "Then you'd better come, because I can't hold on much longer."

Derrick squeezes my balls before his finger travels back and strokes against my hole.

I lose whatever semblance of composure I have left.

I thrust roughly into his mouth a few times before I'm spilling down his throat, chanting pleas and swears as I empty myself.

I'm coming down from the high when Ariana gasps, and I watch as her eyes fall closed, her head rolls back, and the sweet sound of her pleasure fills the bathroom.

She nearly melts against Ivan as he swears and bites his fist with a groan.

"Does it count as coming in my pants if I am not wearing them?"

Chapter Eighteen

"TELL THE CAMERA WHAT HAPPENED, Ariana. Spare no detail."

Bridgette was waiting on the television when I entered my room to get changed after leaving the pack suite. She told me where to find the interview room, saying I had to go there right away while everything was still fresh in my mind.

Like I could ever forget what just happened.

I'm pretty sure the image of Derrick on his knees in front of Grant will live rent-free in my head for the next fifty years.

I thought the room she directed me to was a broom closet when I first explored the house. I'm surprised that it's actually a small room with green walls, and a single chair with a camera pointed directly at it.

It's uncomfortable. Almost clinical. I feel like I'm on trial.

Why bother calling it an interview room if no one is here talking to me?

I adjust myself uncomfortably in the chair. What do I even talk about? Where do I start?

This is the first time I've been acutely aware of what I look like in the house. The camera directly in my face makes it hard to forget that people will be watching my every move once this airs.

I should've brought some water or something. Just to hold onto and keep my hands busy.

"Uh. Yeah. I don't know what to say here. How much detail do you need? Everyone saw that I had a heat spike. Which, if I have any say in it, can we please minimize the airtime that gets? I know being an Omega is nothing to be ashamed of, and going into heat and having spikes is part of it, but damn. Does anyone want their coworkers to see them try to ravage the guy who lied to them for years?"

I run my fingers through my still-damp hair and sink a bit deeper into the chair. I should've put on makeup. I am sure I look wrecked.

"I guess that's unfair to Derrick. Reducing him to 'the guy who lied for years' is an oversimplification of who he is to me. Yeah, he lied, but he's still Sax."

It's his face I saw, his voice I heard.

But the filthy words Ivan whispered in my ears in the bath are not the type that were whispered over the phone.

What does it say about me that I'm starting to differentiate who I was talking to by their dirty talk? Shit, if I'm not careful, that won't be my only heat spike this week.

"But it's not just Derrick that is Sax. All three of them are. It's weird to look at Ivan and Grant and know we've talked before and yet feel like we haven't. They know me, but I don't know them. I love Derrick. I can admit that. And by extension, doesn't that mean that I love Grant and Ivan, too? It's the transitive property or whatever."

It's like my knowledge of Sax is a rope, and they're

each a strand, and now I'm going to have to figure out how to unweave it even though it's knotted and frayed. It's like doing a puzzle backward, which doesn't sound that challenging, but this isn't a case where I can push it off the table and watch as the pieces scatter. In that scenario, I'm the pieces, and they're the table, right? Fuck, I don't know. I'm not making sense."

A slush of Omega hormones has emptied my head of all rational thought. I've never spiraled after an orgasm, but that one I just had may have changed my brain chemistry. All of their scents were smothering me, pushing me higher and higher, and watching Derrick and Grant was almost a religious experience.

It wasn't just the eroticism of watching two people together. There is a natural intimacy between the four of us. It's history, even if I don't know who is mentioned in the books.

"I didn't cross any boundaries. I'm not going to let myself feel bad about it. They wanted me to watch. Who wouldn't like to watch two people they love together?"

"Uh. Ariana? We have no idea what you're talking about." Drew's voice from the small speaker on the wall startles me. *"Can you tell us what happened during your bath?"*

"No. That's between the four of us. You don't need those details."

I can hear his frustration in a sharp exhale. *"Yes, we do. Don't forget that you signed a contract. In areas where there are no cameras, you have to give us the details of what transpired."*

My head is starting to hurt, and I want nothing more than to go lie in my bed. It's making me a little whiny. "Seriously, Drew? Screw the contract. This is my life. This is their life. Why do you get to know the intimate details of how we try to figure out our relationship?"

My bare feet barely reach the wall when I'm turned

sideways in the chair, so I stretch out the best I can to support myself. If I close my eyes, I can pretend I'm lying on my bed, talking to Marlie.

"I don't know what I'm doing here. I don't know where to go from here. My life has changed forever because of this experience. I'm not being a drama queen right now. This isn't in the 'Knowing you has changed me' romance novel way. This is the 'Life as we know it has ended' zombie movie way."

I'm pretty sure there are zombie romance novels. There's a way to combine those two things into a happily ever after, isn't there?

"I'm scent matched and will have to be around them for the rest of my life. Why should I give even more of myself to the producers? To the viewers? Haven't I given up enough of myself for this show?"

"Ah, I understand the defensiveness now. Which one did you sleep with?"

My feet hit the floor. I wish Drew were here so I could poke him in the chest. "Excuse me? I didn't sleep with any of them. Not that it's any of your business. No one touched me but myself."

I realize, as soon as the words are out, that this is exactly what the producers wanted. I let Drew bait me into giving them the exact sound bite they needed.

"Tell us about it."

My body feels heavy as I bury my face in my hands. There is no more pretending that I'm not here. "Do you understand how uncomfortable this is for me? I'm... I've never been with anyone, okay? Not a whole lot of chances to fuck people when you won't leave your house. And now you want me to come here and tell you I got myself off watching them together?"

"I'm sorry, Ariana." His voice is softer now, less argumen-

tative. *"I know this isn't what you thought you were getting into when you joined the show. But this is what it is. This is reality television. We put on a good show for our viewers. You don't have to admit to anyone that what happened is real. In fact, most viewers assume it's mostly scripted."*

"Am I done?"

"Yeah. You're done."

DINNER IS AWKWARD.

Or rather, I'm awkward. The guys are fine. They're laughing and cutting up, trying to include me in the conversation. They're kind enough not to push for more than a few grunts from me as I stuff my face with pasta.

I opted to cook dinner for all of us tonight, if only so I didn't have to look at them or participate in the conversation. Every time I look at Grant, I see his head thrown back, eyes closed in bliss. When Derrick smiles, I can picture his lips wrapped around Grant's swollen dick. And every time Ivan speaks, I remember his words tickling the back of my neck and can almost feel his hardness digging into my ass.

I need to think about anything other than what happened in that bathroom if I am going to get out of here without melting into a puddle.

A soft bing from the living room draws my attention as the TV flickers, the show's logo fading and revealing Bradley's smiling face.

"Hello, lovebirds!" Holy shit, did they adjust the volume remotely? Why is he so loud? "While you didn't quite use the spa basket how we intended, production has decided that you did, in fact, earn your reward. It's outside the door. Why don't you go collect it, Derrick?"

And then the logo is back, Bradley gone.

Derrick pushes away from the table and goes to collect whatever it is they decided to grant us.

The rewards in this show are a double-edged sword. They're always enjoyable, but it's another opportunity for the show to get footage of us that makes for good television. I want to go to my room and hide under my blanket for the rest of the evening, but there is no way I can opt out of whatever they planned for us.

The Alpha comes back with a box roughly the size of a shoebox tucked under his arm. He silently offers it to me to open, but I shake my head.

It doesn't matter who opens it. The contents stay the same.

Derrick sets the box on the table in front of me and lifts the lid.

"Oh, no way." His face lights up with a massive smile as he pulls out several clamshell cases. "It's DVDs of *Unexplainable and Bizarre*."

"Seriously?" I lean closer and yank them out of his hands. Sure enough, it's the first two seasons of the paranormal show that was the catalyst for our relationship. It was a comfort watch for me for a long time, but it was taken off streaming services last year.

Derrick leans over my shoulder to read the back of one of the cases. "Season two is when they visited the shipyard, right? That one's the most obviously fake."

I smack his chest with the case. "It is absolutely real. None of them are fake."

"They embellished a lot—especially that one. You expect me to believe that there are poltergeists that imitate the sound of ships' horns and not that, I don't know, someone is playing recordings of the horns in the distance for dramatic effect?"

"Are you serious right now?" His words light a fire under me, and I jump to my feet. I do *not* play when it comes to the supernatural. "Listen here! I'll tell you the same thing I told you a decade ago, *Sax*. Why bother watching a show if you think it's fake? Suspend disbelief for a moment and accept that there is more to this world than what we can explain. If a duck-billed platypus can exist, why can't a poltergeist?"

"A platypus is a marvel of evolution!" He threw his hands up in exasperation. "And I'll tell you the same thing I told *you* a decade ago, Onion. I like to be entertained, and part of that is seeing gullible people believe the obvious lies."

"Yeah, well, I guess I am pretty fucking gullible, since I fell for you!"

Grant is on his feet, touching my forearm as soon as the words fall from my lips. "Hey, hey. He didn't mean anything by it."

"Maybe I did!"

"He didn't." Ivan places a hand on Derrick's shoulder and puts some of his weight into it, anchoring the other Alpha to the floor. "Do you know how many times we watched that episode before it was taken off of streaming?"

"Shut up, Ivan." Derrick elbows his packmate in the gut.

"No, you shut up, Derrick. You're picking a fight for no reason."

While they argue back and forth, my eyes drift to the DVDs of the old, cheesy show.

This was our reward.

A reminder.

Of where we came from, of who we used to be.

We argued for ages, as Sax and Onion, about whether the show was real. Even after we left the forum, we still watched the episodes together until the show was cancelled a year later. Neither of us would give up our position in the debate.

An incredulous laugh bubbles out of my throat. Well played, Bridgette and Bradley. Well played.

I slip away from the table and put one of the DVDs into the gaming system hooked up in the living room, and plop myself down in the center of the couch. As the familiar, haunting title music plays, the guys stop their bickering.

"Did you know, they had a budget of only two thousand dollars an episode in season one?" I look over my shoulder and gesture for them to join me. "It's why it looks like one of those spooky found footage movies. After they got picked up by a network for season two, the production value increased dramatically."

Ivan vaults over the back of the couch and takes a seat beside me, and Grant sits on my other side. Derrick lowers himself into the chair across from me as I point the remote at him.

"*That* is how I know it's not fake, Sax. The shipyard may have been in season two, but they still didn't have the money for crazy special effects." He's got a strange look in his eyes as he listens to me, and the corner of his mouth is ticked up in a small smile. "What?"

"I... this is better than I could've ever imagined."

"What is?"

"Arguing with you. Seeing your passion in person."

I duck my head, cheeks hot, and try to ignore the way his words make my stomach flip.

Because I was thinking the same thing.

Audience Reactions

EPISODE THREE

snowyreads > *Knot What You Expected*

SHUT UP. SHUT UP. Listen to them argue like they're kids again 😭😭😭 They love each other SOOOO much. Derrick and Ariana are TOTALLY endgame.

thatbeccagirl_reads > *Knot What You Expected*

Okay, but I need more DETAILS about that bath!! Grant was BLUSHING soooo much in his interview.

yikes!Rutherfordium > *Knot What You Expected*

DAE think that Ariana is being kind of a baby? like boo hoo, you're scent matched to three impossibly hot men. cry me a river.

ultracrepidarianbetaboy> *Knot What You Expected*

That heat spike was fucking hotttttttttt. Derrick is a #consentking for real. All the producers need to do to get more viewers is put that scene in an ad, and they'll have people tuning in every night. Anyone else hoping she goes into heat while they're in the house? 😏

Knot What You Expected

EPISODE FOUR

BRADLEY: THINGS CERTAINLY ARE *HEATING* UP, AREN'T THEY, BRIDGETTE?

BRIDGETTE: THEY SURE ARE! I DON'T KNOW ABOUT YOU, AMERICA, BUT THE WAY DERRICK HANDLED HER SPIKE MADE MY HEART MELT.

BRADLEY: ME TOO, BRIDGETTE. BUT WHAT REALLY MELTED ME? THAT ARGUMENT OVER *UNEXPLAINABLE AND BIZARRE*. DID YOU EVER WATCH THAT SHOW?

BRIDGETTE: I CAN'T SAY I HAVE. BUT AFTER HEARING THE TWO OF THEM ARGUE ABOUT IT, I DEFINITELY WANT TO! I FELT LIKE IVAN AND GRANT, ALL HEART-EYED OVER WITNESSING WHAT IT MUST HAVE LOOKED LIKE WHEN THESE TWO FELL IN LOVE FOR THE FIRST TIME.

BRADLEY: THOSE TWO DID LOOK PRETTY SMITTEN, DIDN'T THEY? I HOPE THEY STAY THAT WAY WHEN THEY LEARN WHAT WILL HAPPEN IN THE *EXPECTED* HOUSE TODAY…

Chapter Nineteen

α Ivan
pumpkin bread

YESTERDAY WAS CLOSE TO PERFECT.

Ariana, naked and wet, writhing in my lap as we watched my Beta getting pleasured? Holding her as she trembled through an orgasm?

Amazing. Perfect. A show stopper of a moment.

No notes.

Things got a little awkward over dinner, but it wasn't too bad. And my girl can *cook*! She really is an Omega of many talents. How did I ever get so lucky? I met two guys at a party, and now we're a pack scent matched to an Omega who couldn't be more perfect for us.

Listening to Derrick and Ariana argue over that cheesy paranormal show was the icing on the cake of the day. All I could do was imagine them at our dinner table, lobbing half-hearted insults and threats at one another after a long day at work for all of us. Grant and I would laugh at their antics as the argument got increasingly silly.

Seeing them both regress into angry teenagers was amusing and endearing, and it highlighted why these two fell in love. When I met Derrick and Ariana, they were already in love. I was stepping into an established relationship. Getting to see a glimmer of what it was like at the beginning makes me feel like I'm a part of that love story now, too.

There are so many ways to love someone.

There is a desperate love, where you feel like your life is going to end if you're not with the object of your affections.

Some people love passionately, dripping with desire and sweeping the other person off their feet. That's Grant. He's a true romantic at heart.

Others, like me, show their love through service, whether that is cooking, giving them backrubs, or even making them laugh and cheering them up when they're a bit blue.

But Derrick? Derrick loves furiously. He's argumentative and challenging, and he doesn't let anyone off the hook easily. Arguments between him and Grant, not that they happen often, regularly devolve into a furious fuck fest on the dining room table.

And Ariana went toe to toe with him easily.

They weren't actually angry at one another. If they had been, their scents would have given it away. Instead, both of them were pumping light, airy pheromones into the air that spoke of humor and nostalgia.

We went to bed after three episodes of the show, when Ariana started to nod off on the couch. She let Derrick guide her to her room and tuck her in, the lucky fucker. He came out preening like a peacock.

I'm cautiously optimistic about how the day is going to go as I swing my legs over the side of the bed and stretch out my stiff body.

The TV on my wall chimes.

"Ivan, good morning!" Bridgette's perky, smiling face fills the screen. *"How did you sleep?"*

She's never appeared only on my screen before. I don't mean to be short with her, but something in my gut tells me I'm not going to like this conversation. "Fine. What's up?"

"The producers have been in contact with a FOS specialist, and the specialist has confirmed that we need to reduce Ariana's exposure to scent matched pheromones to minimize her risk of developing the condition. Now, we can't remove you and Derrick from the show, because only Ariana and Grant wouldn't make for a positive viewing experience for our audience. We do have to ask either you or Derrick leave the house."

My stomach bottoms out.

She's joking, right?

This is a joke.

We've only been here three days.

It's not time to leave the house. She's not ready for that. I'm not ready for that. I need more time with her to show her how much I love her. How important she is to me.

We can't turn back now, not when we finally made some headway yesterday.

"We'll leave it up to you two to decide who stays and who goes. We'll unlock the door, and when the decision is made, just head on outside, and we'll take it from there."

I don't say anything. I can't. My words get stuck in my throat as Bridgette stares at me with a blinding white smile plastered on her face.

I hate her.

After a long pause, I find my voice. "Does Ariana know?"

"She does not. Bradley is informing Derrick right now. Your pack can decide as a group how you'll tell Ariana. Good luck!"

Chapter Nineteen

The screen switches to the logo before I can formulate a response.

"Fuck!"

I collapse onto the bed, my heart threatening to beat out of my chest.

One of us has to leave.

Ideally, both of us would leave to keep Ariana safest, but the show must go on.

How are we going to decide?

I don't want to leave. I love her, and I need her to realize she loves me, too.

But I'm practically a stranger to her. She knows Derrick, even if she's pissed at him. She's heard his voice, seen his face, for years.

And, objectively, he's more handsome than me. He'd look better on people's TVs than I do. Better for ratings.

It's going to have to be me. It makes the most sense.

The door to my room opens as I'm throwing my clothes into my suitcase. I look up from the sloppy pile of t-shirts, and Derrick and Grant are there, both with stricken looks on their faces.

Derrick's voice is raspy and strained. "Are they fucking with us?"

"I don't think so. They wouldn't mess around with something like FOS." I can't look at my pack as I continue loading my things into my beaten-up suitcase. "I'm going to finish packing, then we can tell her together what's going on."

"You're going to leave?" Grant's voice is strangled.

I cross the room and wrap one arm around his waist and cradle the back of his head with my other hand. I push my forehead against his, breathing in his sweet, orchid scent. "It needs to be me. Derrick has the most distance to make up with Ariana. I can figure out my relationship with her once all of this is over."

We may not be romantically involved, but Grant is my Beta. We're best friends, and we're platonic lovers. He's my rock as much as I am his. He exhales sharply, hands shaking as he places them on my chest. "I don't like this. I don't want any of us to be separated from her. She needs all of us."

"This is what's best for her."

Her safety comes first. Always.

Derrick is quiet, leaning against the doorframe. I didn't expect him to volunteer to leave, and wouldn't want him to. If he can repair his relationship with her, then I should have no problem developing one once they're out of here.

I hop in the shower, trying to spend as much time as possible in here and drag the day out, but I know it's a bad idea. It needs to be like ripping a bandage off.

Just one tough pull, and it's over.

My stomach is twisting like I had bad seafood, but I need to do this now. I'll lose my nerve if I put this off any longer. I don't want to stick around for the whole day, knowing that, at the end, I'll have to leave. It feels dishonest to keep something like this from her all day.

My nervous hands are shaking as I brew coffee. I'm just pouring it into espresso cups when Ariana leaves her room.

She's the most beautiful woman I've ever seen.

Her hair is slightly frizzy, the waves untamed, and her skin is glowing. Her eyes are sleepy behind her glasses, and she's wearing a pair of linen pants, a plain white t-shirt, and a single sock.

The Omega of my dreams. What if, once I leave, she never wants to see me again? What if she decides that Grant and Derrick are all she needs, and I don't add anything to their dynamic?

Chapter Nineteen

I don't want to give up Grant, but I won't force him to choose between the two of us. I'm going to do right by my Omega and Beta. If it comes down to it, I'll make the decision for him.

"Coffee?" Her voice is thick as she sits down in the chair I've quickly come to think of as hers. "Is there something we need to talk about?"

I chuckle awkwardly. "We'll wait until the guys get here."

Her back stiffens as her delicate fingers wrap around the tiny cup. It's only been a couple of minutes when Derrick and Grant join us, neither smiling. They look like they took quick showers, and Grant's hair hangs wet and limply around his face.

I can count the number of times he didn't style his hair after a shower on one hand, and each time he was sick.

They take their places at the table and accept the cups I slide to them.

I take a deep breath. Here goes nothing.

"I got a message from Bridgette when I woke up."

"And Bradley contacted me." Derrick talks over me and turns his body slightly to face her better. "They said that they consulted with a Foresaken Omega Syndrome specialist about your situation."

She leans her elbows on the table, and her eyes bounce between us. "And? What did they say?"

I can't look at her. If I see that she wants me to leave in her eyes, I'm not sure if I'll ever recover. "In order to give you the best chance of avoiding contracting the illness, either me or Derrick needs to leave the house."

Grant sniffles, not looking up from his cup. It makes my chest ache.

I've imagined the moment we all would be together for so long, and now it feels like my hopes of being a proper pack are being dashed before we even get off the ground.

I drain my coffee. The cup clanks loudly as I place it, too roughly, onto the tabletop.

Now or never.

"I'm going to go, sweetie."

She doesn't move.

Doesn't react.

I don't know what I expected. Tears? Begging me to reconsider?

Why would she, when she barely knows me?

How is she to know that I'm the one who always loses to her in chess? I can't help but feel like I'll never have the chance to tell her.

After a tense silence, I walk around the table and press a kiss to the top of her head. She doesn't flinch away from me.

I don't think I would've handled it well if she did.

"We'll talk when this is over."

No one says anything as I go to my room and grab my bag.

No one reacts as I drag it past the table and through the living room.

I'm steps away from the front door when she jumps to her feet.

"Ivan! Wait."

I worry that I'll spook her if I make too many sudden movements, so I'm careful and deliberate as I let go of my suitcase and walk back to the table. She's wringing her hands together, not looking up from her feet.

A white sock with little pink bows on one foot. Chipped black polish on the other.

"I think you should stay."

Chapter Nineteen

Her soft words have air rushing out of my lungs. "What?"

After too long a beat, she drags her eyes up to meet mine. "I think you should stay."

"But-"

"Derrick should go."

Chapter Twenty

"DERRICK SHOULD GO."

The words are a knife to my heart. I bite my cheek to keep from crying out in pain.

She wants me to leave.

I don't know why I'm surprised.

I guess that I thought that, because she knows my face and voice, she'd want me to stay. But knowing my face doesn't make her feel comfortable with me, it would seem.

Maybe a better packmate would have fought Ivan, saying I should be the one to leave, not him, but I never claimed to be a selfless man. If anything, I've proven that I am selfish to my core when it comes to Ariana.

I didn't think she'd tell me to go. The possibility of it never crossed my mind.

"What?" Ivan's voice reveals his desperation to stay, and I don't have it in me to be mad at him for it. Of course, he wants to stay. Who wouldn't? Now that I've met her, any time away from Ariana will feel like I've lost a piece of myself.

"I think it's better for Derrick to go. I…"

Chapter Twenty

She won't look at me. At least look at me in the eye when you break my heart, Onion.

"I think it's better for all of us if I get to know you two away from him."

That's it, then. At least I didn't ruin everything for my pack with my lies.

Just for myself.

My body is on autopilot as I push myself to my feet. I have to pack. I can't stay in this house any longer, knowing she doesn't want me here. Maybe, when I'm out, I'll break down.

But not before then.

I have to hold it together for her. I won't let her feel guilty for making this decision.

After all, I am the face of her deception.

I'm the villain in her story.

Grant follows me into the room, hovering over me as I pack my clothes.

"Derrick. Say something."

"What is there to say? She doesn't want me, Grant. The least I can do is step aside so you and Ivan can be happy."

He slaps his hand onto the doorframe. "Fight for her! Tell her you want to stay!"

"What's the point of that? One of us needs to leave to keep her safe! I won't let Ivan leave knowing she wants him here. This is what has to happen. It makes the most sense." The tremor in my hands makes it hard to zip up my suitcase.

I'm trying to hold it together, but Grant is not making it easy.

"This is bullshit!" He crosses my room and slaps the screen of the TV like it'll wake it up. "I know you assholes are listening! This whole thing is bullshit. If this is really in

Ariana's best interest, to keep her safe, then let us out of the contract. We'll all leave. You're splitting us up for ratings, not for her. At least admit it and don't pretend you're being altruistic. If you cared about Ariana, you'd send her home, not Derrick."

They don't answer him. The TV doesn't flicker on to one of our hosts' faces.

I didn't expect it to.

Maybe asking one of us to leave is for ratings. A way to add dramatic tension. Will they make Ariana look evil for sending me away? Maybe they'll edit Ivan as the martyr and me as the jilted lover.

It's possible that they were telling the truth about the FOS specialist's advice, and this is a legitimate way to reduce her risk of contracting the disease.

Either way, I have to go.

"We can refuse." Grant is grasping at straws, and his eyes are red. "We can refuse to send either of you out of the house. What are they going to do, come in here and drag you out? They wouldn't dare."

I take his cheek in my hand. His skin is so soft. He'll say that it's his fifteen-step skincare routine, but that's his way of discrediting how beautiful he is.

They'll look amazing together. Grant's Achillean beauty wrapped in Ariana's goddess-like allure is the stuff of fantasy. What the ancient Greeks wrote poetry about, carved statues of.

"We're not going to refuse. If they're telling the truth about the specialist, then I need to do this for her. I'm not going to ruin her life any more than I already have."

He places his hand over mine, holding me there. "Please, Derrick. If you leave, I don't think we'll be able to come back from this. How is she going to become comfortable with our pack if a third of it is missing?"

Chapter Twenty

The emotion that's been threatening to boil over is barely contained. I squeeze my eyes shut, hoping to prevent it from overflowing. "We will. This isn't forever. It's just a few days. I'll figure out how to get her to forgive me. I'll think of something, and I'll be waiting as soon as you guys leave, okay?"

"You promise?"

I press my lips against his. It's a silent plea for him to trust me. "I promise."

Suitcase in hand, I make my way to the front door. Ivan and Ariana are exactly where I left them, and neither looks happy.

For some reason, that makes me feel better. At least I'm not the only one torn up about this. If Ariana were continuing her morning as usual, it would destroy me.

"Ariana?" She looks at me, and for a moment, I see regret flicker across her features. "I'm not upset with you. I need you to know that. I love you. I'll see you when this is over, okay? We'll pick up where we left off."

I don't wait for her to speak. I don't know how I'll react if she tries to apologize or starts asking me to stay. It's better not to give her that opportunity.

I can't lose my nerve now.

The door looms ahead of me. In this moment, I feel like it's not just to the house. If it closes, will it ever open again?

No one speaks when I wrench it open and step out into the sunlight.

"WE UNDERSTAND that this is an unusual circumstance. The network believes that making this change will maintain the integrity of the show while also highlighting how seriously we take Ariana's health."

Bradley has been kind to me, explaining why they removed me.

It doesn't make me feel any better.

I'm glad that they're taking her health seriously, but it hurts that, in doing so, I have to leave her behind. I know she's safe with the guys and that they'll take care of her, but I should be there with them.

I need her to see that I may have lied about a lot, but my feelings are true.

"We'd like you to call in every night to talk to her. We think it'll allow your relationship to reset. She can get to know you as Derrick instead of Sax, in the same way you two fell in love in the first place. It'll be incredibly romantic, and we can use the conversations throughout the episodes as a voiceover. I think it'll be very compelling."

My head is pounding with every beat of my heart that feels trapped in that house, so it takes a moment for me to process what he's telling me.

"I'll still get to talk to them?"

"Not the guys. Just Ariana. Since it's better for her health that you're not there, we think the audience would react well to your relationship going digital. If you talk to your pack, they could make the assumption that you three are working together again to make her fall in love with you. We'd like to remove that thought as a possibility by keeping Ariana your only point of contact."

It takes my brain a few moments to catch up. "So I need to stay here?"

"No. We'll do your exit interview this afternoon, and then you're free to return home."

Chapter Twenty

Home.

Now that I've been under the same roof as Ariana, will Virginia ever feel like home again?

"Okay, yeah. Sure. That sounds great."

I can't go home. I can't sit in that empty house, knowing she won't ever be there beside me. Her laughter will never bounce off those plain white walls.

But where am I going to go?

Waiting for them to leave the house doesn't feel right, either. Staying on this complex, knowing that they're all steps away and I can't be with them, sounds like hell.

I need to do something with this time. Something productive. Figure out a plan to earn her forgiveness. A way to show her that she can fall in love with me, the real me, again.

"We'll call you from this number and patch you into her every evening, okay? Probably around nine, but it may be later depending on what they're doing in the house." Bradley slides a white card across the table to me. "I know this feels like a major setback, but I think this will be a good thing for you."

"A good thing. Sure."

I don't feel as optimistic as Bradley does. When I picture the three of them in that house together, I can't help but think that they're going to look like the perfect pack now that I'm gone. A beautiful Beta, a strong, kind Alpha, and a gorgeous, delicate Omega. A fairy tale of a pack.

I'm sure the viewers will be happy to see me leave. Cheering for it, celebrating that the liar is gone.

I'm going to have to stay off the internet while the show is airing. My self-esteem isn't strong enough to handle the commentary people will have about me.

God, my parents are going to know what a piece of shit I am.

Bradley leaves after a few more encouraging words that I barely respond to. What am I supposed to say? I'm never going to feel good about leaving her behind.

It's not long before an interviewer and a camera crew come in and set up. The man introduces himself to me as Drew. He's a Beta, handsome, with a soft, unobtrusive scent.

"Alright, we're going to get set up. This will be a pretty straightforward process. We're going to edit out my questions and make it look like you're monologuing, so try not to talk to me, but to the viewers. Directly into the camera."

"Sure."

"Tell us how you're feeling right now, Derrick."

Hollow. Empty. Devastated. I should ask for a thesaurus so I can say every word that means hopeless.

"I came here wanting Onion to know the truth, and I got that. She knows. I wanted the opportunity to introduce her to my pack and me, so she could see how perfect we all are for one another. I wish I had more time. It felt like she was just warming up to me, and now I'm back at square one. But I'm not going to whine about the situation. Ariana's health is the most important thing, first and foremost, and if I have to leave for her protection, I will."

Scrubbing my face with my hands does little to relieve the pressure behind my weary eyes. My mom is going to give me a long lecture about my posture, I'm sure, but I can't straighten my shoulders. The weight of my decisions won't allow it.

"This is a setback. But I know this isn't the end for us. It can't be. She's a part of me. Before I knew the type of man I wanted to be, I knew that I wanted to be hers. I've done a lot of things wrong, but... I won't regret what I had

Chapter Twenty

to do to keep Ariana in my life. It's impossible to explain just how much she means to me. I love her. I love her the way the moon loves the sun as she chases her through the sky. I love her like the world begins and ends with her smile. And I'm going to show her that. I don't know how, yet, but I will. I trust my pack to take care of her while they're in there. I know she will realize that she loves them as much as they do her. And when this is over, when we can all be together?"

I don't bother wiping the hot tears from my cheeks. Let everyone see. I don't care what they think of me.

"When we can all be together, I'm going to earn her bite. Whatever it takes."

Audience Reactions

EPISODE FOUR

weaselgromitsandwich > *Knot What You Expected*

I… was not expecting that. Shit, that was heavy. I was never Derrick's biggest fan, but this really sucks for him. I'm not surprised that Ariana spent the rest of the day crying in her room. I probably would have, too. Even though she told Derrick to leave over Ivan, I don't think she really wanted him to go.

cheesesticks..icecream.. > *Knot What You Expected*

How is Derrick supposed come back from something like this? She TOLD HIM TO LEAVE. He was already fighting an uphill battle to win Ariana's forgiveness for what he did, and now he's not even going to have the chance. I am not a fan of the direction this season is going. I can't see how they're going to work this out. Is it possible they were lying about the FOS specialist for ratings?

omegalimepioneer10 > *Knot What You Expected*

From the previews of this episode, I was expecting Ariana to be throwing Derrick out, furious at him for something. Or maybe he's leaving because he broke her heart since they used that clip of her falling to her knees and crying so many times. Kind of deceptive on the network's part, considering it's no one's fault he needed to leave. But if it was sooooo important that she be removed from the Alphas, they both should've gone. Tbh, that feels like a cop-out for dramatic effect.

thebadscientist99 > *Knot What You Expected*

Here's my take on what happened in tonight's episode, from a scientist:

I don't necessarily think the show was lying about Ariana being safer with one Alpha gone, but the better course would have been to send them both away if that was the path they wanted to go down.

Derrick was the obvious choice if someone had to leave. It was not addressed because maybe the pack doesn't think about it, but Derrick is clearly the Prime Alpha, so his pheromones would be stronger.

Research is all over the place and filled with speculation on how to reduce the risk of FOS. The only sure-fire way is regular pheromone exposure to a compatible Alpha, preferably a scent matched one.

What does this mean for someone like Ariana, with a family history of severe presentation? She's going to need to be watched closely for the rest of her life for symptoms if she doesn't want these Alphas. Which is exactly what Ariana was worried about, and why she went to such extremes not to be exposed to one. I can't say I would have made the same choices she did, but I completely understand why she did. That's the unfortunate reality of FOS. It can happen to any Omega, for any reason, at any time. Until we perfect the creation of synthetic pheromones that match a specific scent profile, many Omegas will continue to suffer from FOS with little hope for a full recovery.

Knot What You Expected

EPISODE FIVE

BRADLEY: Last Thursday's episode was devastating, wasn't it?

BRIDGETTE: I sobbed at Derrick's exit interview. He was never given the chance to open up to Ariana like that, and they needed that. When we were told that one of them needed to leave, it destroyed me. I was so worried about giving them that news.

BRADLEY: Me too, Bridgette. But ultimately, this decision is what's safest for Ariana. At least they're halfway through the stay and can meet up with Derrick as soon as they leave the house.

BRIDGETTE: But will she want to?

BRADLEY: That's the question, isn't it? I can't decide if it's promising or problematic that she spent the rest of the day in her room alone.

BRIDGETTE: They certainly earned their reward yesterday, that's for sure. Maybe she will perk up when she sees what awaits them today.

Chapter Twenty-One

I AM SO pissed at Derrick. How could I not be, after a decade of lies? I don't think anyone would blame me for that.

But that doesn't mean I liked seeing him walk out that door.

I can't even articulate why I thought Ivan was the better choice to stay. I didn't want either of them to leave. But for some reason, I felt safer letting Derrick go.

Maybe it's because I don't know Ivan that well, and I want the opportunity to.

Or maybe it's that, deep, deep, *deep* down, I love Derrick and know that this won't change things between us.

Guilt is weighing me down, making it nearly impossible to leave the bed. I know I need to shower and to eat, but the idea of walking out into the living room and not seeing Derrick makes me feel ill.

This is my fourth day in the house, and yet it feels like a month has passed. We're over halfway done and will only be split up for a few days.

Why does it feel like forever?

"Baby?" Grant's voice is slightly muffled on the other side of the door. "Are you hungry? Ivan is making lunch."

I don't answer him. I don't know what sound will come out when I open my mouth.

Will I sob? Scream? Whine?

Better not risk it.

The door opens slowly, even though I didn't call him in. My Beta's face is drawn into a frown as he sticks his head through the crack. His hair lacks its usual luster, and he's not wearing the black eyeliner I was growing accustomed to seeing smudged around his eyes.

I forgot that, with Derrick leaving, Grant lost his Alpha. It's only for a few days, but when we're cut off from the outside world, it isn't easy to keep it all in perspective. It feels like so much more than that.

I pull back the covers and pat the bed next to me without saying a word. I don't know what makes me do it, only that I've felt better every time I've been around Grant.

I can tell myself it's because he's a Beta and that means he's safe all I want, but it's more than that.

He's mine. He was always meant to be mine. He will always be mine.

I don't have it in me to deny that right now.

Grant crawls into bed next to me, his body heavy as he slides beneath the covers. He wraps his arms around my waist as if he's afraid I'll reject him, and when I don't, he buries his nose in the crook of my neck.

"Tell me that this isn't going to ruin everything. That you'll still give us a chance. Because now that Derrick is gone, it feels like he took our chance at winning you over with him."

"I..."

How do I put into words that I know he and Ivan were

Chapter Twenty-One

a part of the lie, but that it doesn't hurt the way it does with Derrick?

It feels like Sax betrayed me, and Sax is Derrick. He was from day one. Sure, they went along with it, pretending the conversations I was having with them were with Sax, but he was the one I talked to the most. He's the one I watched smile on video.

It feels easier to separate that hurt from the other two. Whether that's fair to Derrick or not, it doesn't matter.

"I'll still give you a chance, Grant," is what I settle on.

His heavy exhale brushes my neck as he pulls my body closer to his than I thought possible. We press flush against one another, and I can feel every hard edge of him.

"I hate history," he whispers against my hair. "Ask me when the first season of *Expected* aired, and I can tell you the exact date. Don't bother asking whether I know about one of the wars. I don't. I fell asleep in history class."

His broad hand begins rubbing soft circles on my stomach as he speaks.

"It was me who shaved half of my head because I thought I was edgy. Eventually, I had to take it all off because it looked ridiculous. It's why I wear my hair long now. Well, that and it gives me a defined *look*. And if I want to make it as a model, I need one of those, apparently."

It wasn't a surprise that Grant models. He looks like he belongs on the streets of Milan, not here in bed with me. Even with his eyes shadowed and hollow, his hair hanging limp, he's still one of the most beautiful people I've ever seen in my life.

"I can't sing. It sounds like a dying cat. Or maybe an elephant whose tail got stepped on."

I'm not able to smother my laugh, and his hands tighten around me as my chest bounces.

"I'm an exhibitionist, if you didn't realize. Plus, I'm

weirdly into ears. Like, I want mine chewed on, and I want to chew on yours."

"I think a lot of people are turned on when their ears are nibbled on."

He shrugs and places a soft kiss on my neck. "Maybe. Derrick hates it. Ivan is indifferent. But me? Shit, that's the fastest way into my pants. Something about the breathy noises has my knees weak. Is that what ASMR is?"

Our conversation flows so naturally that outsiders might think we've known each other all our lives. "I've never understood ASMR."

"Me neither, but if that's what it is, I may have to subscribe to some accounts."

His proximity and the conversation have my body heating, and it's impossible for me to ignore. "Why are you telling me this?"

"Because I know so much about you, and I need you to know me, too. I want to level the playing field. It's not fair to you that I know that you want to be blindfolded, so now you know I want you to bite the fuck out of my ears." He clamps his teeth onto my lobe with gentle pressure and groans, the sound ghosting across my ear and lighting my body on fire. "And to bite yours."

I can feel him hardening, but he doesn't grind against me or try to initiate anything. He seems content just holding me close.

"Tell me a secret. Something you didn't even tell Sax."

My stomach does a flip.

I told Sax almost everything. Of course, a lot of it was whispered in the dark over the phone, but I don't know what he shared with the others.

Except for one thing.

Can I share my deepest, darkest secret with Grant?

Chapter Twenty-One

I don't really know him. He might as well be a stranger.

That doesn't feel right. I'm not sure which parts of him I know, but Grant is not a stranger. He feels more like a lover I've forgotten.

My mouth is opening before I can talk myself out of it.

"Calvin and I got in a fight before he fell into a coma. He never woke up."

Maybe that's why I haven't been able to move on from his death like everyone has expected me to. If I had kissed his forehead and told him how much I loved him instead of arguing with him, would I have been able to heal? Would I have opened his letter sooner?

"What about?"

Now that I've started the conversation, it's impossible to hold my secret in.

"He said that he deserved to die with dignity. He was suffering, Grant. The pain meds weren't touching what he was going through; he was lucid for less and less time each day. I refused to leave the hospital. I didn't want to miss a second with him. Even if he was out of it most of the time. It hurt so much when he asked for his Alphas, and I had to continuously tell him they were on their way back. I wasn't going to tell him every twenty minutes that they were dead. It would've been cruel."

He squeezes my waist, but doesn't interrupt me. A silent sentinel at my back.

"He…"

Am I going to do this now? Open my mouth, admit my darkest secret to the world? My parents?

Fuck, what are my parents going to say?

"He asked me to unplug his respirator. He wanted to choose when he died, how he died. I was sixteen, Grant. I couldn't. How could he have expected that of me? We fought over it for hours. It was one of his longest periods of lucidity there at the end, and instead of enjoying it, we were yelling at each other. He called me selfish. I said he was the selfish one. It was bad enough I had to watch him die, but he wanted me to be responsible for it?"

I'll never forget the way he looked at me from that hospital bed. He cried so much, his voice was hoarse from begging. All he wanted was to choose when he left this world.

And I couldn't do that for him.

I couldn't give him the last thing he asked of me.

"Even though we were pissed at each other, I didn't go anywhere. I fell asleep with my head on his lap, like I had every night. When I woke up, he was in a coma. And his opportunity to die with dignity was gone."

Maybe that's why the letter hit me so hard. He talked about his dying wish in it, but it wasn't actually his dying wish.

That was written before we fought. Before he begged me to help him die.

"There was a PS on the letter he gave me asking me to forgive him. He wrote that letter while he was still lucid and setting up his estate. Was he asking me to forgive him for dying? Or did he plan this? Did he know he was going to ask this of me?"

"He was selfish." Grant's voice is hard. When I pull away from him, he looks furious. "Asking you to do that had to have been the most selfish thing he could have ever done."

"But-"

"No. You were sixteen. You were a child. He shouldn't have put that on you. You have five parents, and he asked you?" He grabs my cheeks with both hands. "You were going to feel guilty no matter the outcome."

"He was hurting. I owed him that."

"And you weren't? You may not have been the one dying, but you were the one who had to continue living. And sometimes that's harder."

Chapter Twenty-Two

β Grant
orchids

ARIANA CRIES in my arms for over an hour. When I asked her to tell me something that no one else knew, I didn't expect it to be something so deeply personal.

It feels shitty to be upset with a dead guy, but I am.

She has been torn up about this for ten years. She's trapped herself in her home to avoid the same fate, and no one could tell me that part of that didn't stem from the fact that her brother asked her to kill him.

The words can be dressed up, but that's what he asked of her.

Every state should allow death with dignity, but they don't. What he was asking her to do could have gotten her prosecuted for murder. If he wanted to go out on his own terms, he should have talked to his doctors to see if there was anything else they could do.

Instead, he went to his sister, a sixteen-year-old, newly presented Omega, who was watching someone she loved face the worst fate possible for Omegas, and asked her to make it worse.

Asked her to carry the burden of his death with her for

the rest of her life. How could he love her and do that to her?

It makes my being upset about Derrick having to leave the house look minuscule. It's not like I'll never see him again. It'll only be a few days.

Sure, it feels like a few steps backward in our relationship with Ariana, but it's not the end of the world.

When the tears dry and her shaking stops, she looks at me like I am her hero. Her face is red and splotchy, the deepened color making her pretty green eyes stand out like jewels.

She reaches out and cups my cheek in her hand.

"Thank you, Grant."

"For what?"

"For listening. For being here for me."

I take her hand in mine and kiss her palm. "I'll always be here for you, Ariana, even when you don't want me to be. You're my Omega. I know we didn't get off on the right foot, but fuck, I love you so much. I can't imagine not having you in my life."

"Why were you okay with Derrick's relationship with me when you first met?"

It's something I've asked myself a hundred times, so I'm not surprised she wants to know.

"Honestly? I'm not sure. I wish I could wax poetic about how the first time I heard your voice, it spoke to my soul, but that wasn't it. I hadn't read any of your text messages or listened in on any phone calls when I told him he should continue his relationship with you. But when my Alpha talked about you with stars in his eyes? When he would pick up his phone twenty times at dinner, hoping for a message from you, even though he was the one who put the distance between you two?"

I wiggle a bit and sit up more, propping my back on the headboard before I pull her closer, halfway on my lap.

"He needed you. I have always known that I'm polyamorous. A lot of Betas are monogamous, but that never felt right for me. So when I met Derrick and discovered he was my scent match, I knew I wanted to share him with an Omega at some point. And the way he glowed when he talked about you? God, anything other than encouraging him to explore things with you felt wrong. I'd hoped that I would get the opportunity to know you, too, but the most important thing was seeing my Alpha smile like he did whenever he said your name."

Ariana traces her fingers up and down my arm, leaving goosebumps in their wake. "So what you're saying is I need to give him a chance?"

"That's what you took from that?" She chuckles as I ruffle her hair playfully. "That wasn't my point, but I won't say no to you giving him the opportunity to redeem himself. Derrick is a good man, and he loves you. You know all of us better than you think, but Derrick most of all."

"How did you all… share me?" She wrinkles her nose and shakes her head. "No, that sounds wrong. How did it work, all of you talking to me?"

I purse my lips, trying to put into words exactly how our relationships with her evolved. It was never a simple delineation of roles, or anything like that.

"Sometimes, when you were struggling with something and needed advice or encouragement, the three of us would sit together and figure out how to handle it. And when Derrick was swamped with work or visiting family, Ivan and I would step in to pick up the slack and make sure you never felt abandoned. But really, it flowed naturally. I'm the one

Chapter Twenty-Two

who talked you down from your fears and comforted you when you were sad. It was Ivan who reminded you how brilliant you are, who encouraged you to strive for more, and made you laugh when things looked bleak. And it was Derrick who embraced your fantasies and helped you feel like an Omega. He was also the logical one. Most of the advice you hated? Yeah, that was his. The arguments? Derrick."

She makes a soft huffing noise, no doubt about to argue with me about how she doesn't argue with Derrick, but I talk over her.

"We're a pack. You're included in that, and you always have been. We can't all be everything for each other. You got everything you needed from Sax, but that's because he was all of us. We can still be here for you in the same ways we have been from the beginning. Only this time, you know who we are. I can hold you when you cry, or Ivan can make you laugh when you've locked yourself in the bathroom. Derrick can argue with you about an old TV show, but I will never tell you whether I think it's real or fake."

Her stomach growls before she reacts to what I've said, reminding me that she hasn't eaten since breakfast yesterday. I push her shoulder, encouraging her to move toward the edge of the bed.

"Come on, you need to eat." I slip out of bed and hold my hand out to her. "I'm sure Ivan has a whole spread waiting for you by now."

She grasps my hand, stilling my movements. I'm taller than her, and from this position, me standing and her sitting, I feel like I'm leering over her. A soft, beautiful smile plays on her lips as she stares at me.

She looks at me as if she could love me one day.

"Thank you, Grant. For telling me everything and not

hiding the truth. And for talking me off the ledge six years ago. That… that was you, right?"

I hate that memory.

There aren't many moments in my relationship with Ariana that are bad, but that's the worst of them all.

It was the anniversary of her brother's death, and she was feeling particularly hopeless. I wanted to call her, but I couldn't, and Derrick was at work, so he couldn't talk to her, either. I had to do the best I could through text messages.

That day was the final straw. We decided to force her hand and get her to a psychiatrist and on medication, because she needed help that we couldn't give, and her therapist couldn't prescribe them.

"Yeah, that was me."

She's on her feet, throwing herself into my arms. If this is the only hug I ever get from her, I'll die a happy man, because this is the type of hug that changes lives.

"Thank you."

GOD, Ivan is a fantastic cook. While Ariana and I were having our heart-to-heart, he was pickling red onions and making blackened chicken tacos.

"I fucking love tacos," Ariana says around a mouthful of food. "Seriously, these are so good."

Ivan preens under her praise and pantomimes tossing his hair over his shoulder. "Why, thank you, sweetie. I thought you could use some comfort food."

Ariana loves tacos of all kinds. She makes them at least

Chapter Twenty-Two

once a week. Ivan is pulling out the big guns to cheer her up with this spread.

I'm tucking into my food, enjoying the litany of flavors that explode across my tongue, when Ivan grabs the seat of Ariana's chair and pulls her closer to him.

"The producers delivered today's challenge while you guys were resting. I didn't open it. I thought we could read it together?"

She swallows thickly and wipes her mouth with a paper towel. "Yeah, sure."

Ivan pulls an envelope from his pocket. He must have shoved it in there without care because it's wrinkled and smushed.

"Do you want to do the honors?" He holds it out to our Omega.

She shakes her head and waves him on.

He rips open the envelope, almost tearing the paper that is inside, and clears his throat.

"'Read this out loud.'" He looks up with a flush on the apples of his cheeks, sticking out from the top of his beard. "Right, carrying on. 'Today's challenge is simple. We've hidden something from your lives inside the house. Find it, and tell the others what it means to you. Having to choose which Alpha to leave the house was yesterday's challenge. Since an award could not be given, your reward for this challenge will be doubled.'"

Huh. That sounds easy. I have nothing to hide from Ariana, and Ivan knows basically everything there is to know about me.

My packmate shoves the paper at me and raises his eyebrows. I skim through the words my Alpha read outloud, my eyes stopping on what he didn't say.

Do NOT read this out loud:
Derrick chose to leave the property. He will not be here when you leave the house. We need America to be shocked about this, but we did not want to catch any of you off guard.

Derrick left?
Why wouldn't he wait for us?

Chapter Twenty-Three

α Ivan
pumpkin bread

IT'S NOT the time to tell Ariana that Derrick left, but she's looking at Grant and me through narrowed eyes, knowing there is something on the paper from the producers she's missing.

We're done keeping secrets from her.

When Grant hands her the letter, I brace myself for more tears.

But there are none.

She looks almost relieved. She folds the paper with a gentle hand and places it on the table.

"Well, it's nearly three. I suppose we should get started on this scavenger hunt so we have time to enjoy our reward, right?"

Grant's jaw is a little slack as he stares at her. He looks as surprised as I am that she isn't torn up about Derrick leaving the property. It makes me nervous to think that it may be because she doesn't care about him.

But she has to, right?

Feelings like that don't go away overnight.

After a moment, I clear my dry throat. "Yeah, I'm curious what they hid, and how they got it."

"I bet they got mine from Marlie, since she's the one who applied for me. And now I'm worried about what she could have given them." She jumps to her feet, eyes wide. "Shit, what if she gave them my vibrator or something?"

"I doubt it. That doesn't feel like something you'd need to explain to us. Now, if you wanted to give us a demonstration…"

Grant smacks me on the chest. "Don't be gross."

I hold my hands up in defense. "I'm just saying!"

And to my surprise, Ariana laughs.

I'm gonna be smug about that laugh, too.

"I'm sure both of you are well aware how they work, but if you want a demonstration, Ivan, I bet I can rig a strap out of something…"

Grant's ears perk up. "Was that a pegging joke? Don't tease me, Ariana."

She tosses a saucy grin over her shoulder as she walks away. "Wasn't *not* a pegging joke."

My Beta clutches his chest, dramatically falling out of his chair like she shot him with Cupid's arrow. "I knew you were the girl of my dreams, but this just proves it!"

I lean close to him and keep my voice down. "She seems like she's in a good mood. It was a good talk?"

"It got heavy for a bit, but I think she's starting to understand how we ended up here. And that she knows us better than she thinks."

I am of the opinion that if you cook, you shouldn't have to do the dishes, but I still stand and gather the lunch plates so I can toss them in the dishwasher. "Do you think this is going to work out?"

Ariana shouts from the other side of the house. "Hah! Found it!"

Grant's smile is blinding. "Yeah, I think it will."

IT DIDN'T TAKE LONG for Grant and me to find the items the producers had hidden once we started looking. I don't know how we missed them. They didn't try very hard to keep them out of sight.

Unless they snuck in here while we were sleeping to hide them.

They're not that creepy, are they?

Ariana sits on the floor of the living room, spinning a trophy in her hands. "I guess I'll go first."

"You don't have to." I hold up my item. "I can."

"I found mine first, so it should be me. Did Derrick tell you guys anything about when I presented as an Omega?"

"I don't think so. Only that it happened shortly before Calvin died." Grant makes a strange face when I mention Calvin. I'll have to ask him about that.

She hums to herself, looking at the plate on the trophy with an odd expression on her face. "It happened in front of the entire school during the junior debate. My scent spiked, and I slicked through my pants."

"Holy shit. That's awful." Grant took the words right out of my mouth.

"Yeah, it wasn't great. I still won the debate."

"Wait." I hold my hand up, my brain still processing what she said. "You continued? You didn't run off the stage?"

"It was mortifying. But the debate was about Omega rights, and I figured it would be more impactful if I kept going. I regretted it as soon as I was done. I didn't want to go back to school the next day, but Calvin convinced me to."

I don't blame her for wanting to hide underneath a blanket. Kids can be cruel, and to have a vulnerable moment like that in front of everyone?

"But you won." Grant leans forward in the reading chair and props his chin on his hand as he gazes upon her with pride. "Despite how uncomfortable you were, you won."

"I won."

"No wonder Derrick enjoys arguing with you. You're a worthy opponent. Not like our Beta over there. He shows his neck every time."

She rolls her eyes, dismissing my words. "It's hardly a fair fight. I wipe the floor with him every time."

I won't deny that, but I'll keep to myself that it may be more because she's our Omega than just her convincing arguments.

"Okay, someone else go. I hope y'all's are better memories than mine."

Grant tosses the red disc he's holding in the air and catches it deftly. "I hooked up with a guy on a disc golf course and got my pants stolen by an alligator."

Ariana and I go still, staring at our Beta. Then she laughs, hard. Tears spring to her eyes because of the force of it.

"Wait. Back up. How. How does that even happen?"

"The hooking up? Well, when a Beta and an Alpha…"

She tosses a pillow at him, smacking him in the face. "You know that's not what I meant."

"Okay, okay. An Alpha asked me on a date, and he was really into disc golf. I suck at it, but I was trying to impress this guy. I missed the pole hole-"

Chapter Twenty-Three

"It is *not* called a pole hole!" I'm struggling to breathe at how hard I'm laughing. "I refuse to believe it."

"Laugh all you want, but that's what it's called! Disc pole hole, pole hole, basket. All mean the same thing. Whatever you wanna call it, I missed. The disc went wide and landed a little too close to the marsh. When I went to pick it up, he came up behind me-"

"The gator came up behind you?" Ariana interrupts.

Grant chuckles and shakes his head. "The guy I was on a date with. He wrapped his arms around me and started kissing my neck and chewing on my ear…"

She nods solemnly. "Ah, yes. The ear thing."

He told her about the ear thing? I waggle my eyebrows at him, and he throws the pillow Ariana had hit him with at me.

"Anyway, my pants were removed hastily, and landed close enough to the marsh that a gator snagged them and took them under. I had to walk back in my boxers."

"There's an important detail I believe you may have left out." His expression is unreadable as he turns to me. "Did you still fuck him?"

Grant's face turns bright red, and he tries to hide behind his hair. Ariana claps and points at me. "The Alpha asks a valid question!"

"Yes."

"Couldn't hear that. What did you say?" This teasing, playful side of Ariana is so nice to see after how tough it's been getting her to open up to us these past few days.

"Yes, okay? I did. My pants were already gone. I didn't have much else to lose." He grabs a blanket from the couch and tosses it over his head. His voice is muffled when he continues talking. "Okay, time to laugh at Ivan."

I hope she doesn't laugh at me. It may break my heart if she does.

I hold up the Christmas ornament. At first glance, it's nothing special. Just a snowflake with a year printed on it. "Mine isn't embarrassing like Grant's, or empowering like yours, Ariana." I extend the ornament to her and drop it in her waiting hand. "But it is personal, which I think was their goal, and does tell you a lot about me."

She turns the ornament over in her hands, squinting at the date on it.

"That's the year I 'met' you. I've gotten you one for our tree every year since." Her eyes grow soft, but she doesn't raise them to meet mine. "In my family, we all got a new ornament each year. It's a tradition on my mom's side. I didn't think it was right for you not to have one, too. You're my Omega, a part of our pack. I wanted you represented on my tree, too."

I never told Grant and Derrick what the ornament was. I think they thought it was simply an ornament for each year our pack was together.

But that wasn't it, even if the dates do coincide.

"Family is the most important thing to me. And you're part of mine, Ariana, even if I'm not a part of yours yet."

She holds it against her chest. I don't know how production got this, but I'm glad they did. I never would've thought to admit this to her, but I think it's something that will help her start to understand me.

"Thank you, Ivan, for including me in your tradition."

"You don't have to thank me for that, sweetie. You're my Omega. Even before I caught your pheromones, I knew that I wanted you. That I love you."

The way she looks at me makes me think she may be starting to believe me.

Chapter Twenty-Four

THE DINNER they sent as our reward was amazing. It was clearly from a high-end steakhouse, because the filet melted on my tongue. And the creme brulee we got as a dessert?

Heavenly.

I'm not sure if I consider the silk pajamas "doubling" the reward, but they are the most comfortable ones I've ever worn.

And now the three of us match, which is cute.

I wonder if they'll have a set for Derrick?

I'm cuddled up in a blanket on the couch with my e-reader when Bridgette's face replaces Ivan's video game. Grant looks up from his puzzle at the ping.

"Don't you all look cozy! You look great in the pajamas."

"Thanks for the compliment, but you totally made me lose that race. What's up?" Ivan leans back on his hands and peers up at the screen.

"I need Ariana in the interview room right now."

My back stiffens, and I brace my feet on the ground. "Why? We've kept the cameras on."

"It's nothing bad, hun, we just have some things we need to talk about privately."

The churning in my gut makes me think it will be bad, but I can't turn her down. I'm slow to stand, but I nod at Bridgette's image.

"Yeah, okay, sure."

As I pass Grant and Ivan, they each make sure to touch me in some way, helping ground me. I make the short walk to the interview room and pull the door open like I'm the final girl in a horror movie.

There's no television in here where Bridgette can appear. There's a camera for me to stare into awkwardly, and a speaker on the wall that Drew talked to me the last time I was in here.

"Okay, Ariana, patching you in now." Bridgette's voice is bright and cheery. They must be planning to keep her part in the episode, then.

I barely have time to adjust myself and get comfortable when I hear him.

"Hey, Ariana."

Derrick's voice is jarring in this situation because he sounds like Sax, sending me right back to all of those late-night conversations. My talk with Grant helped me conceptualize Sax as three people, and it's making the whole thing easier to swallow, but my heart is struggling to reconcile this voice with the man who lied to me all of those years.

"Uh. Derrick. Hi."

"How are things in the house?"

"They gave us matching pajamas."

Out of everything that happened today, the secrets I shared with Grant, Ivan's confession about the ornament, the jokes we told each other, and the pajamas are what I mention?

"Oh, that's fun. I'd ask you what they look like, but that veers really close to a 'what are you wearing' conversation."

A conversation we've had several times over the years, and then pretended we didn't.

"Yeah, maybe we can skip that for now. What are you up to?"

"I was tidying up before they called me, but now I've got some tea, and I'm taking a break."

"Cleaning? At this hour? Where are you?"

"Virginia, so same time zone. I like cleaning at night, especially when I need to think. Idle hands make the devil's playthings or whatever it is that they say."

Virginia. That's where he's been all this time? It's far from South Florida, that's for sure.

"So you live in Virginia, then?"

"Yeah. Ivan is from here, so after college, we moved here. If I had known where you lived..." His words trail off, but I know what he didn't say.

If he had known where I lived, they would have come to me.

We were teenagers when we met, and not only did we keep our names anonymous, we kept our locations secret, too. It was never a conscious decision. By the time either of us would've felt comfortable meeting up with someone from the internet, it had been so long that we just didn't tell each other.

I never asked, and neither did he.

People watching the show are probably going to think we're weird as fuck. Not knowing each other's names or even the states we live in, and yet we claim to have fallen in love with one another?

"I'm from Hollywood, Florida."

"Ew."

"Like you have much room to talk. Virginia is not better than Florida. And our weather is nicer."

"At least we don't have iguanas falling from trees and people who get arrested for stealing fried chicken while pantsless and wearing flippers."

I cross my arms over my chest and glare at the speaker, forgetting that the camera is there for a moment. "Okay, look. People love to shit on the weird stories that come out of Florida, but it's only because we have laws that make all arrest reports accessible to the press. I'm sure you've got plenty of weird shit happening there, too."

"Mmmm, I don't think so."

As I open my mouth to argue back, my conversation with Grant plays through my mind.

Derrick was always the one I argued with.

A strange warmth fills me, and I pull my knees to my chest, resting my chin on them. "Maybe you're right. Do you at least like it there?"

"Hate it with a passion."

"I don't think you do anything without passion."

Derrick's voice is soft when he answers me. *"Life's too short for half measures."*

We're both quiet, but it's not uncomfortable. In a way, this feels like we're starting over. Like we're back to before the lies.

It's easier for me to accept the designation lie than I thought it would be. When I look at it objectively, his choice makes sense. I would have cut him out of my life and been alone if I knew he was an Alpha. Sure, I was friends with Marlie, but our friendship wasn't like things were with Sax.

I won't say I forgive him for it yet, but at least now I can understand why he did it.

"Grant told me about how y'all split responsibilities for me."

His sharp exhale has me picturing him rubbing the back of his neck and squeezing his eyes shut. *"You were not a responsibility."*

"You know what I mean."

"I do. It wasn't a conscious decision. It evolved over time, as pack dynamics tend to. It felt natural to us."

Pack dynamics. When the guys speak about all of this, they talk as if we are already a pack. It's not that I think it's presumptuous, even though it is. It's more that I never pictured myself in a pack.

But I never pictured myself with an Alpha either, and now I'm scent matched to two of them.

"For what it's worth, I am sorry that we kept you in the dark, but I don't regret it, nor do I regret lying to you about my designation. As we grew up, there were things I couldn't, can't, be for you. Even if I had never met Grant or Ivan, I'm not able to be everything you need."

That assumption annoys the shit out of me. "Bold of you to presume you know what I need."

"I know better than you do, honey. You're the one who is so terrified of getting FOS that you haven't done any other research into being an Omega beyond what you learn at school. You're so focused on not getting sick that you've forgotten how to be an Omega. You don't have a nest, for fuck's sake."

I wince. "I don't need a nest."

I've had one nest. Shortly after I presented, Calvin took me shopping for the things I'd need. Omegas do better with Alpha input on their nests, but I was a kid. I didn't have an Alpha.

What I did have was my older brother, who took me and dealt with my teenage frustration and got me set up with the perfect little nest.

And then he died and I couldn't look at that nest anymore. It held too many memories. It still smelled like his grassy green tea pheromones.

I've never built another.

"Just because you don't want one doesn't mean you don't need one. You're suppressing your Omega tendencies. Every time you called me, delirious with heat, you'd beg me to mail you shirts of mine. You want to nest, but you're burying that instinct down. Just like I know that you want Ivan or Grant to hold you while you sleep tonight, but you won't ask, because you've convinced yourself that if you don't embrace being an Omega, you won't get FOS."

"I don't…" The words get stuck in my throat.

I do deny myself my Omega instincts. It's so second nature to me that sometimes I forget this isn't how it's supposed to be.

"It's easier this way."

"Bullshit."

I doubt an argument between us was what the producers had in mind when they set up the call, but tough shit. This is who Derrick and I are.

"How would you know, Derrick? You haven't exactly embraced being an Alpha."

"How do you know I haven't?"

"You lied and convinced me you were a Beta."

"Think hard on it, Ariana. Can you actually look at our relationship and tell me I'm not your Alpha?"

"That's ridiculous."

He's not been my Alpha.

He hasn't.

Except…

He eased me while I was in heat.

He supported me through everything, but challenged me when I needed it.

He formed a pack and didn't let his jealousy keep me from developing relationships with them.

He's been my safe space.

They all are.

"A Beta could have done those things."

He grunts, dismissing my statement. *"But it wasn't a Beta doing those things. It was an Alpha who knew from the beginning that you were his. Every choice I have made as an adult was made with you in mind. Our house has a nest, Ariana. An entire room filled with all the gifts I couldn't send you because I had no idea where you lived. We all took classes on how to care for an Omega because we wanted to make sure that when we finally got to meet you, that we would be the pack that you deserve."*

I have no idea how to respond to any of that. I don't have the emotional bandwidth to address how those things make me feel.

Instead, I lash out. I'm not typically so bullheaded, but it's easier than examining how his admission makes me feel.

"I never asked you to do those things for me! I never asked you to be my Alpha."

"You didn't have to!" I can hear his panting breaths, recognize the tone he always takes when we argue.

Except this isn't an argument over a ghost-hunting show.

This is my life.

"I never made a conscious decision made to put you above all else. I just did. It has been killing me not to ask where you live, knock on your door, and tell you everything these past few years, but I didn't want to rush you. I wanted you to come to me and say you were ready. When we were told you applied for this show, I took that as you being ready to take the next step."

"I didn't apply for this!"

"I know that now, but at the time, I didn't. It doesn't change anything, though. I love you so much, and I knew that there was no other Omega out there for me. I was so scared when I presented as an Alpha. I didn't want to lose you. I couldn't lose you. So I lied, knowing it might mean I would never be able to meet you in person. But that was okay, as long as you were in my life. I'll take any part of you you're willing to give me, Ariana. You're my Omega, and you always have been." He sounds choked up, like he's crying, and I find myself aching to hold him in my arms. *"And if you never love me back, that's okay. As long as you're happy, I'll deal with whatever the consequences of this lie are."*

Sometimes, my brain and my heart are perfectly in sync.

This is not one of those times.

My heart bulldozes over my brain, taking the reins.

"I love you too, Derrick."

Audience Reactions

EPISODE FIVE

brittneedsbooks > *Knot What You Expected*

AHHHHHHH how could they end the episode like that? What do you mean we don't get to hear how he reacts to her admitting she loves him? WHAT DO YOU MEAN? Do they hate us or something?

floofymoose > *Knot What You Expected*

That phone call, her talk with Grant, the show and tell? God, I can't stop crying. I knew it was going to be bad when I saw the commercials for this episode, but for once, they downplayed it. They all deserve so much happiness. I hope Ariana doesn't stand in her own way.

cowbellenthusiast > *Knot What You Expected*

That moment between Grant and Ariana had my heart about to explode. I cannot get over how he looks at her.

bookishlymacbre> *Knot What You Expected*

Oh my god, have you seen the fan edit of Grant and Ivan when Ariana made that pegging joke? I swear it's going platinum in my house.

Knot What You Expected

EPISODE SIX

BRIDGETTE: WELL, TUESDAY'S EPISODE HAD A DIFFERENT TONE THAN LAST WEEK'S, THAT'S FOR SURE.

BRADLEY: IT REALLY DID. I FELT LIKE WE FINALLY GOT TO KNOW EVERYONE AND SEE THEIR RELATIONSHIPS FORMING. EVEN THOUGH DERRICK LEFT, THAT PHONE CALL MADE IT FEEL LIKE HE WAS STILL THERE.

BRIDGETTE: I HAD NO IDEA WHAT TO EXPECT WHEN I LEARNED THEY'D GET TO TALK ON THE PHONE, BUT I AM SO GLAD THEY WERE GIVEN THAT OPPORTUNITY. I THINK THEY BOTH NEEDED TO GET THOSE THINGS OFF THEIR CHESTS, AND I DOUBT THEY WOULD'VE BEEN ABLE TO HAVE THAT CONVERSATION FACE-TO-FACE.

BRADLEY: IT WAS PRETTY MEAN OF US TO END THE EPISODE RIGHT WHEN THE CALL GOT TO THE GOOD PART.

BRIDGETTE: I THINK OUR VIEWERS WILL FORGIVE US. I

wonder what Ariana is going to tell Ivan and Grant about what happened on that call.

Bradley: Let's find out.

Chapter Twenty-Five

I DROP my suitcase on the floor of the generically decorated living room.

Everything has happened very fast, but apparently, I can get a lot accomplished in a day when I'm appropriately motivated.

And hearing Ariana tell me she loved me? That is the ultimate motivator.

As soon as we hung up last night, after she stumbled over an awkward goodnight without giving me the chance to reply to her declaration, I booked a plane ticket.

And I emailed my clinic and quit my job.

And I booked a vacation rental.

Florida is a great place to start over.

It wasn't the first time she'd said she loved me. But it was the first time it was said without frustration, without qualifiers.

Without calling me Sax.

How was I going to stay in Virginia, knowing that she loves me?

Moving to Florida was the only option.

I've only been here a few minutes when there is a knock on the door.

"Sax." Ariana's best friend, Marlie, stands on the stoop with her fists on her hips. "As I live and breathe."

It wasn't hard to get her contact information. All I had to do was join Ariana's chat server, reach out to a few of her friends, tell them I was planning a surprise for her, and I needed Marlie's help, but lost my phone and didn't have her number.

They didn't have it, but they did have *her* gamer tag. Once I reached out to her, she didn't hesitate to agree to a phone call.

She was shocked when she learned that I was already out of the house and Ariana wasn't. I bet it violated my NDA to tell her anything, but oh well.

"Thanks for coming, Marlie. I've heard a lot about you."

The Omega is cute, like a doll, and short, but she doesn't hold a candle to Ariana.

"I bet you have. I've heard a lot about you, too. Not what I should've, though. Really wish I had known you were a lying liar who lies before I signed her up for that show. You're a fucking *Alpha*."

"In my defense-"

"There is no defending this. None."

"She's my scent match."

Marlie's puffed chest deflates. She looks a bit like a fish out of water, the way her mouth opens and closes. I guide her into the house to the kitchen table. I'm sure they have some coffee here.

As I make a pot, she starts talking again.

"Oh, I fucked up."

I slide a mug to her with a wry smile. "No, I believe that was me."

"I'm the one who told her to go on the show!"

"And I'm the one who she's going to have to be exposed to for the rest of her life. I think my fuck up is a bit bigger than yours."

"But you couldn't have known." She doesn't drink her coffee. She fidgets with the cup, spinning it in her hands. "Yeah, you lied about your designation, but you couldn't have known that you'd scent match to her and present her with her literal nightmare."

I don't drink my coffee, either. I don't even know why I went through the motions of making it, honestly. Maybe I just needed something to do with my hands. Plus, Ivan always says hard conversations are easier over coffee.

"I suspected. I can't explain how or why, but I was fairly sure she was my match. I had to leave to reduce her risk of contracting FOS, but the rest of my pack-"

"The rest of your pack?" She stands so quickly that her chair falls back, and she spills coffee all over the table. "What the fuck do you mean? You told me she was held up for a few days doing interviews. God, do you lie like you breathe?"

"I didn't think you'd meet with me if you knew the extent of everything. I have a scent matched Beta who is matched with another Alpha, too. We're all Sax."

"I hate this, I hate this. She's never going to talk to me again. I'm going to lose my best friend. Why the hell did I sign her up for that show?"

She doesn't seem to care that the coffee is dripping onto her sneakers.

Can she smell the shame that is seeping out of me? I know how much I fucked up, but I have a plan to win Ariana back. Moving here is the first step.

I don't think Ivan and Grant are going to mind being closer to our girl.

Once Marlie calms down from her freakout, she leans across the table, getting in my face. "What is your plan? I know you have one. You will not abandon her to her fate. What is your plan, Derrick? And how can I help?"

Chapter Twenty-Six

IT TOOK me ages to fall asleep last night. How was I supposed to relax after telling Derrick I love him?

Oh my God, I told him I love him.

It wasn't even a conscious decision. It just fell out of my mouth.

There was no way I could stick around on the call after that. I don't have any answers to the questions he was sure to ask.

Love does not equal forgiveness. I can separate the two in my head. My heart? That's a different story.

But I recognize the undeniable affection I have for Derrick, even as I need to keep him at arm's length. The difference between this morning and the last is that now I know I have the capacity to forgive him.

It's going to take some time.

But it's possible.

Just like it's possible that I already love Grant and Ivan.

Sometimes, when Ivan talks, I can recognize it as something Sax said.

Ivan calls me sweetie.

Grant calls me baby.

Derrick calls me honey.

Sax called me all three.

If I had my phone, I bet I could scroll up and point out messages from each of them because of that.

"It's going to be okay, baby. I know you can handle this."

"Sweetie, you're the smartest person I know. You have nothing to worry about."

"Alright, honey. I'll agree with you. This time."

"You awake, sweetie?" Ivan is at the door, and his use of the pet name has my heart fluttering.

"Yeah, let me get dressed."

"Oh, don't put yourself out on my account. I'm happy to come in now."

God, his flirting is going to be the death of me. Since the heat spike, I've fought not to think about the guys that way, but it is really hard.

"Don't be weird!" Grant's voice sounds far away, but I can still hear him chastising his Alpha.

Five minutes later, I've brushed my teeth and put a bra on and head into the living area. I don't bother with my contacts. I'll do that after I shower.

"She's alive!" Ivan dramatically throws himself at me, stopping short of falling to my feet. "We worried that something was wrong when you ran straight into your room after the interview."

Right. I need to tell them about the call.

"I didn't mean to worry y'all." Grant hands me a coffee before my ass hits the chair. I don't have to sip it to know he made it exactly the way I like it. "It wasn't an interview. It was a phone call from Derrick."

My Beta's eyebrows shoot up into his hairline. "Shit, really? What did he say?"

"A lot. We argued a bit, too."

Chapter Twenty-Six

Ivan snorts into the espresso cup that looks like a toy in his big hands. "I expect nothing less."

Do I tell them I told him I loved him?

Shouldn't they know that? They're in a pack. Don't they share everything?

"I don't know how packs work. Like, is it an everything is an open book thing? No keeping secrets?"

Grant waggles his hand. He doesn't seem put off by my question. "We don't like keeping secrets, but we don't have to tell each other everything, either. It's kind of a need-to-know basis. Like, if it will affect us all, we'll tell each other, but if it doesn't? There's nothing wrong with holding some things to your chest."

So that's the question. Will my telling Derrick I love him affect the guys?

It will, won't it?

He's their packmate, and he loves me, and I told him the same. Regardless of how much his lies hurt me, I cannot imagine my life without him. All of them, if I'm being honest with myself.

They're all Sax. I love parts and pieces of each of them.

It's easier to admit it about Derrick, since he was the first, and his is the voice I heard and face I saw.

But when I reminisce about those moments, Ivan and Grant are now there too.

"I told Derrick I love him."

It's like ripping off a bandage. The words leave me wincing with their sting.

When I get up the guts to look at the guys, I'm not sure what I expected to see.

It wasn't to see Ivan's face lit up, his smile so wide I can practically see his molars, and Grant gazing at me with soft, wet eyes like I am a miracle, a soft smile curving his lips.

It's not long before Ivan's excitement spills out into crowded words.

"So you forgive him? This… we can work? You're willing to give us a real try?"

"I don't think I forgive him, not yet. But I am not opposed to it. I'm willing to give him a shot at making it up to me."

Grant adjusts himself in his chair, opening his chest up to me. "What does that mean for us?"

I run my fingers through my unruly hair, looking everywhere but either of them. "It means I want to know you. I want to… date? Court? Give this the good ol' college try."

Oh my God I need to stop talking.

I can hear Grant smothering a laugh. "Take a crack at it."

"Oh, I'll crack something for you." Ivan winks at me, overexaggerated and flirty.

A laugh bursts out of me, and it quickly devolves into a fit of giggles that I cannot seem to stop. Tears are streaming down my cheeks, and I'm clutching my stomach as I bend over.

Grant smacks Ivan's chest with the back of his hand. "You broke her, you weirdo."

"I did not. I made her laugh. Which I've done several times now, thank you very much."

"By being crude. Again. She's going to think you're a pervert."

Ivan shrugs. "I am a pervert. For you. For her." He wiggles his eyebrows and leans across the table. "I cannot help it that I'm surrounded by sexy people. I only have so much self-control. You get it, right, Ariana? I mean… look

Chapter Twenty-Six

at him." Ivan gestures up and down Grant's body, making the Beta flush red. "I am but an Alpha, after all."

There's only one part of their pack dynamic I never got around to asking about. "So, Ivan. Do you and Derrick…"

Ivan looks like he caught a whiff of something bad. "Ew. No. I'm not into Alphas. It's hot to watch the two of them together and share Grant, but Derrick and I are strictly platonic."

This conversation is only possible because the two are unashamed about how they feel for one another. There are so many ways to be together, especially within a pack, that being shy is doing everyone a disservice.

Not that I know much about relationships.

In our culture, sex doesn't matter much when it comes to people's preferences. Designations drive attractiveness, and there tends to be little preference for the genitals a person has.

There are groups that are trying to change that. One Alpha, one Omega purists who don't believe in packs. And there are people who think Alphas and male Betas shouldn't be together because there is no chance for procreation.

Not that I thought the guys would be like that, but it's nice to have it confirmed.

"It works out well," Ivan continues. "I'm a voyeur, Grant is an exhibitionist. Everyone wins."

This is news to me. Derrick was the one I had *spicy* conversations with, and he didn't share either of those things with me.

But he did share something.

"Is Derrick the only one who is into, uhm…" I can't believe I'm asking this on television. This is essentially admitting I had phone sex with Derrick multiple times. Do they know that? I'm sure they do.

I clear my throat and take a sip of my coffee before I continue. "Is he the only one into orgasm control and bondage?"

"Oh, yeah, that's all him." Grant's voice is dreamy, almost nostalgic. He's obviously been on the receiving end of that more than a few times. "Ivan is the exact opposite."

"What's the opposite of bondage?"

Ivan perches himself on the table in front of me. "Liberty, I guess." How he says that with a straight face is beyond me. "Freedom to move around. But that's not really what Grant meant, because I also enjoy having someone tied up and at my mercy."

My Beta's cheeks turn a pretty shade of pink. "Forced orgasms. Probably more than you could ever want. It's a fun but frustrating tag team they play. Derrick is refusing to let you come, but Ivan is trying to pull as many out of you as he can. They make it a competition."

I cannot imagine how that works, and if I try, I'm going to have another heat spike. I don't want to go through that on camera again.

Oh. Shit. We're on camera.

I point at the camera mounted on the front of the fridge, even though there are hidden ones all over. That one is just the most visible. "Guys, we've been talking about this on camera. America is about to know what you're into in bed."

Grant shrugs and places his empty mug on the table. "I'm not ashamed of it. If someone wants to talk shit because of something consensual and fun that we do, that's on them. We're all adults. Besides, you haven't told us yours yet. So you're still safe."

Chapter Twenty-Six

Ivan leans forward and brushes some of my hair out of my eyes. "Don't use the camera as an excuse not to reciprocate, Ariana. We showed you ours, now it's time for you to show yours."

Chapter Twenty-Seven

ARIANA CHEWS on her lower lip, and I want to take over for her. They're just so biteable, plump, and look ridiculously soft. I bet she uses one of those weird lip glosses that have sugar pieces in them, so it feels like sand got kicked onto your mouth. That's gotta be why they look so good.

Will she taste like the sweet cream and citrus scent that I can't get enough of?

"You don't have to tell us anything, baby." Grant takes her hands in his. "This isn't a quid pro quo thing."

"I'm a pervert, but not that much of one. A consensual pervert, if you will." I lean back on my palms, still perched on the table in front of her. If she moved her chair a little, she'd be between my knees.

I hope she does it.

My Omega takes a deep breath, and when she exhales, her green eyes meet my dark ones. "No, I should tell you." She looks nervous to, but she's a big girl. If she thinks she needs to, I'm not going to stop her. She's allowed to make decisions for herself.

"You guys know I'm a virgin, right?"

"Not a lot of people to pick up when you're stuck in your house." Grant says it without judgment and squeezes her hand. "That's not something that matters to us. Virginity is a social construct invented to make people feel like their worth is between their thighs."

She turns her hand over, lacing their fingers together. It makes my heart want to explode. I think she actually meant it when she said she was going to give us a chance if she's holding his hand.

People don't just hold hands all willy-nilly.

"Oh, I know. I bring it up because… This is theoretical, okay? I've never done it, so it may need to stay in the realm of fantasy."

I scoot closer to the edge of the table, because I already know this is going to be good. "Yeah, some things don't translate out of fantasy, I get that."

"Right. So you know how, when in heat, an Omega is begging, desperate? Like insatiable? Maybe even a little annoying? I want to be treated like that all the time."

Grant's eyes dart to me with a glare that tells me not to speak right now, which is fair. The things I want to say would have her running.

He pulls their hands to his mouth and kisses the back of hers. "You want to be horny all the time?"

She tugs on the ends of her hair, looking up at the ceiling as if she can't bear to look at us. "No. I want to be treated as if I am begging for it at all times. Kind of like free use, but add in a little degradation about how needy I am." She drops her voice and closes her eyes. Does she think that if she can't see us, we can't see her?

"I want to be told how much I want it. How you're a little annoyed with me because I wouldn't stop pleading to be fucked, and that it seems like that's all I'm good for."

She is too close to being between my knees when my

cock is this hard. My knot is already trying to swell. If she were to glance down, there is no way I could hide the impact her words are having on me.

I try to hold my tongue, but I can't. I can't let the three of us sit in silence when she was so vulnerable with us.

"I haven't heard of that one before, but I don't think any of us will have a hard time accommodating you."

Grant mouths '*Accommodating?*' at me. I'm trying to be a gentleman, here. I think if I told her that if that's the case, I'm going to take her right fucking now, she'd run away.

Wait, would she want to be chased?

Oh fuck, I hope she wants to be chased.

"As I said, it's all theoretical. But yeah. That's my 'thing', I guess."

I can't help myself. I thought I didn't want her between my thighs, but I have changed my mind. I hook my legs around her chair and haul her closer. "And Derrick knew?"

"Yeah. I brought it up once when I was in heat, apparently. I don't remember telling him, but I knew that he was not making it up."

Oh shit, orgasm denial as punishment for the imagined begging.

Forced orgasms to help satisfy her because she's so needy.

There are so many opportunities to be had with this. Is it presumptuous to say I know I can help her out with this fantasy?

Probably.

But I definitely can.

"Thank you for telling us." Grant squeezes her hand and gives her one of those coy smiles that photographers love to see when he poses for them. The one that says, "I know you want to fuck me, but I'll let you pretend you don't."

Chapter Twenty-Seven

I clap, startling both of them. "Well, I think we gave the show some good footage. We could hide out in the bathroom for the rest of the day, and they'll still be able to fill an episode, no problem. I wonder if that means they'll let us skip today's challenge."

Ariana stands and gathers our empty cups. "No way they'll let us skip. Have you ever even watched the show?"

"In fact, I have not." I shrug and trot after her like an obsessed puppy. "I didn't even know about it until they contacted us."

"And you didn't think to binge older seasons to know what you were agreeing to?"

I'm doing my best not to stare at her ass while she fills the dishwasher, but it is a futile effort. Even in baggy pajama pants, I can see its delicious shape.

Would she squeal if I sank my teeth into it?

Grant follows us into the kitchen and leans against the fridge. He's blocking the camera on the door, but I don't think he cares. "The others didn't care what the show was like because we'd get to meet you. It could have been one of those shows where we have to eat pie with our hands behind our backs, and they wouldn't have cared."

Ariana tosses a rag at him, hitting him square in the face. "Don't put that out there, or that may be our challenge! That sounds like my nightmare."

I pinch the bridge of my nose. "Guys. You know they're going to do it now, right? You put it out there. They're gonna do it."

She waves off my words. "Nah, it's highly unlikely. That is too lowbrow for the show."

THEY DID, in fact, make us eat pies with our hands behind our backs.

When Bradley came on the television and told us to check outside the door, he had this glint in his eyes that told me it was exactly what we didn't want.

At least the prize was worth it.

A phone call home. Ten minutes in the interview room. And Grant and I got approval to combine our time to call one person.

Grant is sitting on my lap in the tiny interview closet as we wait for the producers to patch Derrick into the speaker system.

"What are you going to ask him?" He wiggles deeper into my lap. I'm so on edge from our conversation with Ariana that I don't know if I should force him to sit still to avoid riling me up again or pull him closer and grind him against my cock.

"No idea. I figured he'll have more questions than we do."

Before Grant can respond, the line clicks on.

"Guys!"

"Hey, Alpha." Even though it's only been two days, I know Grant is missing Derrick. He's crawled into my bed to sleep both nights. "Are you doing okay?"

"Uh... Well. Define okay."

"Not broken? Not crying? What else could it mean?" I try to turn so that Grant and I face the camera, not the speaker, but it's hard not to look at it when I talk.

"Well. I quit my job."

Grant's jaw drops open. "Why would you do that?"

"Ariana told me she lives in Hollywood, Florida. So I'm moving to Hollywood. I've got a short-term rental right now."

"Oh, hell yeah." I can do my job from anywhere. And if, for some reason, my company doesn't accept a change

Chapter Twenty-Seven

of address, data analyst jobs aren't that hard to find. "So we need to put the house on the market."

"I'd love it if you guys came with me, but I'm not going to force you. Grant would need a job transfer, and he'd lose his modeling gig."

Our Beta does not look bothered by that at all. "Hollywood isn't far from Miami, right? Miami is kind of a fashion hub. They have their own fashion week. And I'll apply for a transfer at work. Let's do it."

"Just like that? You two are sure you're all in?" I'm a little offended that Derrick feels the need to ask that. We've all been in love with Ariana for years. Why would that have changed while spending time with her?

I run my fingers through Grant's hair to give me something to do. "Of course we are. She's everything. We've really been connecting."

"Good. Because the movers are already on their way."

Chapter Twenty-Eight

"OH MY GOD! *Tell me everything! I've missed you so much.*" Marlie's voice reverberates around the small room.

"I only have ten minutes, so you'll have to settle for the top line."

"Spill, spill, spill."

I press my feet against the wall and slip a little down the chair into a reclining position. "Well, Sax is real, but he's three people. And he's an Alpha."

"Oh, no, I can't believe it." Her words are a little strangled, which is an odd change from the exuberance she possessed just a moment ago.

"Yeah. Imagine my shock. Add in the fact that he's my scent match…"

Her horrified gasp is a little validating, honestly. *"I need you to know that I am so sorry for signing you up for this show, Ariana. This was your worst fear, and I'm responsible for making it happen."*

"I appreciate the apology, and I'll figure out a way to get you back one day, but I've had to admit to myself that I wouldn't have held out much longer without meeting Sax.

Chapter Twenty-Eight

At least you helped me do it in a controlled environment where I was forced to hear them out."

I would've run in any other situation.

"Then tell me all about them."

"Grant is a Beta, scent matched to Derrick, who's the one from the pictures. He's gorgeous, Marlie. Like, an actual model. And he's also scent matched to Ivan, another Alpha who is so hot. Pure masculine perfection, I swear. And they're all my scent matches."

She makes a clicking noise with her mouth that almost sounds like she's grimacing. *"What are you going to do?"*

That's the question of the week, isn't it? What am I going to do? It's easy, in the vacuum of the *Expected* house, to say I'm going to give them a chance and get to know them. What is going to happen when we're out of here, and everything is long-distance again?

"I'm getting to know the guys." I have to make sure that I don't mention Derrick leaving the house. Even though she signed a non-disclosure agreement and they'll edit out a slip, they want to make extra sure that doesn't leak before the episode airs. "I'm learning which parts of Sax each of them is. And honestly, talking to them feels like talking to Sax. It's like I know them, their souls, even if all the facts aren't there."

"So you love them?"

"Possibly. The foundation is poured, and the frame is up, but we're not a house yet."

"Uh." Marlie pauses, as if she has no idea what to say. *"I don't watch those home makeover shows as much as you do, but aren't there a lot of steps after framing the house?"*

If I close my eyes, I can almost see us stretched out on my couch together. I didn't know I needed this so much. "Yeah. The roofing and rough-in and the rest of it are forgiveness and falling in love."

"Weird analogy just to say that."

"Bonding is giving them the keys." I think I can hear her eyes roll, which makes me laugh. "I didn't realize how much I miss you. I needed this."

"I miss you, too."

"What have you been up to?" It's only been a week since I left home, but I'm still two or three days out getting home, and it feels like so much has happened.

"Oh, nothing much. Nothing out of the ordinary at all. But let's talk about you! Tell me more about this pack…"

I FEEL LIGHTER than ever after my conversation with Marlie, even if it was way too short. I could've spent another half hour describing the way Grant's silvery lavender hair reflects in the light, or how comfortable I was when Ivan held me in his lap in the pack tub.

But I can't think about that. Not after everything we talked about today. I feel like I'm on the edge of a cliff, a step away from falling.

And it didn't help that after dinner we all cuddled up on the couch and watched more *Unexplainable and Bizarre*. Not that it's a particularly arousing show, but having my feet in Ivan's lap while he rubbed them, and Grant holding me against his side, meant I was having trouble paying attention to the show. The heat of their bodies and Ivan's pumpkin bread and Grant's orchid scents combined into something unexpected and delicious.

I was grateful for a little space to clear my head when I got the notification from Bradley that Derrick was ready for our call at eleven on the dot.

Chapter Twenty-Eight

"How are you today, honey?"

Has Derrick's voice always had that low purr in it?

"I'm okay. It's been a long day, but not in a bad way. Well, the pie-eating thing wasn't great."

"Pie eating?"

"Didn't the guys tell you when they called you? We earned the privilege by eating pies with our hands behind our backs."

"That is ridiculous. Why would the network want you to do that?"

I'm so used to having conversations with him on the phone that I don't pay attention to my mannerisms. I fall back into our old pattern, folding my legs under me in the chair and chewing on the ends of my hair.

"It's a long story that ends with Ivan saying if we didn't stop talking about that, they'd make it our challenge."

"How does that even come up in conversation?"

"Well…" Do I tell him about our sexually charged conversation? It's not like I've never talked about this stuff with Derrick before, even if we always pretended it didn't happen afterward. "It started with me telling them my fantasy." My voice gets quieter as I speak, but it's nothing compared to the silence coming out of the speaker.

When Derrick finally responds, the purr in his voice is richer, his tone deeper. *"The one about how you want to be treated like you're in heat and free to use?"*

I try to silence an aroused whine, but I don't think I manage. "That's the one."

"I bet they loved that. I know I have spent years imagining taking advantage of it."

Slick gathers between my thighs, and I drop my feet to the floor to squeeze them together. "You have?"

"Oh hell yes. Taking my Omega whenever I want, and punishing

you for being desperate for me? God, the possibilities. I could fuck you all day and never let you come."

Yeah, how am I supposed to think about anything other than that ever again? My whole body is hot just listening to him.

"Ivan would take care of me." I don't know why I bring it up, and I worry Derrick is going to be upset that I brought his packmate into it.

His laugh is throaty and so sexy I feel like I'm going to spontaneously combust. *"He won't have a chance if I keep you stuck on my knot all day."*

Oh, fuck.

Derrick has a knot.

Not one of those knot sleeves I've fantasized about him wearing when I thought he was a Beta, but an actual fucking knot.

What would that feel like? The toys are great, but I doubt they hold a candle to the real thing.

"Imagine it. I wake you up with my cock, and when you try to come, I pull out, ruining your orgasm, because you're a selfish Omega who thinks if she asks for it, she should get a knot whenever she wants. And you're so needy all day, begging for me, but I push you away before you can come every single time. Maybe Ivan will be there trying to get you off, but I think my bark could convince him to leave you alone. At least until I'm done with you. When I've decided you earned it, I'll turn him loose on you, and you'll regret asking for us because he'll give you every single orgasm I stole from you and then some."

Oh fuck fuck.

I am throbbing between my thighs, slick soaking through my leggings, and my flesh is so heated that I feel like I need to do a polar plunge.

"Maybe I'll let you watch me fuck Grant, but have Ivan hold your arms so you can't touch yourself like you did in the tub. Oh, I

could edge you while Ivan gives Grant so many orgasms he's begging to stop, and you have to watch, helplessly, knowing you won't be allowed even one."

"Derrick. Please." At this point, it doesn't matter that there is a camera in here. I don't care that others will see or hear this. I need him, or I am going to lose my mind.

"Please, what, Omega?"

Holy shit.

He's never called me Omega before, and I'm realizing why. There is no way to deny he is an Alpha when his words rumble like that.

"Help. I'm so... I..."

"Oh, did I get you worked up, honey?"

"Yes!"

"If I was a mean Alpha, I'd leave you hanging. But I'm not mean, am I? I'm a good Alpha. Aren't I?"

"You are a good Alpha." My mind may be foggy with a heat spike and arousal, but I know the words are true. After ruminating on the conversation last night about how he's always been my Alpha, there is no denying he has been in everything but title all of this time.

"Go ahead and slip your hand into your panties, Ariana." I follow his command without protest, groaning as my fingers slip through the slick. *"Good. One finger. That's all you're allowed right now. One finger on your perfect little clit."*

The moment I touch my clit, my body jerks. I'm so worked up that it won't take much for me to come. I rub slow circles with the pad of my index finger, and I don't try to stifle the pathetic whimper that slips from my lips.

"It sounds like you're getting ahead of me, Omega. You wouldn't do that, would you? You're going to listen to your Alpha, aren't you?"

"Yes." I groan and have to force myself to stop my finger from massaging my clit. He never told me I could move it.

"Good girl. I can tell you're worked up, so I won't torture you too much. You can use two fingers and rub yourself, but I want you to stop before you come."

I waste no time moving a second finger to my clit and making circles on it. "Why do I have to stop?" God, my voice doesn't sound like my own. It's wanton, pleading. I don't typically get like this outside of my heats.

"Because you need to ask permission, honey. That's the rule."

This isn't the first time we've had phone sex, but it is the first time outside of heat and that we've incorporated either of our kinks into it. I am so into it, I can't see straight.

It's only a few moments before I can feel the tidal wave of my orgasm growing. "I'm going to- I need to-"

"Oh, already? Desperate, needy thing, aren't you? As long as you say my name, you can come."

As soon as the permission is granted, my legs shake, and tension coils in my lower belly. "Oh, fuck, Derrick," I moan, thrusting my hips into the air. "Holy shit. Derrick, I'm coming, I-"

"Come for me, Ariana. Come for your Alpha."

And I do. The orgasm pulses through my body, leaving me weak but satiated when it's done. "Alpha." My voice is barely more than a sigh, but I know he can hear me.

"Such a good little Omega."

Maybe tomorrow, when I wake up, realize I had phone sex in front of a camera and that it is highly likely America is going to see footage of me masturbating, I'll regret what happened.

But I can't bring myself to right now. Right now, I feel satisfied in a way I'm not sure I've ever been before.

Because that orgasm didn't come from me. It came from my Alpha.

And I never realized how much I needed that.

Audience Reactions

EPISODE SIX

pastel_p1xel_punK > *Knot What You Expected*

I don't know if I'll ever forgive them for cutting the show as soon as Derrick and Ariana were getting to the good part. I was just as revved up as she was at that point. Fucking hell, that was hot.

blink_glitch > *Knot What You Expected*

Was that episode sponsored by Knots-A-Lot? Because that was the horniest episode of TV I've ever seen. I can't believe they showed that on network television.

omegavibes > *Knot What You Expected*

They had to have known what was going to happen when they put an Omega not on suppressants in a house with men that hot, right? I'm sure they didn't expect the scent match, but it looks like Derrick doesn't have to be there to get Ariana's engine running.

..psycho..alpha..4real > *Knot What You Expected*

I kinda feel bad for Grant and Ivan. They had to have been worked up from their earlier conversation, and she gets taken care of on a phone instead of sliding into their beds. That would hurt my feelings, honestly. I hope that booth is soundproofed.

Knot What You Expected

EPISODE SEVEN

BRADLEY: WOO, OUR LAST EPISODE WAS HOT AND HEAVY.

BRIDGETTE: IT SURE WAS, BRADLEY. I THINK WE MIGHT BE STARING DOWN THE BARREL OF AN OFF-CYCLE HEAT AT THIS POINT.

BRADLEY: HOW OFTEN DOES THAT HAPPEN?

BRIDGETTE: WHEN MEETING A SCENT MATCH? I HAVE TO IMAGINE IT'S NOT UNHEARD OF. EITHER WAY, IT SURE DOES MAKE CENSORING THE EPISODE HARD FOR OUR TEAM!

BRADLEY: IT'S DAY SIX, WHICH MEANS TODAY'S CHALLENGE IS THE LAST THEY'RE GOING TO GET. WITH EVERYTHING THAT'S BEEN HAPPENING, THEY'RE GOING TO NEED TO MAKE SURE THEY COMPLETE THIS ONE.

Chapter Twenty-Nine

β Grant

I WAKE with a hard cock pressed against my ass, moving up and down my crease. I can't hold back a sleepy moan.

"Morning, Beta." Ivan's voice ghosts against my neck. He drags a hand down my stomach, stopping right at the top of my boxers. "You smell so good this morning. I don't think I'm going to be able to keep my hands off of you."

"What about Ariana? She'll hear us."

He dips his fingers beneath my waistband, massaging the base of my cock. "And if she does? You love to put on a show."

"I don't want to make her uncomfortable." He grips my cock so tightly that I groan and throw my head back on the pillow.

"She enthusiastically watched you and Derrick. I think our Omega may surprise you. Besides, it's early. She stayed up late talking to Derrick. I'm sure she's still sleeping." Ivan slowly strokes me, teasingly, as he grinds his cock into me.

It's been a bit since I was with my Alpha, and I have been craving him. He's a much softer lover than Derrick, and that's what I want right now.

"Come on," he growls in my ear. "I want you, Grant."

My body grows loose as he pumps his fist up my cock. I can barely get the words out because I'm struggling to hold back my sounds of pleasure. "I want you, too, Alpha."

His hand on my dick speeds up, and the other presses me tighter against his body. He rubs himself between my cheeks, driving me closer to the edge. "Then you need to come for me, because I forgot to pack the lube." My Alpha continues rutting against me and pulls my earlobe between his teeth. My entire body grows stiff as my orgasm barrels down on me.

Ivan's pumpkin bread scent is so rich, so spicy, as it wraps around me, that I want to do nothing more than swallow it down. The only thing that would make it better is pecans and creamy oranges.

My Alpha chomps down on my ear, his breath shallow, growly pants, as he swipes his thumb over the tip of my cock. I lose myself in the sensation, my cum dripping down my shaft. My Alpha catches it all in one hand and pulls my boxers down with the other. He doesn't say anything as he teases my entrance with one cum-covered finger. I can hear him slather his cock with the rest.

Damn, that is so hot.

It doesn't take long for him to stretch me, and when he notches his cock against my softened hole, I let out a loud whine. "Fuck me, Alpha."

My dick is already hardening again as he slips past the outer ring, and a keening sound escapes me. Ivan slaps his hand over my mouth, and I taste myself on his palm.

"Shh, don't wake her up." His words flutter over my ear, and shivers wrack my body. "Unless you want our Omega to see how needy you are. How you fall apart with the smallest amount of attention."

He's a passionate lover, not pounding into me, but his

pace is enough to leave me with a pleasant ache. When he adjusts his position and his dick slides against my prostate, my eyes roll into the back of my head.

"You needed this, didn't you, Beta? You needed reminding of who you are now that our Omega is here. You're mine. And Derricks. And hers. You're going to take as good of care of her as you do of us, aren't you? No one will be left wanting when you're around."

I whimper against his hand, and he pulls it far enough away from my mouth, allowing me to answer. "Whatever you need from me. I want to give you all everything. Take what you want from me. I'm yours."

Ivan growls and slams into me, pace growing frantic. He decides to leave my mouth uncovered so he can grab my cock and jerk it in time with his thrusts.

I'm on the edge, close to coming again already with the dual pleasure, when the door opens.

Ariana stands there, with one sock, messy hair, her glasses on, and pajama pants so low on her hips that I can see the top of her pretty pink panties. Her eyes widen at the sight of us, but either Ivan doesn't see her, or he doesn't care because he's still fucking into me without stopping.

An explosion of citrus and creamy vanilla fills the room. She grabs her neck, chest rising and falling rapidly as she watches us.

She doesn't say anything.

Two thrusts later, and my orgasm hits me like a freight train.

My body tightens and twitches as my cock empties itself onto the bed in front of me. I groan her name, long and loud.

"That's right, you love putting on a show for our Omega, don't you?" Ivan's growled words prove he's known she was here. But I cannot deny them.

Chapter Twenty-Nine

"I do. So much."

My body is lax, and at this point, I am just a hole for my Alpha to use. He presses my head down into the pillow, hiding my view of Ariana, and pumps hard into me. His knot bumps against my rim, but he doesn't try to force it in. I have no interest in being knotted, but I won't deny that the extra stimulation feels great.

With a groan, Ivan's hips stutter, and I feel his dick twitching in my ass as he fills me.

The room is quiet as he collapses on top of me, the only sound our heaving breaths.

And then our Omega breaks the silence.

"Goddamnit, I cannot continue to get horny in this fucking house."

BY THE TIME Ivan and I are cleaned up, Ariana is at the stove making breakfast, her back to us.

"Hey, Ariana, I'm sorry about that."

Her voice is strained when she answers without looking over her shoulder. "No need to worry! I shouldn't have entered without knocking. That's my mistake! I'm the one who should be apologizing."

Ivan snickers and slides beside her. She startles as he leans around her and picks something out of her pan and tosses it in his mouth.

"Did you enjoy the show, at least?"

Though I only see a sliver of her face when she looks at him, I can tell how red it is with embarrassment. "How could I not? You've seen yourselves."

"And now you've seen us, too." He leans over and kisses

the tip of her nose. "Plus, you know Grant likes to be watched. He enjoyed that more than he'll admit."

She clatters around in the cabinets for plates. They hit the counter with a thunk, and she starts plating the food she made.

I grab my plate and look to see what she made. "Fried rice?"

"Yeah. We had leftover rice and eggs. It's one of my favorite breakfasts." She places a handful of forks on the table before grabbing the mug of coffee she left beside the stove.

"Well, I for one am stoked." Ivan snags the chair next to Ariana and pushes it so close to her that they're almost on top of each other.

"It smells delicious." My first bite confirms that it tastes even better than I thought it would. It's the perfect savory breakfast that will fill me up until lunchtime, for sure.

We eat in a not-quite-comfortable silence for a few minutes before the TV pings and Bridgette's voice fills the room.

"Good morning, lovebirds!"

Ariana wrinkles her nose in displeasure. I don't know if it's the interruption, calling us lovebirds, or just Bridgette in general that she dislikes.

"Sup, Bridgette?" Ivan doesn't turn to the television, but he does stare at the camera on the fridge with unnerving eye contact. "What have you got planned for us today?"

"As I'm sure you're well aware, you will be leaving the house tomorrow. That means you'll recieve your last challenge today. If you successfully complete it, you'll recieve our grand prize."

My Alpha's back goes ramrod straight. "There's a grand prize?"

"Told you you should've watched the show," I mutter.

Ariana nods and turns toward him. "Yeah, not every group is keen to complete the challenges given to them. I mean, some people are lied to by their moms, their bosses, whoever. Once, they even had the jealous best friend who was pretending to be a famous Alpha in an attempt to make her Omega friend cheat on her partner."

That was a crazy season.

She pushes her hair behind her ear. She hasn't changed out of her pajamas or put her contacts in yet. I love this soft look on her. It's what I want to wake up to for the rest of my life.

"They do a grand prize if you complete all the challenges. There's only been two or three seasons where someone's got it. Honestly, our challenges have been fairly easy in comparison to a few of the seasons."

Bridgette interjects as soon as Ariana finishes speaking. "Which was a decision made by production since you all were already going through so many difficulties with the accidental scent matching and heat spikes."

My Omega buries her face in her hands with a disdainful whine.

"Aren't you curious about the prize?" Bridgette may not have access to our live video feed, or she might be bad at reading the room, because she embarrassed the shit out of Ariana.

Ivan rubs his hand over our Omega's back as he answers her. "Yeah, sure."

Bridgette squeals in excitement. "Round-trip, first-class flights to Vegas, premium tickets to see the incredible Cirque de Mordu, and two weeks in the penthouse suite at the luxurious resort Hedonistic Heat!"

Oh, shit. That's a great prize.

Hedonistic Heat is a resort that caters specifically to

Omegas and their packs during heat. Two weeks is more than enough time to get through a heat and do some sightseeing. I've never been, but I've heard people talk about it. It's all-inclusive, with a nesting space, jacuzzi tubs, and food and drink delivered.

It takes on many of the difficult parts of a heat and outsources them, while offering beautiful views and luxury accommodations. There's one in most major cities.

But the one in Vegas? That's the pinnacle. And the penthouse? That has to be tens of thousands of dollars a night. Plus the flights, the circus tickets, and all our expenses?

This is an incredible prize, and I want to earn it for Ariana. She deserves to be spoiled.

"What will we need to do to earn that?" There is no way that this is going to be an easy earn, and I need to know what they're expecting of us.

"Oh, well, that's the question, isn't it? Your challenge should arrive soon." Her Cheshire grin is practically burned into the screen as the TV turns back to the show's logo.

We've barely had time to look at each other before a knock sounds at the door.

"I guess I'd better get that."

I snag Ariana's forearm as she tries to pass me. "No, I'll get it. We don't know what it is, and if it's heavy, I don't want you to have to carry it."

I'm not particularly muscular, but I am stronger than I look.

She sighs in relief and falls back into her chair.

I rip the door open, blinking against the morning light before registering what I'm looking at.

Chapter Thirty

"AND YOU DIDN'T LET her know that you've met me, did you?"

Marlie's voice is snippy through the phone. *"No, I didn't, and I hated it. I hate lying to her."*

I pull my glasses off and pinch the bridge of my nose. "You agreed that this is one of those times where a little lie is worth it. That it's better for her not to know what we're doing. Do you not feel that way anymore?"

"Maybe it's my guilt over putting her into this situation to begin with."

Marlie has been beating herself up over applying for the show for Ariana, and, in the process, exposing her to her scent matches, but how would she have known? She was trying to do right by her best friend.

Besides, she's doing what she can to help me make it so that Ariana never feels trapped with the guys or me.

"It'll work out. She'll understand."

"I just can't believe she forgave me. I don't know if she's going to be able to give me any more leeway."

I rub my temples. We've been going around in circles

about this for ten minutes, and it's giving me a headache. I don't have time to manage her spiral. I have things to do. They're out of the show tomorrow, and I need to be ready. The movers should be dropping the temporary storage pod off today, and I've hired a real estate agent to get the ball rolling on putting our house on the market.

We don't have a permanent place to live right now, but that's okay. The vacation rental agreed to let us stay here for three months, and hopefully, by then, we will have figured out our next steps.

It's too much to hope that Ariana will let us move in with her, but an Alpha can dream.

And after our call last night?

I was so hard I thought I would fall into a rut. Listening to her sweet, breathy sighs as she touched herself to my words? I must've gotten off three times since then.

I'm getting hard again just thinking about it, and now is *not* the time.

"Are you still there, Derrick?"

I clear my throat, trying to shake off the dregs of arousal. "Yeah, sorry. Got lost in thought for a second. If Ariana gets upset, blame me. She's going to need you when she gets back. Especially when the show airs."

Are we going to have to sequester ourselves entirely so we don't spoil how the season ends? Or will it be enough to ignore everyone on social media?

After all the episodes air, there is a live reunion show where we sit in front of an audience and talk about our experience.

I hope to have earned her bite by then.

But it's not going to be easy. Nothing worth having is.

I'll get there. I'm determined to earn her forgiveness.

We love each other, and while love may not be the only thing you need, it's a great start.

Chapter Thirty-One

GRANT COMES BACK to the table, a manila envelope in his hand. I expected a lot more than a single envelope, given the buildup Bridgette did.

"What's that?" Ivan leans over his shoulder, trying to see what Grant is holding.

"I haven't opened it yet. Can't be much."

I reach over and put a hand on top of his. "Do you want to do the honors?"

Instead of answering, Grant opens the envelope. He pulls out a single piece of paper and places it in front of me. "You read it."

READ THIS OUT LOUD:

ARIANA, GRANT, AND IVAN,

ARE YOU READY FOR YOUR LAST CHALLENGE HERE IN THE *EXPECTED* HOUSE? WE'RE THRILLED BY THE WAY YOU'VE BONDED AND SHARED SO MUCH OF YOUR-

SELVES WHILE HERE, DESPITE THE SOMEWHAT ROCKY START. EVEN WITH DERRICK HAVING TO LEAVE THE HOUSE, YOU HAVE STILL MANAGED TO MAKE REAL CONNECTIONS.

YOUR CHALLENGE FOR TODAY IS TO MAKE SURE THEY LAST. TO WIN THE GRAND PRIZE, YOU WILL NEED TO BITE ONE OF THE MEN INTO YOUR PACK, ARIANA.

YOUR CHOICE. YOU HAVE UNTIL MIDNIGHT.

THE LETTER WEIGHS a hundred pounds in my hands.

"Can they do that? Have they done this before?" Ivan snatches the paper from me, as if it will say something different when it's in his hands.

"No, they haven't." Grant's voice is shaky and weak.

I don't say anything.

I can't.

The prize is huge, the biggest they've ever offered.

But I don't need a trip to Vegas.

I don't want a fancy trip.

Not when it comes with strings like this.

The prize is not enough to bind me to someone for life. They could reject the bond once I bite, but that's almost guaranteed to be a one-way ticket to an FOS diagnosis.

Ivan and Grant are wonderful. Getting to know them has eased much of the heartache of discovering that Sax wasn't real. But we're not there yet.

Are we?

Some Omegas bond their scent matches immediately. I have always thought that was a bad call. We're all human.

Chapter Thirty-One

Some matches could be awful people. Being a scent match doesn't mean that they're going to be good to you. And while the chance of meeting multiple scent matches isn't high, it's not impossible. Especially when, like Grant, Derrick, and Ivan, they're already tied to one another in some way.

No one actually knows what draws Alphas to packs. A lot of the time, packs form around Omegas. But so many Alphas give up their dream of having an Omega and pack up for companionship.

But the guys aren't awful people. They lied and deceived me, sure, but it was never for malicious reasons.

In their own way, they were protecting me. I didn't want to expose myself to Alphas, and they respected that, but they wanted to take care of me, be my emotional support, so they made it work.

My mind is reeling, my thoughts a jumbled mess, when Ivan's hand claps down on my shoulder.

"Sweetie, you do not have to do this. The prize is not worth your discomfort. But you should know that, if you're ready, so are we. We want this."

I peer at him over my shoulder. "You do?"

Grant huffs a quiet laugh. "Yeah, baby. That's why we did what we did. We've always wanted you. I have loved you since the first time I heard your laugh through a video call with Derrick."

Ivan turns my chair gently until I'm facing him. He cups my cheek in his large hand. "For me, it was a voice memo you sent. You were pissed, ranting and complaining about that game you play and how your raid partners fucked everything up. I had no idea what you were talking about, but I knew that kind of passion was something I needed in my life. I've always been told I'm a little too much. Too loud, too touchy-feely, too much to handle. And when I heard you so pissed over a video game? I knew that you wouldn't think I was too much."

I place my hand over his. "Of course you're not too much! You're wonderful."

"Yeah, Alpha. You know we love you." Grant reaches around me and feeds his fingers through Ivan's empty hand.

Ivan grins and kisses the back of his Beta's hand. "I know. But that's how I knew she was the perfect fit for our pack. She's got Derrick's passion, my exuberance, and your kindness. She can argue with him, play with me, and find comfort in you."

All of this has my mind reeling. They want me to bond them.

They're okay with this.

I haven't slept with them, haven't even kissed Ivan, and he's saying he wants my bite. That he wants to be tied to me forever. I suppose that he could get tired of me one day and wants to spend a lot of money getting the bond dissolved, but I can't see him doing that.

"You could reject my bond. We'd still get the prize." My voice is barely above a whisper.

"Why would we do something like that? We want you, sweetie."

This challenge is forcing me to think about something I would have put off for as long as possible.

"I need a minute."

I'm on my feet, rushing into the room that looks like mine but isn't, before they can speak. I shove the door closed and lock it, needing to think about all of this without them staring at me.

I wear tracks in the carpet, my mind whirling.

Do I want to bond them?

Chapter Thirty-One

If there was none of the Sax baggage, how would I feel about them?

I think I'd trust them.

Even though I carry so much-

"Ariana, could you process this out loud?" Drew's voice through the television startles me into silence. "It gives us more to work with."

"Ugh, Drew. Can't I keep some things private?"

He rolls his eyes. "You had phone sex in front of a camera last night. I think privacy is out the window."

My face turns red, and I fall face-first on the bed. The reminder that people were watching me get myself off makes me a little sick.

"Don't worry, it'll be censored and cut off before it gets too saucy. Can't show that much on network television."

A small consolation.

"But, please. We need this footage. This challenge was given so you can confront your fears and reservations about pack Sax. It doesn't work if we can't hear what you're thinking."

Pack Sax. I kind of like that.

"Fine!" I roll over onto my back and wave at the camera in the corner of my room. "Hi, America. I don't so much care about the prize on offer, even though it's a massive one, but now that they've put the thought into my head, I can't stop thinking about how the natural end to this, to meeting my scent matches, is bonding with them. I feel like I'm on a time limit. The guys would never, ever, force me to bond with either of them, and I know the show can't make me, but now I'm having to ask myself if I ever want to bond at all. They deserve to know that before we leave and go our separate ways."

It's the big question.

Will I ever feel comfortable enough to give someone my bite?

"My brother died because his bonded Alphas died. Worse, they were his scent matches. I've done extensive research on FOS, but it's an underfunded area of medicine. So maybe some of the rich people watching this can make donations to a research foundation in Calvin's honor, yeah?"

An Omega can develop FOS in a few ways.

Spending a long time on high-dose suppressants, which lock up their Omega pheromones.

Being exposed to scent matches and losing access to their pheromones.

Having a bonded Alpha die.

"Calvin never stood a chance. It wasn't an if he got FOS, but rather a when."

I stand and resume my pacing. The TV has replaced Drew's face with the show's logo, so there are no responses to my words. However, processing out loud is actually helping me.

"That's why I stayed locked in my house for so long. If I stepped out of those doors, I could meet my scent match. If I never met my scent match, I never had to worry about something happening and not getting their pheromones. If I didn't take suppressants, I couldn't get FOS, either. And if I never fell in love with an Alpha, I'd never want to bond them, and that risk would be gone, too. It wasn't like I was scared of the world. I was scared of the potential the world held for ruining my life."

I'm scared of death. It blows my mind that some people aren't. Eventually, after so long locked in my house, I had convinced myself that the moment I was outside of those doors, an Alpha could come strolling past, and I would be trapped.

Chapter Thirty-One

And as terrified I was getting here, as devastated I was when I realized who the guys were to me, I haven't gotten that itchy feeling I used to get whenever I thought about leaving my house.

"I'm not cured of my anxiety by any means. And I much prefer being in my home rather than anywhere else, but the worst has already happened. I met my scent matches. What's the point in keeping myself locked up anymore? Maybe, when I'm no longer in this house with just them, I'll lose my shit in a crowd. But right now? I have to decide how I want them in my life long term, because they're going to be. Even if it's just meeting up once a week for a pheromone infusion. Fuck, that would be hard, though. Seeing them that often. I'm already falling in love with them. I already love them, I think. Seeing them, and not having them as mine, would probably kill me."

I stop pacing and look up at the camera again. "Okay, listen to me, America. I'm falling in love with them. I'm definitely in love with Derrick. It's easier to admit that because I've seen his face and heard his voice so much. Ivan and Grant, though? I didn't even know they existed. It doesn't matter, though. Meeting them has been like having deja vu. I know they're mine."

My hair is still an unwashed mess, so my fingers get stuck while I drag them through it. "Mistakes were made, but shit. My *soul* knows theirs. I can already feel them here." I hammer my fist on my chest. "They're here, and they'll never go away. It would kill me if they did. And that's the problem, isn't it?"

I think back to the letter from Calvin, to all the conversations we had after his pack died.

"Even though I lost my Alphas, being their Omega for any amount of time was better than never knowing them. You'll understand one day, when you find those people for you."

"I don't want your fear and anger to force you to forget all of the wonderful, beautiful things that have happened to me over my life because of my designation."

I have let fear run my life since my brother took his last breath.

And honestly? Fear's done a pretty shitty job.

Anger hasn't done much better.

"Being their Omega for any amount of time was better than never knowing them."

My heart aches at the thought of him. It always does.

But I think I'm finally realizing what he wanted me to know. What he hoped I would find.

With my hand over my heart, tears falling down my cheeks, I open the bedroom door.

"I've made my decision."

Chapter Thirty-Two

"WHAT DO you think is going to happen?" I have felt as if I am going to crawl out of my skin since my Omega locked herself in her room.

Grant runs his fingers through his hair, not looking away from her door. "I don't know. I think it was really shitty of the producers to ask her to do this."

"It wouldn't be a grand prize if it were easy." Bridgette's voice surprises me. I hadn't seen her face pop up on the screen or heard the bell sound that precedes her. "You're not being forced to do it."

"Even putting that idea out there was unfair. Her worst fear came true, and now you're asking her to bond with one of us?" It's not anger that flashes in Grant's eyes, but devastation. "This could push her away from us for good."

"I don't believe that will happen. Everyone can see how much you care about one another. Things will work out. And when it does, I want an invitation to your bonding celebration."

The TV goes black, with only the logo bouncing around on the screen.

Before we have time to process the interaction, the door to Ariana's room opens.

"I've made my decision."

When I get her in my sights, my stomach bottoms out. She's crying, clutching at her chest as if there is a physical ache.

Fuck.

This isn't good.

If she rejects us now, I worry there will be no second chance. And she's not ready to bond us.

I would have shown her my neck the moment I first laid eyes on her if it wouldn't have made her run away screaming. I'm all in. And I know Grant is too. Either of us would let her sink her teeth into us right now.

But to do it for a prize makes it feel cheap.

Forced.

And the last thing I want is to take this decision from her. We've hurt her so much with our deception already, I won't let her do something she'll regret.

Before I can open my mouth and tell her to forget it, we're not doing this, she speaks.

"I opened the letter from Calvin when I first got here. And it hurt so much to read. It was like he was sitting there with me. I could hear his voice in my head. Not that it ever left. But he told me not to let his death be the most memorable thing about him. And honestly? It has been. It's driven every decision I've made since I was sixteen." She sniffles and wipes the tears off her face, and I want nothing more than to pull her into my arms.

But I won't. I want her to be able to say her piece before she rejects us.

"Except coming on this show. When I accepted their invite, I wasn't thinking about Calvin's death or all the Alphas I'd come into contact with getting here. It still scared me when I had to make the journey, but that didn't play into my agreeing to come here. To meet Sax. I knew that meeting him would make the risk worth it. That if I was ever going to put myself in danger of meeting a scent match, it would be for him. For you guys."

Grant reaches out and grabs my hand, squeezing it and seeking reassurance from his Alpha. Ariana is still half a room away from us, and I can't smell her scent, but somehow I know it'll be bitter and sour. My Beta's typically sweet floral scent smells more like the soil an orchid grows in.

"*'I want to be the reason why you take a chance on something. I want to be the reason why you follow your heart. I want to be the reason why you trust yourself enough to fall in love.'*" She fists her hips and looks up at the ceiling, but it doesn't stop the tears that track down her cheeks. "He wrote that in the letter. One of the things I kind of glossed over. I tried to pretend he hadn't said it. He also said he didn't want to be a ghost that haunts my footsteps, and he has been. For ten years, his death has followed me everywhere."

I can't help myself anymore. I'm on my feet, crossing the room, and pulling her into my arms. Grant is right behind me, embracing her from behind. A sob cracks her chest, and she melts into our arms.

"My big brother was amazing. He was strong, loving, and brave. And he wanted me to take a chance. To follow my heart. And I owe that much to him. I deserve to have the kind of love he got from his pack."

My breath catches.

"He said that he knew that they were his pack immediately. He just knew, even without catching their scents and having that confirmation. He knew. And I know. I've always known. Whether you're three people or one, you're my pack."

Grant is smothering silent tears against her back, his shoulders bouncing as he wraps his arms tighter around her.

I'm crying, too.

Because she called us her pack.

"I want to bond. Both of you."

Our Beta loses control of his knees and drops to the ground, arms banding around her knees as his quiet sobs become loud in relief.

"You don't have to do this," I tell her, grabbing the back of her neck. "We can wait."

She tilts her head and presses our foreheads together. "We could. I'm sure people will judge me, thinking I'm doing this just for the prize, but I'm not. Why should we wait when we know what we are to one another? You're mine, and I'm yours. That won't change when we leave this house. It will never change."

Then her lips are on mine, and I am kissing Ariana for the first time.

I've heard my entire life that my Omega would change everything for me. Older family members would grab my hands and tell me the right Omega for me is just waiting to be found. Even as a kid, our fairy tales and movies make the bond between an Alpha and an Omega seem like the stuff of dreams. And she is. She didn't even know who I was until six days ago, and yet she knew I loved her. She may not have said that she loves me, too, but I don't need that. Offering me her bite is the highest honor she could bestow upon me.

Love isn't everything. But a house is only as strong as its foundation, and it makes a pretty fucking good one.

She pulls away, leaving me panting and chasing her lips. Before I can catch them, white-hot pain in my neck almost brings me to my knees.

Chapter Thirty-Two

The bond rolls through me instantaneously. I can feel her everywhere. Her sweet, cool presence wraps around me, and nothing will ever be the same again. The bond waits for me, and I know that I could reject it, like slamming a door in her face, but I would never.

For the seven years I've known her, this is all I ever wanted.

I open my heart and soul to her and let our bond settle right where it belongs behind my heart.

"Ariana," I whisper as I stroke the back of her head. "Hey, sweetie. I feel you."

She looks up, face still streaked with tears, but her eyes are bright, and her smile is blinding. "I can feel you, too. You're happy. You're actually happy."

"Happy doesn't begin to cover it."

Happy is how you feel on your birthday. It's laughing with a friend in the park as someone trips over their rollerblades. It's getting a surprise day off from work.

That's not what this is.

My soul is singing. The world feels different. Lighter. There is nothing I cannot accomplish with Ariana by my side.

I am not happy.

I am forever changed.

Things are going to be different moving forward, and I am so excited to embrace every change. I wonder how my scent is going to morph now that I'm bonded to her. How will Grant's? Derrick's?

My swirling thoughts quiet, and my mind goes blank when she pushes her hips against me. Pleasure zings through me, swelling my dick, at the softest touch from my Omega. I've heard from people that bonding can make you weepy, or horny, or both. I assumed we'd be weepy, and this turn of events has taken me by surprise.

It takes her pushing me toward the couch to notice that Grant had stepped back and given us some space. He's been waiting for us on the arm of the plush sofa, never taking his eyes off of her, when she shoves me onto it and straddles me.

The cameras that dot the room become an afterthought in the pleasure of the moment.

Let them watch.

The producers, the crew, America.

I don't care.

I've got my Omega on my lap and my Beta beside me. All that is missing is my best friend, and our pack would be complete.

Desperate hands plant on my shoulders, heat radiating from them. Ariana uses them as anchors as she grinds against my cock and makes the sweetest little whining sounds. I want to pull the front of my basketball shorts down and push into her, knot her, give her everything she wants. My instincts are going haywire with the need to take care of my Omega.

My voice is thick with arousal as I call to my Beta. "Grant. Help her with her pants."

A lascivious grin splits his face as he moves behind her and slips his hands under the waistband of her leggings. I pop her butt so she rises onto her knees, and he makes quick work of pulling them down her thighs. As she's revealed to me, I can feel myself slipping closer into a rut.

It takes some maneuvering for the two of them to get her pants off, but she's soon bare to me from the waist down. The scent of her slick is thick in the air. Creamy vanilla and tart citrus combine in a way that makes me desperate to get my mouth on her. Grant works her shirt off, and once he undoes her bra and leaves her naked and

Chapter Thirty-Two

wanting on my lap, he kisses and nibbles up the side of her neck.

As much as I want to feel her slick heat, to have her squeeze my knot, I am not going to take her virginity on television. She deserves better than that. Something intimate, where she's not entertainment for a horny crew watching through monitors.

I'll still take care of my girl, though.

I snake one of my hands between her legs, finding her slick with need, and gently stroke her lips. Her head snaps up, eyes wide as she stares at me in slack-jawed amazement.

"I'm the first person to touch this pretty pussy other than you, huh?" She sucks her lower lip into her mouth, cheeks flushed with embarassment but her chest painted pink in arousal. "I'm going to take good care of you, Omega. All you need to worry about is enjoying yourself."

Derrick would deny her until he was ready to watch her explode. Me? I'll give her as much pleasure as she wants, and then some. I want to see my Omega shatter into pieces.

My aching dick is jealous of my finger as it slips inside her. The vestibule inside her meant to catch my knot is one large pleasure center that I seek out and give attention to as I keep my thumb on her clit.

Our Beta grabs her hips and helps her rock against me. I can't wait to watch them together. Knowing the gentle, passionate lover he is, the way the two of them will move together will be art come to life.

My dick is so hard it feels like it may explode, but that's of no matter to me. I'm going to make sure our girl knows exactly how much she means to me and show her the pleasure she deserves. I'll worship her on my knees. I'll say my prayers against her flesh. I'll pledge myself to her with every flick of my tongue.

Ariana's breathing turns into pants as I curl my fingers and stroke inside her. She throws her head back onto Grant's shoulder as her legs shake, and slick floods my hand as she reaches her release.

That's one.

Omegas are always easier to get off when they're in heat, and I'm sure our bonding triggered another spike, but I didn't expect her to come already.

It makes me want to play a game.

"Hey, Grant." I don't remove my fingers from her as she comes down from the high. "How many days have we been in this house?"

"It's day six, Alpha. Why?"

I stretch Ariana with another finger. She clenches around me but doesn't protest. "Just trying to decide how many times to make her come. Six seems like a good number."

She shakes her head, unruly waves smacking me in the face. "No, no. Six is too much."

I kiss her on the tip of her cute little nose. "Hhhmmm. Maybe, but I think you can handle it. If it gets to be too much, just call out 'Red'. Red means stop, yellow is back off a bit, green is enthusiastic consent." She whines a little, but doesn't protest when Grant resumes grinding her against me. "Do you understand?"

She chews on her lower lip, eyes going hazy. "Red means stop."

"Red means stop."

I know this spike, the bonding, and making her come several times is going to bring on her heat faster than we expect. I can't wait to see her needy and desperate, wanting nothing more than to live on my knot.

Chapter Thirty-Two

Grant dips his head and sucks our Omega's neck between his lips. It's not gentle. His teeth flash as she gasps and moves against me. Her second orgasm takes over, and I kind of feel like I'm not doing enough for her, despite how much slick has seeped down my hand and onto my shorts.

Her body is eager for her Alpha after waiting for me for so long.

I take one of her nipples into my mouth, suckling and nibbling it as she continues to chase her pleasure on my hand. I love a woman who takes what she wants without shame. Grant licks and kisses her ear, and the combination of sensations has her rolling from her second orgasm into her third.

Oh, Derrick is going to struggle to deny her. Her greedy body takes what it wants.

This is going to be so much fun.

Ariana stills her hips with gasping, panting breaths. She exposes the long, creamy skin of her neck as her body shudders with her release, and I'm worried that she's done and is about to call her safeword. I shouldn't be. My girl takes what she wants, and right now, she's got her sights set on Grant.

She grabs his hair and pulls him away from her neck. He braces his hands on the couch on either side of my thighs, looking at our Omega with stars in his eyes. Without warning, she wrenches his head to the side, leans in, and bites him on the ear.

It's a delicate bite in an awkward place, but she does her best to have it curve with the shell of his ear. Hopefully, the scars will look like white studs around the edge.

I doubt he cares much about the aesthetic. Our Beta is panting, one of his hands gripping his cock through his pants, which now have a wet spot on the front, while the other is clutching onto the soft flesh of her hips for dear life.

Holy shit, did he come in his pants? Oh fuck, that is so hot. Knowing that he was so overwhelmed with pleasure while receiving our Omega's bite that he couldn't control himself, makes me want to lick him clean.

Ariana and I must be on the same page, because she climbs off my lap and kneels before him.

"Baby…" Grant's voice is strained as he looks down at her with reverence. She's slowly inching his pants off, the base of his cock barely visible.

She doesn't respond as she pulls his spent dick from his pants and licks and kisses around the head. Grant's refractory period has been trained by me to be short, and I'm sure he appreciates that now as he starts to stiffen under her attention.

When she gets brave and pulls his head into her pouty mouth, he feeds his fingers through her hair, moaning in a way I love to hear.

Yep, just as gorgeous as I thought they'd be together.

I want to stroke myself and watch the show, but I owe her three more orgasms, and I always pay my debts. I fall to my knees behind her and pull her hips up until she's kneeling, bracing herself with one hand on the floor and the other wrapped around Grant's shaft.

I slide my hands up the back of her thighs. "Show me that pretty pussy, sweetie. Spread your knees for me."

My perfect Omega gives me exactly what I ask for. Her slit drips with slick, and I am so fucking excited that I get to finally find out if she tastes as good as she smells. I spread her wide from behind, one hand on each cheek, before bending and licking her from front to back. Ariana has to drop her hold on Grant to brace herself with both hands as soon as my tongue finds her clit.

Chapter Thirty-Two

As I'm lavishing attention on the firm spot, Grant takes control of her mouth by carefully weaving her hair between his fingers.

I could live between her thighs. She tastes like a hint of her scent and feminine musk, and it is better than I ever could have imagined. Her body moves with my attention with fluid grace until she's grinding herself against my tongue with desperate mewls muffled by Grant's cock.

Orgasm four hits, and her elbows give up. Grant steps back, cock hard and dripping as she falls into submissive Omega presentation, chest on the ground, and ass up.

"Fuck me, please, Alpha." Goddamn, she is hard to deny.

"I'm trying to be good here, Omega. I don't want your first time to be on camera." She whines at my perceived rejection. I place a hand between her shoulder blades, anchoring her to the floor. "Open our bond and feel me, Ariana. I want nothing more than to take you just like this, knot you, and keep you stuck on me while our Beta fucks your throat."

Grant kneels beside her and strokes her hair, murmuring soft words of reassurance. "Our Alpha is going to take care of you, baby. You can have his knot when we're out of here."

While he coos at her and strokes her hair, I slide three fingers inside our Omega to give her some of that pressure she is begging for. As I curl my fingers inside her, her body quivers. I fuck her with my fingers to the erotic soundtrack of her keening moans.

Her fifth orgasm comes just as easily as the ones before. I know she can take a lot more than six, and I look forward to finding that limit. But not this time. I won't push her for more yet.

But soon? All bets will be off.

Grant leaves Ariana's head to slide underneath her hips. He has to put himself in an uncomfortable position, but he manages to get her clit between his lips, where he sucks gently as my fingers continue to massage her where she wants me most.

By the time her sixth orgasm hits, she is practically made of rubber, unable to maintain the position any longer. I ease my hand out of her, and Grant and I help her stretch her weary limbs. She mumbles something about taking care of us, but neither of us is worried about that. Grant grabs a blanket from the back of the couch and throws it across her naked body before we both snuggle up beside her on the floor.

This is better than I could've dreamed.

If only Derrick were here.

Audience Reactions

EPISODE SEVEN

SilentStream > *Knot What You Expected*

I did NOT expect her to go through with the bonding. But when she was looking at the camera and talking directly to us? God. I've always thought reality shows were scripted, and if they are, she needs to win some awards because that was so good.

GlowRush.89 > *Knot What You Expected*

Why the hell did they cut the episode *there*? I want her phone call with Derrick! I need to know how he's going to react to her bonding his pack!!

bitten+beautiful+disaster > *Knot What You Expected*

I'm surprised they showed as much of the intimacy as they did. I'm not exactly sure why they think we want to see that. We're here for the drama, not the smut!

beta4hire > *Knot What You Expected*

I don't normally watch reality TV, but my boyfriend told me I had to check this out, so I figured, what the hell? Oh my god, why am I now more invested in Pack Sax than I am in my own relationship? I have to see them get their happily ever after. I neeeeeeeeeeeeeeed it.

Knot What You Expected

EPISODE EIGHT

BRADLEY: DID YOU THINK THEY WERE GOING TO GO THROUGH WITH THE BONDING?

BRIDGETTE: I HOPED SO. IT'S SO OBVIOUS HOW MUCH THEY CARE ABOUT ONE ANOTHER, AND I THINK SOMETIMES WE ALL NEED A LITTLE PUSH TO TAKE THE NEXT STEP.

BRADLEY: THAT WE DO. AND I THINK THIS IS THE FIRST TIME I FEEL LIKE WE'VE BEEN LEFT ON A CLIFFHANGER!

BRIDGETTE: I KNOW! OUR AUDIENCE IS CHAMPING AT THE BIT TO HEAR THE PHONE CALL BETWEEN ARIANA AND DERRICK. IS SHE GOING TO TELL HIM? IS SHE READY TO BOND WITH HIM, TOO? OR WILL SHE KEEP IT A SECRET UNTIL SHE SEES HIM IN PERSON AGAIN?

BRADLEY: IT'S TIME TO FIND OUT, ON THE FINALE OF KNOT WHAT YOU EXPECTED.

Chapter Thirty-Three

"WE'RE PATCHING *you in now, Derrick. How are you feeling about them getting out tomorrow?*"

I stretch out on the rental couch, phone propped on my chest on speaker as I stare at the ceiling and listen to Drew's voice. "Weird. Excited. I'm ready to see all three of them. It feels like it's been longer than just a few days."

"I bet it does. Ariana's in the interview room. Sending the call in."

I hear the tell-tale click of the line switching, and my smile broadens even though she can't see me. I'm so glad I've gotten these phone calls. I needed this connection to her, and I think we've made a lot of progress. I didn't realize how much better things would be as Derrick than they were as Sax.

"Hey, honey."

"Hi, Derrick."

Her voice is soft, nearly blissed out. All I've ever wanted is for her to be happy, but I can't help but feel a little jealous that my packmates are the ones doing it while I'm stuck here on the sidelines.

Chapter Thirty-Three

But that's what a pack is for. With three of us, she'll always have someone on her side, someone to be with her. If I can't be the one holding her, I'm glad it's Grant and Ivan.

"How was your day?"

"Uh. Eventful. Today's challenge was intense."

There's something in her tone that has me on edge, and my back is locked tight as I perch on the edge of the bed. "What was it?"

"The prize they offered is massive. Two weeks in Vegas, first class flights, a penthouse suite at Hedonistic Heat." She stumbles over her words in a way she only does when she's anxious. I've heard that tone enough to know she's holding something back.

"That is a good prize. But what did they ask of you guys to earn it?"

"They challenged me to bond with one of the guys."

I'm pretty sure my heart has stopped.

I can't tell if I'm breathing.

They wanted her to bite one of the guys into her pack?

Did she? Which one?

"Oh. That's a wild challenge."

It kills me, but I don't ask her if she did it. I want to live in ignorance just a little longer, because the answer to that question will change everything. If she wants me to know, she'll tell me.

"I bonded with both of them."

I'm on my feet so fast my phone tumbles to the ground. I want to scream, to celebrate that we're going to be a real pack. She's going to accept me as her Alpha.

Until reality comes crashing down.

She doesn't have to bond me, too. There's nothing that says she has to keep our pack together. She can choose the two of them and kick me to the curb. I wouldn't be upset with them for going along with it.

I couldn't even blame her if she did. I deserve it after all of the lies.

I will never deserve her, but I'm trying to show her that she can trust me with her heart. Maybe, when she learns what I've done, she'll give me a chance to show her that I can be good to her.

All I have wanted for ten fucking years is Ariana Cooley. I wanted her when we were teenagers, learning about ourselves and the world. I wanted her when we were in college, trying to figure out our place in life. I wanted her when I started my job and moved in with my pack.

I have wanted her through every moment, the good and the bad.

Every fight.

Every laugh.

Every sigh.

Every word whispered in the dark against our pillows.

I have wanted her to be mine for ten years.

And it feels like I am on a tightrope, struggling to maintain my balance.

Which way will I fall? Toward being her Alpha, or out of her life?

The elation I felt at her news drains out of me. I'm almost afraid to hear what she has to say next.

Will my heart be broken on television? The viewers may not be able to see me, but there is no doubt that they will hear the despair in my voice.

"Derrick? Are you still there?"

I clear my throat, hoping she can't hear the upset and worry in my voice. "Yeah, honey, I'm here. Congratulations. I'm happy for you guys."

"Thanks. I want you to know that I didn't jump into it. I did a

lot of thinking first. About Calvin. About Sax and you and Grant and Ivan. About the lies. About myself. When I really dug deep, I realized something important."

Her voice carries me to the kitchen, where I grab a beer and take a huge swig. I wish I had something stronger.

Maybe it's a good thing that I don't. I should be sober when I have my heart broken by the woman of my dreams.

"Calvin said his pack was worth the pain he went through when they died. That he loved them so much, he followed them into the next life. I've spent so long being afraid of death. I couldn't think of anything worth dying for. And then I thought about Sax."

I stumble into a chair at the kitchen table. She thought of Sax? What does that mean?

"He was my pack. The only person I loved. I never said it because I feared rejection. How could Sax love someone who wouldn't leave her home? Whether one Beta or two Alphas and a Beta, you three are Sax. I can pretend all I want that Sax is gone to try to heal, but that's not true. Every time I talk to you, I'm reminded of how much you mean to me. And Ivan? I hear Sax in his jokes and encouragement. I can remember so many conversations with Sax when I'm talking to Grant and sharing some of my secrets."

My hands are shaking.

Tears form in the corners of my eyes, and I know that no matter how this conversation ends, they'll spill over.

"Sax was my pack, and Sax is the three of you. You're my pack. I still feel raw over what happened, but not enough to risk losing you. I may have thought there was nothing worth dying over, but I was ignoring that I had something worth living for all along."

"Ariana." Her name comes out like a prayer. "Please tell me you're saying what I think you're saying."

She giggles, then sniffles, and I can picture her with her knees to her chin as she wipes tears from her cheeks. *"I'm saying that I'm going to follow my heart. I'm done letting fear rule my life. You're my pack, Derrick. And nothing is going to change that."*

I wish I could kiss her.

I want to pull her into my arms and hold her so tightly she'll forget every time she felt lonely.

I can't now, but I can tomorrow, when they leave the house.

There is so much I want to say. So many feelings I long to put words to. My clumsy tongue can't find them. Instead, I say the only thing that I can. The thing that has always been true.

"I love you, honey."

"I love you too, Derrick."

The sweetest five words I've ever heard. They're tattooed on my heart, right beside Grant's declaration. Proof of who it beats for.

"Thank you for giving me a chance."

And I'll see you tomorrow.

Chapter Thirty-Four

β Grant
orchids

THERE'S a feeling in my chest that is not my own. It's the beautiful, cool contentment that belongs to my Omega.

She's sleeping in my arms, tangled between Ivan and me, and I cannot remember ever feeling this way before. I have always wanted to protect her, to spoil her, to calm all her fears.

And now I get to.

Forever.

Sure, there are experimental procedures that can be done to dissolve bonds, but they may as well not exist, because she's never getting rid of me. This may seem fast to others, but it's been years in the making.

And I think she finally sees us. She knows the parts of me that made up Sax, but also the real me.

Ivan stirs awake on the other side of our Omega. My heart swells as his sleepy eyes focus and realize who he's cuddling with. He kisses the back of her neck before slipping out of the bed and motions with his head for me to follow.

We cross the hallway to his room, and he closes the door behind us.

"Do you think she told Derrick?"

I sit on the edge of his bed and rub the sleep from my eyes. "I would think so, why?"

"Because what if she doesn't want to bond him?"

A strangled noise escapes me. It never occurred to me that she wouldn't want him, too. "I don't think she would've bonded with us if she didn't want him, too. We're kind of a package deal."

"Okay, but say she doesn't."

I can't choose between my Alpha and Omega. I won't. What am I going to do if she doesn't want him? "He's moving our stuff to Hollywood, right? We can all get an apartment if she doesn't want us to move in. And then we help him earn her trust." I refuse to entertain any other option. My pack needs both Alphas and my Omega. Splitting us up feels wrong.

Ivan paces slowly in front of his television. "Why do you think she trusts us now?"

I rest back on the heels of my hands. "If I had to guess? He's the face. To her, the betrayal came from him. We were background characters. We were his pack, supporting him. That's what packs do. She sees him as being responsible for informing her about us. What were we supposed to do, message her out of the blue and say we were his pack and wanted to get to know her? No, she would've blocked us. I love Derrick, but he messed up. He should have facilitated the introduction, but that would've required admitting that he's an Alpha, which was the original lie."

Ivan throws his hands in the air with a low growl. "We told him to come clean hundreds of times!"

"That anger you're feeling? That's why she forgave us.

Chapter Thirty-Four

She knows that we had no other option if we wanted to know her."

My Alpha lowers himself beside me on the bed, shoulders drooping with the weight of what happened yesterday. "What if she regrets bonding us?"

"I don't think that will happen. I think she-"

A loud, annoying sound comes from the television, interrupting my sentence. Bradley's face appears on screen.

"Good morning, boys! Today is your last day in the house. We'll be bringing you to the soundstage around one for your exit interviews."

I look at the clock. It's just after nine. Ariana is sleeping a lot later than she normally does, but Ivan wore her out last night. We have four hours left before we step into the real world.

Are we going to go home with her today? She doesn't know that Derrick's moved all of our things near her. I don't know how she'll react. I hope she approves of it because I don't want to leave her side. The bond between us is so fresh that I know it would hurt to be away from her.

"We've got the plane chartered and ready to take you where you need to go. Am I safe to assume you'll be flying home with Ariana?" Bradley exaggerates a wink, playing it up for the camera.

"Yeah, we are, unless she tells us not to." I lean into Ivan's shoulder. I know he is nervous that Ariana will regret all of this and won't let us come home with her, but I'm trying to stay positive, because if I let myself ruminate on it, I will fall apart.

"Good. We'll get everything set up on our end and give you all the rules you need to follow until the reunion show."

Once the TV fades back to the show's logo, I rub my hands over my face. Leaving the house isn't the end of this.

"Shit, I forgot we're going to have to be careful about being seen while the show airs. It'd ruin things if we were seen galavanting about as a pack."

The sound of a soft knock interrupts whatever Ivan was about to say.

"Guys? Are you… decent?" I can hear her blush in her voice, and it is adorable.

"Yeah, sweetie, come on in."

She's fully dressed when she walks into the room, which is surprising. We haven't been in here that long. Her contacts are in, her hair styled prettily, and she's wearing tight jeans and a fashionably oversized sweater. She sits on the bed and wedges herself between us.

"This is it, huh? The last day."

I can't tell if she's happy or sad. Things are going to be different once we get out of here, but that's a good thing, right?

Ivan rubs his beard, eyes unfocused as he stares at the ceiling. "Yeah. How are you feeling about everything? About…" He doesn't finish the sentence.

"Are you asking if I regret bonding you?"

Straight to the point, I see. I guess it's better to get this conversation out of the way right out of the gate rather than waiting until we're about to board the plane.

He places his hand on top of mine and squeezes, reassuring himself as much as he is me. "Yeah, I guess I am."

"Then let's get that out of the way. No, I do not regret it. I am still a little sore from the Sax situation, but I'm not going to let that stop me from seeking happiness. Calvin would have approved of you guys."

I still have complicated feelings toward her brother. It makes me sick that he asked her what he did, but I can see

Chapter Thirty-Four

it was a moment of weakness for him. It doesn't matter how I view him, though. It matters that his memory tainted Ariana's view of the world.

Until now.

Ivan grabs her chin and pulls her across me for a delicate, romantic kiss. This is not the type of kiss that makes someone moan or their toes curl. It's the kind that makes you feel safe. She sighs into his mouth, nearly melting into my lap.

When he releases her, I scoot back to give them more space. He presses their foreheads together, and she grabs his bearded cheek.

"We still have a lot to figure out, especially me and Derrick, but I promise I'm not going to run away from you." She releases him and turns to me, caressing her bite on my lobe. "And I hope you don't regret letting me bond you."

"Never." My words ghost across her lips before I press mine against them.

After a few luxurious moments where we fall into one another, she pulls away. "I'm going to go make us breakfast. Do you think they'll have any last-minute challenges or anything they want us to do today?"

I try to think back to the final episodes of the show, but I can't remember if it was just packing up or if the producers tried to sew in a bit of discourse before leaving the house. I come up blank.

"Well, it can't be worse than asking us to bond, right?" Ivan asks as he pushes to his feet. He digs through his suitcase, which he never bothered to unpack when Derrick left, for an outfit to wear today.

"Well, Alpha, now that you put it out there, I bet it will be." He stops short at Ariana's words, spinning around and gaping.

"Say it again."

My Omega wrinkles her brow in confusion for a moment before a sly smile curls her lips. "Oh, that now that you put it out there, it will be worse than asking us to bond?"

He shakes his head and takes two long steps to get to her. "You know that's not what I want to hear, Omega."

A full body shiver rolls down her spine. She plays with the ends of her soft brown hair. "Alpha."

Our Alpha groans and grabs her around the waist, pulling her hips flush with his. "You're not allowed to call me anything else. Fuck my name. Who likes Ivan anyway? I will only answer to Alpha now." He points a finger at me and narrows his eyes. "You never call me Alpha."

"I do too, Left Alpha."

"Not the same," he growls.

"Left Alpha?" Ariana looks at me for clarification. "Why do you call him Left Alpha?"

Ivan tries to answer on his own, but I talk over him. "Because he's never right!"

Ariana rolls her lips inward, trying to hold back laughter. It does no good. She has to brace her hands on his shoulders as her giggles take over.

"You better not start calling me that, Omega, or I'll have to put you over my knee."

She untangles herself from him and takes a few steps toward the door. "Promises, promises, Alpha."

Ivan lunges for her, but she runs out, laughing. He looks at me with narrowed eyes that hold no malice. "If this becomes a thing, just remember I have two knees."

His words light a fire in me, but I do my best to maintain my cool. "Promises, promises, Left Alpha."

Chapter Thirty-Five

I'VE JUST PUT the last pancake on the serving tray when Grant and Ivan come into the kitchen, both freshly showered and dressed nicer than they have all week. Ivan looks delicious in a cream linen shirt that highlights his broad shoulders, and Grant is beauty incarnate in a silken black button-up.

"Those smell good." Grant kisses my cheek as he reaches around me for plates. "What's in the pot?"

"Blueberry syrup. Since we're leaving today, I didn't want to let the berries go to waste." Something innate inside of me said I had to impress my pack this morning. I want them to see that I'll be worth having as their Omega. I recognize that it's my Omega instincts waking up from wherever I shoved them, and it makes me a little uncomfortable.

Putting yourself out there means opening yourself up for rejection. For ridicule.

Not that I think the guys will ridicule me. No way in hell. But they may not like the syrup. And if they don't like the syrup, doesn't that tell me that I'm not a good Omega?

It's a lot of pressure to put on syrup.

I grab a mesh strainer and pour the blueberry maple syrup mixture through it, making sure no berry pulp gets through. Luckily, this house has a gravy boat, even though I cannot fathom why, and that's a good enough vessel to put it in.

Grant made drinks while I was finishing, so by the time I make it to the table with the syrup, a mimosa is beside my plate of two pancakes.

Ivan pours so much syrup onto his pancakes that I fear his plate will turn into pancake soup. Grant is much more conservative with his. I can't tear my eyes away from them as they take their first bite, soft sounds of satisfaction escaping around their food.

"Brilliant. Can this be my special occasion breakfast? My birthday is in two months." Ivan pours even more syrup on his plate as he shovels it into his mouth.

The Beast may have turned into a man, but he still doesn't have table manners.

The line from Calvin's letter floats across my mind, and I don't cry. Since he died, every time I so much as thought his name, I tended to tear up. But this time, they make me laugh. I can think about him and see him through a different lens. He's not the Omega who died. He's the Omega who loved his Alphas so much he followed them into another life. The one who thought one of his Alphas was like the Beast, just as mine is.

"Whatever you want, Alpha."

My eyes burn, and I can't understand why now it feels like tears are going to spill down my cheeks at any moment. I thought about Calvin and the letter and didn't cry, but calling Ivan Alpha and making a plan for the future has me tearing up.

The future.

Chapter Thirty-Five

That's what it is. The thought of a future with them, where I make special occasion meals. Where I wake up next to them in the nest and sneak out to make breakfast after a long heat.

Ivan rubs his chest with his free hand and speaks around a bite of food. "Why are you sad and yet also happy? What's that called?"

"Bittersweet." My voice is scarcely above a whisper.

He's nearly cleared his plate before I even put syrup on my pancakes, and didn't even stop eating to talk to me, but that doesn't bother me. It's who he is.

"Why bittersweet?" Grant leans across the table where he sits opposite me and grabs my hand. "What's wrong?

"I thought about how soon all of us will be able to sleep in the nest, and then I realized I don't have one." My throat catches, and I have to take a sip of my mimosa before I can continue. "Calvin helped me build my first nest, and I destroyed it after he died. I never thought I'd need to build another because I wasn't going to have a pack. I had my heats in my bedroom. And now I have a pack, and I don't have a nest to take you home to."

I don't like the idea of them looking into the nesting suite I've used for storage since I moved in.

"That's not going to be a problem. We have so much stuff for you, and we're never more than fifteen minutes away from a Great Nestpectations. It's time to build your nest with your pack, baby." Grant leans forward, almost brushing his lips over my cheek before he jerks up straight. "Sorry, sticky lips."

I don't let him get away with that. Our lips crash together, and he immediately deepens the kiss as his hand grips the back of my head. I taste the sweet sticky syrup on his lips as he trails his tongue against my teeth, asking for entrance. I welcome him happily.

"I love what the two of you are doing and will require you to let me watch about a thousand more times, so I'm terribly sorry that I have to interrupt, but this episode is going to be boring as hell if we're sucking face the whole time."

Grant pulls away, then dives forward and presses a final quick kiss to my lips. "You think that the people won't want to watch an hour of the two of us? Come on now. We'll melt their screens clean off."

As I imagine what our future together is going to look like, Grant and Ivan are exchanging barbs. Distracted by my plate, I can't keep up with their light-hearted ribbing.

"Aren't you worried she's going to smell your socks and kick you out of the nest?"

My head snaps up. I never thought about the fact that three guys in my house meant three pairs of stinky socks.

Ivan throws his napkin at Grant playfully. "Your socks don't smell much better, Beta! Just because you're pretty doesn't mean your feet don't sweat."

"I don't wear grocery store socks. My feet can breathe. It makes a difference!"

Wait, I wear grocery store socks. What's wrong with those? Do my feet stink?

"At least I don't leave hair swirled on the wall of the shower!"

Whoops, I do that, too.

"And yet your chest hair clogs the drain anyway!"

My head bounces back and forth between them during their verbal tennis match, struggling to smother my laugh behind bites of pancakes.

By the time we finish breakfast and pack up our things, it's just after eleven.

"We still have two hours? How are we supposed to be entertaining for two whole hours? What do they even show

Chapter Thirty-Five

in the final episode?" Ivan's legs are thrown over the back of the couch, and his face is turning red as he hangs his head upside down.

"A lot of it will be our exit interviews. We'll probably all do our own, and then they'll pile us all onto a soundstage and pepper us with questions about our week here." I pause the game I'm playing and pull a leg up on the couch, facing my Alpha.

"I think one season they skipped the individual and did everyone together." Grant doesn't look up from his puzzle as he talks. He's trying hard to finish it before we leave, but I don't know if he'll make it. I offered to help, but he said that he needed to do it on his own and prove he was smarter than it.

Not sure what the guy's issue with puzzles is, but I'm not upset that he said he didn't want me to build it with him. I hate doing them.

Before I unpause my game, I ask a question that I've been wondering about for days.

"Do you think that Derrick will be here when we get out?" They told us not to reveal to the audience that he wouldn't be, but part of me hopes he'll surprise us all.

Neither answer me, probably trying to figure out how to without revealing what the producers told us. I never asked Derrick on our calls if he was going to come back. I didn't want it confirmed that he wasn't. But I also didn't tell him I wanted him to be here, so I can't be upset if he isn't.

Ivan shifts sideways, lying across the couch and resting his head in my lap. "Maybe. If he's not, don't think that's any indication that he doesn't want to be here. Maybe the producers didn't want to pay to fly him in for this when there is going to be a reunion episode."

"I think he'll surprise us," Grant ignores his puzzle to

assure me. "Even if they didn't want to pay to fly him up, I think he'd figure out how to make it happen."

Okay. Hope for the best, expect the worst. If anything, maybe he told the producers at first that he didn't want to come back, but he changed his mind.

I want him here, don't I? Since he left, I've told him I love him and want him in my pack, and I've had phone sex with the guy. Is it going to be awkward to see him? It's probably going to be awkward. And it's going to be televised. That's just great.

"There's no pressure with him. You know that, right?" Ivan stops my hand from where I've been idly stroking his head, and weaves our fingers together.

"I don't think he'll pressure me into anything. But I don't know how to be around him. I told him he was my pack. Isn't that basically a promise to bite him?"

Grant leans over and pretends to chomp my thigh. "No, it isn't. All it is is acknowledgment of who you are to each other. You take things at your pace."

Chapter Thirty-Six

THE STUDIO LIGHTS ARE BRIGHT. I'm back in the room where Bridgette first interviewed me a week ago, but this time, there is an emerald-green couch opposite a love seat where she sits with her husband. I'm in between Grant and Ivan, perched awkwardly on the end of the couch.

Derrick isn't here.

He didn't show up.

But they told us he wouldn't. So it's fine.

I'm fine.

I'm not going to read into it. Even though Grant said he would've found a way to be here. Even though the couch feels like it's large enough for four, I can't stop looking at the place he's supposed to be sitting right now.

Bradley's teeth are somehow brighter than before. He's gotta lay off the bleach. "Well, everyone wants to know. Was that what you expected?"

Grant leans back and crosses his arms over his chest. "Is that really a question? Were you not watching? This episode is the poster child for the whole show."

"We definitely earned our name this season, that is true! It was a shock from our side of things, so I cannot imagine what it was like to live it." Bridgette flips her ponytail, but it doesn't look dismissive like it would on most people. She leaves her head tilted to the side with an encouraging look on her face as she stares me down.

I guess she wants me to answer the question her husband asked, but Grant sidestepped.

"It was painful. I felt so much hurt, so much fear, that I barely even gave myself a chance to know them. I'm lucky I did."

Bradley crosses one leg over the other. "And what made you make that decision?"

My hands are shaking as I push one into my back pocket and pull out Calvin's note, neatly folded.

"Calvin. I'm glad I brought this letter with me, because it helped me realize that I wasn't honoring my brother's memory by living the way I was. My heart knew it was time to take a chance and open myself up to them." Ivan takes the letter from me and stuffs it in his front chest pocket, and Grant weaves his fingers with mine for support. "It may not make sense to some of the viewers how things played out, but it does to me, and that's what matters. I fell in love with them once, when I only had pieces of them. It wasn't hard to do it again."

I spent years not telling Sax I loved him, thinking I was protecting my heart, and here I am, letting it slip out as if I say the words all the time.

There's a smile on Grant's face when he turns to me and cuts Bradley and Bridgette out of the conversation. "You loved me?"

"Love."

Maybe I should have waited until we weren't on

camera. Until we'd been together for the obligatory three to six months that make it acceptable to drop those words.

But I don't need to wait to acknowledge what my soul has known for ages.

"About time you said it. Didn't you tell her on day one, Grant?" Ivan kisses the side of my neck as our Beta chuckles. "I love you too, sweetie. I hope you didn't need me to say it out loud to know."

I didn't. Ivan wears his heart on his sleeve, and I adore him for that.

Bridgette interrupts our moment. "Wow. How incredible it is that we got to witness this! What a one-eighty from that first day in the house!"

Her husband chimes in as well. "It's touching to see, honestly. I was terribly worried about how this was going to affect Ariana."

"I have a question," I interrupt. When they give me their full attention, I ask what I've wanted to know since I got the selection email. "Why did you pick me for this season?"

Bridget's voice goes dreamy. "Your story was fascinating. The producers loved the idea of bringing together two people who had let fear keep them apart. After researching Pack Sax and interviewing them, we knew we had to bring you on the show. But it wasn't just the truth about who Sax was. Something you wrote in the application moved all of us."

Her husband grabs her hand and picks up where she left off. "'I'm terrified of so many things, but I'm starting to think that everything would be less scary with someone I love beside me.'"

Damn, Marlie killed it with that one.

"We insisted, and the producers agreed, that even

though it was going to be a massive surprise to you and put you face-to-face with Alphas, that if you were ready to stop going through life alone, we should help you get there." Bridgette leans over and grabs my hand. "It's not often we have a storybook outcome. A lot of the time, it's such a massive lie that there is no hope for reconciliation, or everyone is exactly who they said they'd be, and there's little excitement in that. But we hoped that even though you had someone who may not have been who he said he was, you'd end up happier because of it."

I'll never know if that was a sincere sentiment or something they were told to say to help the ratings. But I like to think it was real.

Ivan trimmed his beard and shaved his neck before we left the house, and his brand new bite mark shimmers under the set lights. I can't keep my eyes off him. And when he talks in a low, rumbling voice? Oh my God. "While I'll forever be grateful to the show for bringing us together, please don't pretend this was anything other than a strategic business decision."

Holy shit, that tone. He's never used it with me, but part of me now wishes he would.

Bradley clears his throat awkwardly and sits back, pantomiming brushing dust off his suit. "We're dying to know. What is your plan when you leave here?"

I stroke Ivan's back gently. "Since we're bonded now, we've decid-"

"Wait! Before you continue. We have one thing we need to do." Bridgette makes a come here motion, and my hesitant heart stalls.

Derrick steps around the couch, his back to Bridgette, and smiles at me.

And it's a smile I've seen a couple of hundred times.

Chapter Thirty-Six

It's the one that he'd have plastered on when he answered a video call.

It's the one that he'd fall into when I laughed.

It's the one that has warmed my heart for years.

"Hey." He reaches a hand out to me. "Come here."

I let him pull me off the couch, unable to form words. It wasn't until he appeared in front of me that I realized just how much I wanted him here.

And now he is. He looks gorgeous, eyes wet behind his glasses, and his blond hair tousled.

He holds me close, nose to nose, and I breathe in his nutty and sweet scent. I worried about what would happen in this moment, but I shouldn't have been.

My lips find his because they were always meant to be together. Our paths were destined.

Even though I want nothing more than to fall into him, we eventually pull apart. Derrick's eyes are closed, but this close, I can see that he's been crying. Not a lot, but the tears are there. Was he worried before this moment that I wouldn't accept him? Even after I bonded his packmates and told him I wanted him, too?

Being told it is different than feeling it. I pull him into another kiss, making sure he knows he's mine, and nothing will change that.

"Isn't this a nice surprise?" Bradley asks, obliterating the moment.

Derrick guides me back to the couch before sitting and pulling me against his side. "I wouldn't have missed this for the world."

Bridgette claps her hands together in excitement. "You're just in time, too! Ariana was about to tell us what the plan was now that the show is over."

My packmates share a look around me. "You should

tell them, Alpha." Grant clutches Derrick's hand tightly, as if worried he's about to disappear.

"After I left the show, I went back home to Virginia, quit my job, and packed up all of our things. Our pack has officially moved to Hollywood, Florida."

Did he say he's moved? To be near me?

All of them?

The guys and I decided they'd come back to my place for a bit until we could talk this through as a pack, but Derrick moved to be close to me before I even bonded the others. I can't decide if it's beautifully optimistic or a bit presumptuous.

Grant leans around Derrick and ensnares me with his passionate gaze. "When Derrick told us he'd started the moving process on our reward call, both Ivan and I were thrilled. I don't think I could've left you, even before you bonded us."

"I have to confess something." Bridgette waves us closer. We lean toward her, even though the camera is going to pick up everything she says. "I think this may be my favorite season yet. Seeing your love grow has been incredible. I know America is going to eat you guys up."

"It's weird to think that soon people we know are going to get really up close and personal with us," Ivan admits. "We're looking forward to getting to spend time together without someone watching our every move."

"Totally fair! I can't wait until the reunion episode so we can see where you are at in six months."

Chapter Thirty-Six

"NOW, don't forget. You have to do your best stay out of the public eye while the show airs. Hats, sunglasses, and not confirming who you are while you're out as a group. Try not to spoil the outcome of the season." Drew walks us through the compound since none of the golf carts were big enough for all of us. I don't mind. It's nice to feel the sun on my face, even though it is close to setting. "And don't respond to anyone on social media who may reach out to you. And, it goes without saying, but I need to remind you, avoid all contact with magazines or television shows that want to feature you. We'll set up those interviews for you after the reunion episode. You're fine going about your life until the show airs, as long as you don't tell anyone you were filming it."

Ivan holds one of my hands, and Derrick the other, with Grant on the other side of him. Drew looks at me for confirmation that I understand.

"Got it, Drew. We know the drill. Bridgette and Bradley drilled it into us after the interview."

"I just don't want to see you get sued. Better to be told too many times than not enough."

As we reach the gate, a large, black SUV waits for us right outside it. Our ride to the airport.

Where all three of them are flying home with me.

Holy shit, they're flying home with me.

Is my house a mess? I can't remember how I left it.

Do I have any food for us to eat? I probably should do a grocery order.

And my nest. I need to prioritize getting that set up, even if the idea of it makes my stomach churn a little.

Before I can spiral any more, Drew pulls me away from the guys and into a hug. "I told you this was going to be a good thing, didn't I?"

"You sure did."

"Things were touch-and-go for a minute there. I didn't want those boys to make a liar out of me." He pats me on the back and pulls away, a fatherly grin touching his lips. "I'm proud of you, Ariana. You faced a lot of fears this week, and I'm sure you'll inspire plenty of people to face theirs."

We all say our goodbyes to Drew and pile into the SUV, tired but happy in our silence on the way to the airport.

Audience Reactions

EPISODE EIGHT

boys.with.knots.lost.the.plot. > *Knot What You Expected*

Honestly, this is an award-winning season. It was everything that the show claims to be about, and it didn't feel exploitative or cheesy at all. I can't wait for the reunion show. I already applied for the lottery in hopes of scoring a ticket!

stefkittykat > *Knot What You Expected*

I'm glad they saved Derrick's phone call for the finale. I think seeing him at the end of the episode made it that much more powerful. The four of them belong with each other.

SwiftPhantom > *Knot What You Expected*

Okay, but did Sax and Onion make anyone else want to watch *Unexplainable and Bizarre*? I had never heard of it before this, and now I wanna go binge it all.

micachu.reads > *Knot What You Expected*

POLL: Do you think Derrick has groveled enough for Ariana to bond with him?
    Yes
    No
    Someone was supposed to get pegged

Chapter Thirty-Seven

THE FLIGHT IS SHORT. It's only about two hours in the air. I don't know how, but I'm simultaneously amped up and bone tired.

I still can't get over the fact that they're flying us on a private plane. It was surreal on the way here, and even more so with the guys beside me. It's much bigger than we need, so I have to imagine it's the network's and usually transports executives. The interior is chic and modern, with chairs facing one another around a table.

After we've leveled out and can move around, Derrick grabs my hand and tugs me out of my seat.

"Come with me?"

Ivan and Grant both give me encouraging head nods as I trail behind the Alpha.

He pulls me into what I thought was a small closet, maybe a place to store beverage carts or something, but it's actually a cramped bedroom. The bed is bigger than a twin but smaller than a full. It's just enough room for one person to pass out if they need to, but not somewhere I'd want to spend the night.

In the small space, it's impossible to ignore Derrick's mouthwatering, sweet, and nutty pecan pie scent.

I haven't had a good pie in ages.

"Sit with me?" He perches on the side of the bed and pats it. I prop myself on the edge. My teeth find my lower lip as I toy with it in anticipation of what he has to say. He grabs my hand and feeds his fingers through mine. "Let me talk? Don't interrupt me?"

I'm afraid that if I say anything, he'll clam up. I know we have a lot to talk about, but there is pressure in person that wasn't there while on the phone.

"I'd love to talk about our past, to explain again why I made the choices and told the lies I did. But there isn't anything I can say other than every move I made came from the selfish desire to keep you with me, and the fear of what would happen if you knew the truth. But I didn't want to hold you back from finding someone, which is why I kept the little bit of distance I did. I thought that with no real names, no revealing our locations, no telling you I loved you, you'd still be free to find someone who could love you out loud."

My hand tightens around his as emotions clog my throat. I know exactly what he means. I, too, held those things back so he could find someone. I thought there was no way he could love a person like me, who was afraid of everything and swallowed by grief.

"I don't want to look back. I want to look forward. Because Ariana, honey, you're everything to me. I know I haven't done right by you, but I want you to know I'll do whatever it takes to show you how much I love you. I'll never be worthy of you, but I will spend the rest of my life trying to be."

"You don't-"

"Let me finish, please?" His pleading eyes meet mine,

Chapter Thirty-Seven

and I pantomime zipping my lips. "I told you I quit my job. The guys are probably emailing their companies right now. I'm not expecting to move in with you. I got us a short-term rental until we can figure out where to buy. If you want the guys to move in with you, I'll be there whenever you need me. I don't expect you to bond with me or welcome me into your home. I've not earned that yet. And even if you never decide I do, I'll still be there. I won't let you get sick. I'll never abandon you."

"I know you won't."

The certainty with which I do surprises me, but I'm not sure why. He's Derrick. I knew him before Ivan and Grant came into the picture, and I still do. In my heart, in my soul, I've always been his.

Does it matter if it's not perfect? If we don't know every little thing about one another? Can anyone know every piece of the person they love? My parents always talk about how they still find new stories to tell each other, even though they've been together for almost forty years.

Derrick is looking at his shoes, stuffy-looking dress ones that probably squeeze his toes. His glasses are slipping down his nose, and his shoulders are hunched over.

He looks defeated, and I don't like that on him.

I open my mouth to offer reassurances, but my words dry up on my tongue as he continues.

"I love you. I think I loved you from the first private message, when you asked me what I was doing on a forum for a show I appeared to hate. I don't know why that did it, but I knew that I was never going to let you go. Those few weeks after I met Grant, when I pushed you away, were some of the toughest in my life. I'm not meant to be away from you. I need you like sunshine. Like the air in my lungs. But I'd give it to you if you needed it. Every breath I take, everything that makes me me, is yours for the taking."

His eyes meet mine, and I almost gasp at the naked emotion in them. I've always loved a man who isn't afraid to show his feelings, and this pack is not shy about it. Some people may prefer their men stoic, but not me. I love that all three of them don't hide that side from me.

"I'm yours, Onion." I take a sharp breath at hearing that name on his lips again. "Please, please, will you consider being mine?"

I don't answer him.

I can't.

It's not because I don't have an answer for him. It's not because I can barely see straight since my eyes are brimming with tears.

It's because something instinctual has reared up inside me. A part of me that I can't deny. And I'm grateful it has, because it gives me the chance to turn off my mind.

I don't need to think about this. I've always known. Deep down, it was always Derrick who was going to walk this life beside me.

And how lucky am I that he brought two amazing men with him?

He's waiting for me to answer him, and I know words aren't enough. I sling one leg over him and perch on his lap, luxuriating in the way his body feels against mine for the first time. I stroke his cheek before feeding my hand into his hair and yanking his head to the side.

And I bite.

I bite and hold on until the shocked, sticky feeling of his emotions blooms in my chest.

Derrick's mouth opens with a gasp. The desperate, pleading sound sends shivers down my spine. He clutches at my waist as if I'll float away if he doesn't ground me.

Part of me feels like I will.

Our lips find one another, and the kiss quickly deepens,

Chapter Thirty-Seven

as I throw my arms around his neck. I can feel how slick I am already, and the swell of his knot bumps into me every time I move my hips and grind against him.

He swears to himself as he pulls our mouths apart. "If we don't stop, I'm going to take you right here, and I don't think I can stop myself from knotting you if I do."

"Take me, Derrick. I'm yours. Knot me. I want my first time with you."

Surprise flickers across his face, whether at my admission that I didn't fuck Grant or Ivan or that I'm okay with sleeping with him on a plane, I'm not sure.

He picks me up and gently lays me on the bed, bracing himself with his hands on either side of my head.

"Are you sure?"

"So sure."

Derrick, my Alpha, bends and presses a soft kiss on my lips before sitting back on his heels and reaching for the hem of my shirt. He moves with a gentle grace as he pulls it over my head. His follows mine to a pile on the floor.

He worships me with soft kisses and nibbles down my neck and throat, stopping to remove my bra so he can suck one of my nipples into his mouth.

I want him so bad. My body is cramping, aching for him, and I don't think I can wait any longer. Bonding him must have triggered another heat spike, because I'm desperate to feel him inside me.

So desperate that I pull his mouth away from me and work at my pants, wiggling them down my hips and legs. They get stuck on my shoes, and he has to help me slide them off. Then he tugs his belt open and pushes his pants and boxers off in one smooth movement.

I've seen his dick before. He sent me photos. But it didn't prepare me for this. The knot on the base is already swelling, and liquid pools on the tip. My mouth waters with the desire to taste him.

Then another cramp hits me, and I know I need him inside me right now.

"Alpha." The word is a pleading whine.

His grey eyes flash behind his glasses as he pushes me to the bed and crawls over top of me. I can feel his arousal pushing against me, his knot bumping into my clit as he moves his hips in tight circles.

"What do you need, Omega?" Another desperate whine slips out, and I thrust my hips into his, but he silences me with a kiss. "I need to open you up, honey. I don't want to hurt you."

"I was made for you." I put a leg around his hips and try to pull him closer. "I can take you."

"Just because you can doesn't mean you should have to." He reaches between us and strokes a finger through my slick core before pushing it inside me. I clench around him, the intrusion wonderful but not enough.

"I've used toy knots. I can handle it."

A wicked smile transforms his face from soft to predatory. "Oh, you think so? I'm trying to control myself, Omega. I'm trying to make sure your first time is beautiful and romantic."

"Don't control yourself. I want you, not the version of you movies say I should want."

That's all the permission he needs to relinquish control to his hindbrain. He grips himself around the base of his knot and guides himself to my entrance. The feeling that overcomes me as he pushes inside runs all the way to my toes, a shock to every one of my nerve endings at once.

This is nothing like a toy, that's for sure.

The heat of him as he fills me has my eyes rolling back

Chapter Thirty-Seven

in my head. I'm going to combust even though he's holding himself still as I adjust to his size.

I slide my hand down my body to my clit, but he bats it away. "You said you wanted me? Then hands off. This is my pussy. My clit. You'll come when I say you can."

Shit, what have I gotten myself into? Do I want to be edged during my first time?

Yeah, I do. I said I wanted Derrick, and this is him.

"My safe word is red." It's barely more than a whisper, but it's acceptance of what he plans to do to me.

My Alpha grabs my hips and pulls me with him as he rests back on his heels, before finally pulling out and thrusting inside me again. He starts tentatively, watching my face for how I'm feeling, before his pace picks up and his knot pushes against my entrance.

I can feel my orgasm bubbling up and about to overflow. I knew after everything with Ivan that being with my Alpha is nothing like getting off on my own, but this is next level. Every drag of his cock across the vestibule that aches for his knot is enough to make me cry out.

In the back of my mind, I know that Ivan, Grant, and the flight attendant can most likely hear us, but it feels so good that I can't bring myself to care.

"Derrick, please. I'm going to… I need to…"

He shakes his head and squeezes my hip tightly. "No, hold it, Omega. You can do that for your Alpha, can't you?"

I don't know if I can, but I'm going to try. Because I want to make my Alpha proud of me. I want to hear his praise after we're done about how obedient I am and how well I listen.

That praise kink snuck right up on me.

When the tension starts to release, I know this wave has left me. He picks his pace back up, this time resting his thumb on my clit and pressing down. He doesn't rub me, but the weight of his touch is amazing.

"Gonna knot you," he growls in a low, dangerous tone. "Fuck you and knot you and make you scream for me. Can you do that? Can you take my knot, Omega?"

My panting breaths are transforming into moans. "Please. Please, Alpha, I need it."

Just when I think I'm going to fall apart, he starts pushing his knot inside me. It's not fully swollen, but it's big enough to make entry difficult.

And holy shit, it feels so good. My legs shake, and my pussy clamps down on him.

"Don't come, honey. Not yet."

I throw my head back in a frustrated groan. I'm so close. I want to come on his knot, to soak him with my slick, but he won't let me.

Before I can whine and bitch about it, his knot slots into place, and I can feel it swelling, pressing against me and making me feel so full my eyes cross.

He groans as I thrash underneath him. "Oh fuck. I didn't know it'd feel like this."

My Omega nature is smug that I'm the only person he's knotted.

I'm veering close to the edge, unsure if I can hold back anymore. I want to be good for him, to wait until he tells me to come, but with his knot filling me, I don't know if I'm going to be able to for much longer.

My Alpha takes pity on me and strokes my clit with his thumb in time with his shallow thrusts. "Come for me, Omega. Come for your Alpha."

An all-consuming orgasm, made stronger from the two he denied me earlier, whites out my vision. My back bows off the bed, and I pant out his name as the pleasure overfills my body and spills out.

Chapter Thirty-Seven

Derrick's cock jerks inside me, and his knot grows impossibly larger, trapping us together.

He collapses onto the bed, pulling me onto my side so we can face one another. Before I can speak, he takes my mouth with his, twining our lips together lazily. I can feel his contentment swirl in my chest, and next to it are the blissfully happy bonds of my Beta and other Alpha.

Our pack is complete.

Chapter Thirty-Eight

α Ivan
pumpkin bread

DERRICK AND ARIANA left the bedroom at the back of the plane shortly before landing. There was no hiding what they were doing in there. We felt it in her bond, and it was impossible to tune out.

Not that I wanted to.

His scent is already changing. I wondered how our bond with Ariana would morph our scents, and I'm pleasantly surprised with the outcome. My pumpkin bread has taken on a zing of citrus, brightening its spice profile. The soft floral notes of Grant's scent have become more like orange blossoms.

And when Derrick climbs into the ride share next to me, it's obvious that his pecan pie is now à la mode.

When we get to Ariana's house, it's early evening. We place a pizza order, and Derrick heads out to grab it and some of our things from the rental home.

I don't think we're going to be staying there.

Ariana looks nervous to have us in her home, but I don't take it personally. This has always been her safe

Chapter Thirty-Eight

space, and we're invading it. No matter how much she cares for us, it's going to be an adjustment.

Unfortunately for her, she let me in, and I'm not going anywhere. Going to claim squatter's rights. I'm a puppy who followed her home.

She's stuck with me.

I mean, if she asked me to leave, I would, but I'd probably end up sleeping under her porch with the opossums.

My girl looks uncomfortable, and I hate it. She awkwardly wrings her hands as she paces around the cozy-looking living room.

"What's going on?" Grant places a hand on her lower back to calm her movements. "Talk to us."

"My nest is a mess. I've been using it as storage. Now that you're here, I need a nest."

He makes a shushing noise and takes her face in his hands. "We don't care if you have a nest."

She looks outraged at the statement. "Well, I do! What kind of Omega doesn't have a nest?"

I move close and wrap an arm around both of them. "What if we clean it out together while we wait for Derrick to get back?" She chews her lip then nods in acquiescence. "Take us there."

We follow our Omega through the house to a white door at the end of a short hallway. With a fortifying breath, she throws it open.

"Oh my God."

I peer around her to see what the issue is. "Derrick, you dog." The nest has been emptied of whatever she stored there, and a brand-new mattress, still in its plastic, rests in the pit in the middle of the room. Along the walls are boxes swollen with the gifts we've bought her over the years.

"How did he do this?"

"If I had to guess, I bet he had help from a certain meddling best friend of yours." I take her hand and pull her into the room with Grant trailing behind us. "These are things we bought for you over the years. There should be more than enough here to outfit a nest. We can go to the store tomorrow if you don't like any of it."

"I don't need to go to the store. I love it already." She hasn't even seen anything in the boxes yet, but the conviction in her voice tells me she's not lying. "If you guys picked it out for me, it'll be perfect."

Grant snags her other hand and rests his cheek on her head. "How about we wait for Derrick to get back, eat, and then we can come in here and dig around and see what you can find."

She bounces on the balls of her feet like a kid on Christmas morning. "Yes, yes, please! I'm going to call Marlie and thank her for helping him while we wait."

BY THE TIME we're all stuffed, the only thing left is half of the white pizza Derrick got our Omega.

"I can't believe you like chicken and pineapple on pizza," she teases me. "I'm worried about what it says about you being into me when you have such bad taste."

I gather up the empty boxes and plates. "It says that you're the superior choice and anyone who doesn't think so is wrong."

Grant hums as he wipes his face with a napkin. "I'm just happy I don't have to share my pizzas with you monster Alphas."

"Because no one else wants lactose-free cheese."

Chapter Thirty-Eight

Ariana is antsy with anticipation, her eyes darting between the three of us.

"Are you ready to go set up your nest, Omega?" As soon as the question is out of Derrick's mouth, she's on her feet and rushing to the room at the end of the hallway. "I guess that's a yes."

I finish cleaning up the dinner mess with my packmates as quickly as possible and follow her. By the time we push through the doorway, she's sitting in the middle of the room with a large box in front of her.

"This one feels like a good one." She's playing with the edge of the tape, a question in her eyes.

"Go ahead and open it, sweetie."

With a squeal, she rips the tape off, not caring that it takes half of the cardboard flap with it. She turns everything over in his hands, examining it as she pulls them out and lines them up in front of her.

This box is from four years ago. A pair of pajamas in galaxy blue with a matching robe from Grant. A string of lights with butterflies covering the bulbs and soft purple blackout curtains from Derrick. I got her a set of cream throw pillows, one with sequins and the other with faux fur.

None of us speaks, afraid to interrupt her Omega instincts that are taking over. She moves around the nest, staging everything around her nest. When everything has found a home, she pushes a massive box into the middle of the nest.

This one is seven years old. The first birthday I knew her for. And it's not the only box from that year. She's got one from each of us. The one she found is mine, and the guys grab theirs for her.

Derrick's box focuses on decor. It's filled with small paintings, a lamp, more string lights, and gauzy curtains that are meant to hang from the ceiling like a canopy.

When she tears into Grant's, she finds everything she needs to outfit her bathroom. No spa products, since those expire, but it's got fluffy towels and a warmer, washcloths, and apothecary jars to hold her things. At the bottom of the box is a rainfall shower head.

She's thrilled, sorting out Derrick's gifts and dragging Grant's to the bathroom. She bustles around in there, placing everything where it's supposed to go.

She peeks her head through the doorway and waves the showerhead around. "Someone needs to install this tomorrow!"

"On it, baby." The smile on Grant's face is gigantic, his eyes soft with affection. When she darts back into the bathroom, he turns to Derrick and me and whispers, "She's so happy."

"Omegas do better in a nest that their pack helps build. I can feel how giddy she is now that she's let her instincts take over." Derrick pulls Grant into his arms and gives him a sweet kiss. "I didn't get to tell you how much I missed you."

"I missed you, too, Alpha." Grant melts into Derrick as the Alpha palms the back of his head.

Ariana watches them from the doorway of the bathroom, her face soft. When they notice her and smile sheepishly, she crosses the nest and puts a hand on each of them.

"I love that you love each other. I love seeing you together here, in my nest." She kisses them each on the cheek before turning her attention to my box.

When we first started buying her presents, we decided on a color theme for her nest. We didn't want everything to feel disjointed. She doesn't have to use what we bought,

Chapter Thirty-Eight

but I hope she does. We put a lot of thought into choosing things we thought she'd love.

I focused on the linens that year. One by one, she empties the box, lining the items up in front of her.

A navy blue throw.

Two sets of sheets for a nest-sized mattress, one in navy blue and one in cream.

A collection of pillows I had to vacuum-seal to fit the box, in a variety of sizes and fabrics, in navy, charcoal, and lavender.

At the bottom is a small stuffed cat. It's solid black with bright yellow eyes. I don't know why I bought it, but the moment I laid eyes on it, I knew that she needed it.

My heart is in my throat as she looks everything over.

What if she doesn't like it? What if it's all wrong, and the blanket isn't comfortable, or she hates the color scheme?

She doesn't give me a chance to spiral too much, launching her body into my arms. We tumble to the nest, and she kisses me all over my face and neck.

"I love it, I love it, I love it!" She reaches up for Grant's hand, hauling him and Derrick down with us. "You all did so good. It's everything I could've ever wanted."

Pure Alpha satisfaction courses through me. She approves of our gifts. She wants to use them in her nest.

I provided for my Omega and made her happy.

The stuffed cat stays tucked in her lap as she continues going through the boxes, revealing more blankets and pillows, cozy loungewear, and even an entire box of high-fashion pieces from the designer Grant works with.

It's not just nesting material in the boxes. There are gaming controllers, books, trinkets, and silly things we saw over the years that made us think of her.

By the time she's gone through every box, she's practically vibrating with excitement. It's nearly eleven when she pushes us out of the nest, claiming she needs to get it set up before we go to bed.

Twenty minutes later, she throws open the door and beckons us in.

The nest has been transformed, the mattress now covered in cream sheets, piles of blankets and pillows around the edges, and a lamp on a small end table that Grant gifted her one year.

She even managed to hang the string lights and curtains on the low ceiling.

"Do you like it?" The vulnerability in her voice is a fist around my heart. How could she think we wouldn't?

Derrick speaks first. "It's the perfect nest. I love it. You did a great job, Omega."

She turns to Grant next with a beaming smile, craving his assurance. He reaches for her hand and pulls her body against his. "It's the most amazing nest for the most amazing Omega."

Before she can ask me, I press against her back, sandwiching her between Grant and me.

"You're such a good Omega. So clever. It's just missing one thing."

She looks over her shoulder at me, wrinkling her nose. "What's that?"

"Our scents."

Chapter Thirty-Nine

β Grant
orchids

WE FELL into each other's arms shortly after Ariana finished her nest, falling asleep in a tangle of limbs that I have dreamed about for years. I have both of my Alphas and my Omega touching me at once, and it is so beautiful, so grounding, that I don't want to fall back to sleep. I want to live in this moment forever.

I can't imagine it's been long since we passed out. I'm not sure what woke me up.

Just as my eyes start to get heavy again, Ariana groans and curls up on her side. She and I slept head-to-head, reaching out for each other so the guys could touch us both. I roll over on my stomach to get closer and brush her hair off her forehead.

Her burning hot forehead.

Sweat is beading on the top of her trembling lip. She's still asleep but clearly uncomfortable. Her scent has flooded the nest, like a melted orange popsicle drowning in decadent cream. I can't even smell the guys because it's so strong.

Holy shit, my Omega is in heat.

How did it come on so fast? I know she's been having spikes, but those can last weeks before a proper heat hits. Was it bonding all of us? Building the nest?

It doesn't matter. It's here.

I stroke her cheek, trying to pull her out of sleep without startling her. When her pretty green eyes flutter open, her pupils are dilated.

"Grant? It hurts." Her pained whimper breaks my heart.

"I know, baby. We're going to take care of you, okay?"

Our Alphas are stirring awake, even though our conversation is in low whispers. As soon as the fog clears from Derrick's eyes, he growls low in his throat.

"Omega." That one word has her panting, writhing on the soft surface of the nest. I don't blame her, honestly. I'm almost there myself. Our Alpha doesn't waste any time ripping her pants off and diving between her thighs.

Ariana's back bends off the nest as she grinds her pussy on his tongue. He fills her with two fingers and coaxes an orgasm out of her right away. If there is ever a time not to withhold orgasms, it's during heat.

Ivan pulls her shirt off, bearing her breasts to me, before lying down and peppering her with sweet kisses. Not one to be left out of the fun, I take one of her nipples into my mouth. She grabs the back of my head and pushes me into the plush cushion of her breast, encouraging me to suck harder. I angle myself so I can watch as Derrick slips his pants off and notches himself at her entrance.

I'm dying to fuck her. I want to feel how tight and hot she is as she comes. I rut into the nest as I watch Derrick slide into her. I want both of them at the same time. I want Derrick to fuck me into Ariana. I want to be pressed between them.

Chapter Thirty-Nine

Maybe take Ivan into my mouth at the same time.

Oh fuck.

I'm grinding my cock into the nest as I watch them together. Ariana looks so pretty, her chest splotched and red, as she takes our Alpha's cock. Their bodies are moving together in a gorgeous symphony that I can't take my eyes off of. Even Ivan is sitting back, enjoying the sight of them together.

I almost want to cry, watching them. I know how much Derrick wanted this and how long he thought he'd never get it. I was there when he stared at his phone, trying to convince himself to tell her the truth, but terrified that he'd lose her. Ariana has gone through all of her heats alone since she presented as an Omega, and now the Alpha she loves, the person she has fantasized about, is taking care of her.

And I get to watch them come together, Alpha and Omega, the way they were always meant to.

They reach their peaks together, and Derrick pulls her on top of him as his knot locks inside her. His purr fills the nest, and she drifts off to sleep, safe in her Alpha's arms.

"Get some sleep while you can." His voice is soft, even though I don't think he needs to worry about waking her. "It's going to be a long four days."

HOT, wet, and soft. That's what I feel as I'm pulled into consciousness. When the last dregs of sleep clear, I see my Omega with my cock in her mouth, hazy green eyes locked on me.

"Good morning, Omega." I'm trying not to thrust into

her throat, but it's difficult because her mouth may be the best thing my cock has ever been in.

She pulls me from her throat and shuffles up my body to kiss me. "Beta, please."

"What do you need, baby?"

"Please." She throws a leg over my hips and lines herself up with my cock, but doesn't sink down. She watches me and whimpers softly. "Please?"

"Take what you need, Omega." I've barely finished speaking when she lowers herself onto me. Her slick ensures there is no resistance as she takes me to the base.

I grip her so tight that her skin turns white around my fingertips. "Fuck." The word is breathy and drawn out as she rides me. Holy shit, it's better than I ever imagined.

A pleased rumble tells me that Ivan's awake. I find him sitting on the side of the nest with his cock in his hand and a massive smile on his face. "Don't mind me, just enjoying the show."

Knowing he's watching is the icing on the cake, and I adjust our bodies so he can get a good look at the two of us. I lick my thumb and place it on her clit, encouraging her to grind against it. She's panting, sweat dripping between her breasts, when Derrick slides behind her from the other side of the nest and grabs her hair.

He pulls enough to get her head bent backward. "You're not going to come, Omega."

She clamps down on me, and I swear I see stars. Fuck that feels good.

"You're going to fuck your Beta while you suck me off, then I'll give you to Ivan to make sure you've gotten more than enough orgasms. How does that sound?"

I didn't think that Derrick would try to control her orgasms right now, after he let her come so easily before.

Chapter Thirty-Nine

I'm waiting for her to say no, to reject the idea because her heat is riding her hard. But she doesn't. She whines but agrees, letting her mouth drop open for him. He releases her hair and stands over my chest, giving me the most incredible view.

Derrick's ass flexes as he pushes between her lips. Her small hands grip his thighs as he thrusts, gently at first, into her mouth. From my position, I get a eyeful of my Alpha, from his muscular ass to his balls that are already tightening. I wish I could see her right now. The sounds she's making are enough to quicken my breath.

She flexes around me, and I push my hips up into her, losing composure as I chase my release while Derrick denies my Omega hers. I spill inside her, panting and covered in her slick, as I fall limp beneath her. Completely blissed out. When our Alpha's ass tightens and his hips stutter, I know he won't last long either.

By the time both of us have come, Ivan is there, tapping us out. He picks Ariana off of me and lays her on the nest. She's desperate, begging to come, and a wicked smile curls his lips.

"I'll give you what you need, Omega."

He grabs her clit and pinches as he slides inside her, forcing a brutal orgasm out of her as soon as he bottoms out. Once she comes down, he's pounding into her, one hand twined in her hair and pulling tight as he toys with her nipple with the other. When he leans to capture her lips, he pinches her nipple hard and grinds his knot against her.

"Again," he whispers against her mouth. "Now, Omega."

Our beautiful, obedient Omega bucks beneath him, chanting to a God that's not in the room with us.

After several orgasms, Ivan finally allows himself to knot her, lowering himself on top of her as his orgasm overwhelms him. He wraps Ariana in his arms, purring, and she falls asleep, momentarily satiated.

Chapter Forty

BEING a part of a heat is no joke. Ariana is insatiable, begging to be fucked from the moment her eyes open until she passes out again.

And it's only day two.

She's bouncing on Ivan's cock, both of them feral with desire, but my girl can handle more. Maybe it'll help her sleep a little longer if we overload her with pheromones.

I wake Grant with a soft nudge.

"Alpha?"

"Come here, Beta, I have a job for you." He's sleep-rumpled and gorgeous, his pale purple hair shining beautifully in the low light. I pull him into a kiss, and he falls into me, perfectly submissive and gentle in this moment.

I ghost my lips over his ear. "How would you feel about sliding into Ariana's ass while I take yours?"

My Beta makes a needy sound as he throws his arms around my neck. "Please, Alpha."

I guide him over to our packmates, moving him behind Ariana.

"Omega?" I purr. "Your Beta wants inside you. Can you handle them both?"

"Yes, yes, yes." Her cheeks are flushed and her eyes cloudy, the heat in the driver's seat making her bold.

"Do you remember your safeword?" Ivan's words are interrupted by grunts as he thrusts into her.

"Red."

With the confirmation that even in a heat haze, she remembers the word she needs to say to stop us, I slide my fingers between her cheeks, finding her hole slick and soft already.

God, Omega bodies are incredible.

"She's already ready for you." I kiss Grant one more time before pushing him toward her, grabbing his dick, and pumping once before lining him up. He loves it when I manhandle him. As he pushes inside her, she screams her pleasure until he's flushed against her back.

"So tight. So good." Her words are mumbled, but I hear them all the same.

As Ivan ruts into her from below, Grant stays still, waiting for me to get him ready. Reaching between Ariana and Ivan, I'm able to gather enough slick to coat my cock and fingers. I rub Grant's hole, feeling it flex beneath my fingertips, before pushing one in.

He sighs in pleasure as he accepts me.

One finger becomes two, two becomes three, and now I'm sure that my Beta is ready to take me. I grip his shoulder as I guide myself into him. The sounds that Grant makes as he pulses around my cock should be illegal.

"Okay, Omega, I'm going to fuck your Beta into you now. Be a good girl. You can take all of us, can't you?"

"Of course she can. You love this, don't you, Omega?" Ivan's voice is a seductive purr. Dude should narrate audio-

Chapter Forty

books or something, because that baritone, when not joking and laughing, is so sexy.

Our bodies move together in a passionate dance, the four of us coming together as a pack. I feel lightheaded with a blend of pleasure and joy, as I rut into my Beta, slamming him over and over into our Omega. I'm rougher with him than I have been with her, and I know he loves it. He's a whimpering mess as he groans against Ariana's ear.

When she bucks between my packmates, losing control of her body to an orgasm, her Alpha grabs her hips and pulls her onto his knot, groaning out his release.

Grant is panting, clearly nearing his limit, when I grab him around the neck. That small amount of pressure is enough to have his ass choking my cock as he comes in Ariana. It is only a few moments before I'm filling him as well, pulling out before I accidentally knot him.

We fall into a sticky pile of limbs, Ariana already snoring on top of Ivan.

I PULL the door to the nest closed with the carefulness of someone diffusing a bomb. My cell phone and keys are resting on the counter where I left them two days ago, and I grab them on my way out.

The rental is nice but plain, the type of car that was listed as a "mystery sedan" on the website when I booked it. I hate having to leave Ariana while she's in heat, but she just fell asleep, so hopefully I can be back before she notices I'm gone.

I make sure my phone is hooked up to Bluetooth before I call Marlie.

"Uh, hello. What have you done with my best friend?"

"Hello to you, too, Marlie. We got home and got her nest set up. She woke up in heat."

"She's done already?"

I flick my blinker. It's a twenty-minute drive. It'll take thirty minutes to finish, then twenty minutes back. Will she sleep for over an hour? Fuck, I hope she does.

"No, I stepped out. This is the best time to-"

"You left her? While she's in heat? What were you thinking?"

I grip the steering wheel, trying not to snap at the Omega who only has Ariana's best interest at heart. "Do you think I'd leave if I didn't have to?"

"But you don't have to! You can go after it's over."

"This is the best time and you know it. I'm on the edge of a rut, Marlie."

"Ew, TMI."

"Well, what else do you want me to say?" This redlight is taking forever. It needs to hurry the hell up. I don't *want* to be away from my Omega. The farther away from her I am, the tighter and itchier my skin gets.

I have to remind myself that I'm doing this for her. That she'll appreciate what I'm doing. Love it, even.

"Okay, well, are you at least going to tell her?"

"Not yet. I need more before I do." Oh my God, if this car in front of me doesn't move, I'm going to scream. I need to get a hold of myself. The last thing I want is to fall into a rut while I'm driving because I get pissed off. That would be a nightmare to deal with. Someone would have to come pick me up. I focus on my breathing to calm down.

"This is a bad idea."

"I hear you, Marlie, but it's the one I've got."

"You should take my advice and tell her sooner rather than later. I am an Omega, you know. I know something about this shit."

Chapter Forty

Maybe I should tell Ariana. Marlie knows her well, and I know she wouldn't steer me in the wrong direction. But part of me feels like this needs to stay a secret. That the moment she knows, it's going to look like I did this to make her forgive me, to convince her to bond me.

And it's not why. This is me keeping every option open for her. Making sure she never feels trapped. It doesn't matter that we've bonded. She deserves a safety net.

I swing into the parking lot and turn off my car.

"I just wanted you to know she wasn't ignoring you. I'll have her call you when the heat is over."

"You'd better. I miss my best friend."

I end the call without saying goodbye and climb out. The clinic opened five minutes ago. Here's hoping I get back before she wakes up.

Chapter Forty-One

Ivan
pumpkin bread

DERRICK HAS LEFT every day of her heat. He told me why, but it has been hell to distract Ariana enough that she didn't realize he was missing. When he crawled back into the nest the first time, she was asleep again, having drifted off while she suckled softly on my cock. On day three, Grant had slipped her off to the shower before she could notice Derrick missing and cleaned her up. It's day four, and this is the first time he managed to get back before she woke up at all.

"How's she doing?" He strips off his clothes and slips into the nest, curling up against her back. "Did she wake up?"

"No. She's sleeping in longer stretches, so I think she's close to being done."

He sighs in relief as he pulls her closer to his body and strokes her neck.

"She's so perfect, Ivan."

This close, I can see the nearly invisible freckles that dust her cheeks. Her pink lips are parted and swollen, and her hair is a complete mess.

Chapter Forty-One

She's the most beautiful thing I've ever seen.

"Yeah, she is. How did we get so lucky?"

He looks off to the side, eyes wistful. "And I almost ruined it for us all."

I clap him on the shoulder. "It worked out in the end, didn't it?"

"Yeah. We're lucky that she gave us a chance."

We were lucky, that's for sure. In many ways. The odds of our being her scent match were so slim, even though it wouldn't have made a difference if we weren't. And yet here we are, with bonding scars and scents that mark us as hers because even though we lied to her and hurt her, she still trusts us.

If we weren't scent matches, would it have been easier for her to forgive us, or harder? I hate to think that our scents and the fear of getting FOS were what pushed her to accept the pack, but that had to have some bearing on it. Would she have made a different decision if our pheromones hadn't recognized each other?

I know that I'm spiraling. How could I not? Will I ever know if she truly wanted this, wanted us?

My Omega's eyes flutter open as she reaches for my chest. "Your thoughts are so loud, Alpha. I can feel them in the bond. What's worrying you?" Her voice is surprisingly lucid, but she's still warm enough that I know her heat still isn't over.

I shouldn't talk about this. Not right now. It could upset her and make her heat harder.

But I have to know.

"Did you feel like you had to bond with us because we're scent matches?"

Derrick's exhale is loud at my question, and I hear Grant stirring on my other side. They both would have waited to have this conversation until after the heat was over, if they ever asked her at all, but I can't. My hindbrain is out of control, thinking that our Omega doesn't want us.

I can't pull my eyes away from her soft face.

"No. I bonded with you because not only are you my scent match, but you're wonderful. Even if you weren't my match, I think we still would have ended up here."

Does being in heat work like alcohol? Does it lower inhibitions and make someone tell people the truth because it doesn't cross their mind to lie?

Damn, I hope so.

"You're already taking care of me. Already putting me first. Being scent matched doesn't mean shit if you're not a good, loving person. Which you are. You all are." She reaches out for me and cups my cheek in her hand. "I don't ever want you to think I regret this, Ivan. Even if I have moments where I'm pissed at you, I will always want you."

Derrick squeezes her tightly around the waist as I pour my feelings into our Omega through a kiss.

"SHIT," Derrick swears, waking me from a short nap. "Give me one second, Omega."

When I look over at the two of them, I find Ariana on her knees in presentation, backing her ass up to Derrick, demanding to be fucked.

"I've just got to get my pants off." I'm not sure why he bothered putting them on at all. If someone looked through the windows while he was grabbing water for us and got a view of his ass, that's on them for being peeping Toms.

Chapter Forty-One

"No, now. Now, Alpha." Ariana's little Omega growl is so cute, but I don't tell her that. I'm not looking to be on the other end of her wrath. If the frustration that writhes in my chest tells me anything, it's that she's at the end of her rope waiting for him.

When he finally pushes into her, she sighs with relief and flops face down on the floor.

I slide underneath my Omega's raised hips and prop myself up on my elbows. I'm able to reach her clit with my tongue, but it's not comfortable, and I really don't care. The taste of her slick on my tongue is all I need to make me happy. And if I happen to miss and get Derrick's cock? He won't mind.

We've been working her together for a few minutes when I feel Grant's pretty mouth wrap around my dick. His silvery hair is still wet from a wash, his cheeks are flushed, and his cock is jutting out between his legs. The sight of him, combined with the sounds of my Omega being fucked within an inch of her life and her slick on my lips? I can barely keep myself from blowing my load.

Derrick and I are two very lucky Alphas. Probably the luckiest in the world, and everyone is going to know it once the show airs. Our Omega and Beta are two of the most beautiful people in existence. And when they're together? Shit, how can anyone expect us to do anything outside of this nest?

Ariana's panting moans draw my attention away from the Beta shoving his face against my pelvis, swallowing around my cock. I suck her clit between my teeth, and she bucks, nearly knocking me flat on my back with the force of her hips. Derrick grips her tighter to keep her from flailing around.

"Stay still, Omega, and let your Alphas take care of you."

Grant's soft fingertip slips under my balls and strokes my hole, and now I'm the one bucking my hips and losing control. I may prefer to top, but I'm never going to say no to a finger or two.

There are so many things happening at once, so many sensations, that I have no hope of holding back the orgasm as it barrels into me. Grant strokes my prostate as he swallows me down, and with the taste of our Omega on my tongue, I empty myself into the back of his throat with a yelp.

Ariana must have been watching us, because as soon as Grant pulls off my cock and squeezes my knot, she falls headfirst into her orgasm, collapsing on top of me.

I don't mind.

She could smother me, and I'd die a happy man.

After I slide from beneath her, Derrick hikes his leg up and places his foot between her shoulder blades, holding her in place as he ruts into her at a punishing pace. She has to be oversensitive, but he's not letting her come down, forcing her into another orgasm as he pushes his knot into her with a grunt.

She's a limp pile of Omega as he adjusts her to her side so we can all lie together. Her eyes are looking clearer, the red flush fading from her chest as she falls to sleep, and I know that the heat has finally broken.

Chapter Forty-Two

AFTER MY HEAT BREAKS, I take an hour-long shower while the guys strip all the linens and put them in the wash. There are parts of my heat that are blank, but I can remember chunks of it.

My guys took very good care of me.

I'm digging through the pile of clothes that Grant got me, searching for something comfortable to wear, when a throat clears behind me.

I look up to see my Beta leaning in the doorway, his arms crossed over his chest, staring at me with a strange expression.

Before I have a chance to ask him what's up, he's on me, spinning me around and pinning me against the mirror.

"Just finished your heat and already needy again? You just can't get enough of us, can you, greedy girl?" He grinds his hard as a rock cock against my ass. He rips off my towel, kicks my legs apart, and thrusts into me in one stroke. "Since you're so desperate, I'll give you what you want. Don't you dare move."

My mind blanks for a moment, and my body goes completely limp. His grip is the only thing keeping me from collapsing onto the tile.

He's helping me live out my fantasy, and oh my God, it's as good as I thought it would be.

Grant rests a hand that is incongruously gentle with the current scene on my head and pushes me down so my ass sticks out even farther. He pounds into me with no care, just a hard, ruthless fucking.

He's using me, punishing me, and I love it so fucking much.

"Is this what you wanted? You wanted to be our little doll? Our perfect cock sleeve to use whenever we want?"

I can't form words, only whimpers and moans at the idea of being used by all of them. I just finished my heat, and I shouldn't want to fuck right now, but this is what I needed. Grant is taking what he wants from me, and in doing so, giving me what I have fantasized about for ages.

My Beta bends and nibbles on my ear. Keeping his voice low to not break the scene, he asks, "Color?"

"Green." I don't even have to think about it.

That one word gives him the permission he needs to let go completely. "Fuck, you feel so good. So tight and perfect for me. The best little fuck toy."

Yeah, that's doing it for me. I dive my hand between my legs and strum my clit, knowing that Grant is the only one who will let me orgasm whenever and however I want, even in a scene like this.

My toes curl, and I rise up on the balls of my feet. He grabs my hair and forces my eyes to meet his in the mirror. He looks feral, that stunning, delicate face of his twisted in a snarl. His pale purple and silver hair is pulled back at the base of his neck, but several pieces have fallen out and stick to his face.

Chapter Forty-Two

I want to see him like this all the time.

I look wanton, aching for more as he uses me. When he reaches around me and grabs my chin, forcing me to lock eyes with him through the mirror, I lose control. I drench his cock with slick. His fingers tighten to almost the point of pain as he fills me.

It takes us a few minutes to come down from the high. When our breathing has leveled out, and my legs stop shaking, he picks me up and carries me back into the shower.

"How was that?" He turns on the water and lathers a washcloth. "Everything you wanted it to be?"

"And more."

THE GUYS HAVE ALMOST FINISHED MOVING in with me in the two weeks since my heat ended. The place feels more alive than ever, even if it is crowded in a way that I'm not used to. I've never had to share my space so intimately, but I can't say I mind it. I'm getting the best sleep of my life now that we're all piled up together in the nest.

There's one dark spot in all of this, though.

Derrick has been acting shady.

I don't want to accuse him of anything, but it's hard to ignore. I've walked in on him on the phone a few times, and he hangs up as soon as he sees me. He doesn't leave it lying around either. It's always on his person, like he's scared I'm going to grab it and go through it.

I don't want to think he's hiding something again, but there isn't any other explanation. Everyone deserves privacy, even in relationships, but this isn't the behavior of someone who wants privacy.

It's someone who's keeping a secret.

I scrub my face and pause my game. I cannot be a good raiding partner right now. My brain is too scattered. I need some coffee or something.

It's second nature to pick up my phone and call Marlie while I wait for it to brew.

"Hey, lady! How are you?"

"Hey, Marlie. I'm kind of freaking out."

Her voice fills with concern. *"What's going on?"*

"A lot. Ivan and Grant are figuring stuff out with their jobs. Ivan is getting what he needs to set up an office here, and Grant's visiting his company's local branch to work out a transfer. But Derrick is gone too, and I don't know where he is. I thought he was just going to the rental to grab the final load of stuff to move over, but it's been a long time."

Rather than having the movers bring everything here, we had them drop the moving pod in the rental's driveway so we could decide what needed to come and what they'd put up for sale. It's been slow going.

There's a long pause on the line. I have to check to make sure the call is still connected. With a heavy sigh, Marlie says something I didn't want to hear. *"I know where he is."*

Betrayal twists my gut. My best friend and my Alpha? How could they?

"Don't spiral. There is nothing going on between us."

Oh, thank God.

"Then what *is* going on, Marlie?"

"I shouldn't be the one to tell you. It needs to come from him."

"Bullshit. You're my best friend."

I can imagine her rubbing her temples as she ducks her head. If we were together, there's no way she'd be making

Chapter Forty-Two

eye contact with me. *"I really can't. But I can help you get the answers you need. I'll give you the address. He should be there now. But promise you'll keep an open mind and let him explain before you freak out."*

After assuring her I'll give him a fair shot, even though I worry I can't, she texts me the address, and I call an Omega-only rideshare to take me there.

As I stand on the curb, waiting for the blue SUV to pick me up, my breathing grows labored.

I haven't left the house since we got back from the show, and now I'm getting in a car with a stranger.

Fuck, fuck. Can I do this? I can't do this. I just got home. I don't want to leave.

My old anxieties are twisted snakes writhing inside me, and I have to fight to keep my breath steady. I talked to my therapist a few days ago about everything that has happened between the guys and me, and he said that my agoraphobia was less a fear of leaving the house and more of a fear of being exposed to an Alpha.

The world was never the problem. What lives in it was.

Now that I'm bonded, he warned me that it's possible that my anxiety will manifest as a fear of being without my pack.

I think he was right. We've been in a happy little bubble. It's easy to think you're cured when you avoid the cause.

The idea of getting into a car with a stranger without one of them makes me feel like I need to curl into a ball and hide.

By the time the car stops at the curb, I've not calmed down even a little bit. One wrong move and I'm going to bolt into the house and lock the door. The only thing keeping me in place is the desire to know what Derrick is hiding from me.

The driver rolls down the passenger-side window and leans across the center console. "Are you Ariana? You okay?"

I clutch at my throat and shift from foot to foot. "Yeah. No. Yes, I'm Ariana, no, I'm not okay."

He's got to be about forty, with a few stripes of grey at the temples of his dark hair. His eyes are full of sympathy, and he's got a kind smile. "First time without your Alphas?"

"How'd you know?"

"I had a panic attack in the middle of the mall. Got out of the house fine, but when there were a bunch of people around me, and not one of them was my Alpha? Yeah, one of them had to come and pick me up off the floor." He puts the car in park and unbuckles his seatbelt. As he passes around the front of the vehicle, I know I should run away, but something about him is calming my fears.

"I'm Jerome. Is your Alpha home?"

I wave at the house behind me. "No, my pack is out. I'm trying to go meet my Alpha."

"I know this is hard. There's no pressure to get in the car. But you're going to see your Alpha in a few minutes, so there's something to look forward to. Would you feel better sitting up front with me or in the back?" His scent, a soothing limeade, combined with his tender, sweet voice, immediately relaxes me.

"Up front, I think."

Like a gentleman, Jerome opens the passenger door, and I slide in.

On the twenty-minute drive, we tell each other all about our packs. He's got four Alphas, which sounds like a lot to manage to me, and they're not scent matched. None

Chapter Forty-Two

of them cares. They fell in love at school and have been together since.

By the time we pull up to the address Marlie gave me, my anxiety has quieted to only the worry about what Derrick is hiding from me.

I climb out of the SUV and wave goodbye to Jerome before I notice where the address Marlie gave me led. Derrick's rental car is in the parking lot of a health clinic.

What is he doing here?

Chapter Forty-Three

THE NURSE at the front desk waves at me as I exit the procedure room. "Will we see you in two days?"

"I'll be here!"

This isn't a pleasant experience, but I always leave in a great mood. I'm ready to get back to my Omega. I've been gone longer than I anticipated.

I squint against the sun, and when my vision focuses, I see Ariana standing in front of my car.

Oh, shit.

Ariana is standing in front of my car.

She looks like she's upset but also pissed. Upset that she's pissed? Pissed that she's upset? Regardless, I know I'm the one who put that expression on her face.

"What are you doing here?" As I get closer, I can see that her hands are shaking, but she doesn't reach for me for comfort. "What are you hiding from me?"

"This isn't how I wanted you to find out."

That wasn't a smart thing to say. She takes a step back, betrayal painted across her features.

"I forgave you. I looked past your lies, bonded you,

Chapter Forty-Three

welcomed you into my pack and my bed. And now you're lying to me again? How could you?" Tears trail down her cheeks. Ones that I caused, again.

"Please, let me explain." I'm not above begging. This may not be how I wanted her to find out, but I'm not willing to let her suffer or hurt in hopes of hiding what I've been doing. I hold my hand out for her, praying she'll trust me enough to take it. "I'll show you."

Tentatively, she slips her hand into mine and lets me pull her through the doors of the clinic. When we get inside, the nurse looks up in surprise.

"Back already?"

Ariana's hand tightens around mine at the nurse's familiar tone. "This is my Omega."

They know that I've been keeping it a secret from her. The doctor was concerned about it at first, but when I explained that I was doing this to protect her, she stopped asking questions.

"Oh. Well. Come on, then. The procedure room hasn't been cleaned yet. You can go over your file with her." Her fingers dance across the keyboard. The printer beside her whirrs, and she grabs the pages. "Follow me."

The small room still smells like my creamy pecan pie scent, and Ariana's nostrils flare as soon as she crosses the threshold. I don't like how sour she smells. I hate that I've ever given her a reason to think that I'd hurt her, but I know that my lies are still so fresh.

I shouldn't have kept this from her.

I lift her onto the bed and step between her thighs. "When I left the *Expected* house, I didn't know if you'd ever want to see me again, and the last thing I wanted was for you to feel like you had to or risk getting sick." I hand her one of the pages, but she doesn't look down at it. "I've been coming here three times a week to harvest my pheromones. I've had them cryogenically frozen, so they won't degrade over time. I wanted to make sure there was never any reason why you felt like you had to keep me in your life if you didn't want to. If anything happens to me, or you decide you don't want me around, you'll have a stock of my pheromones to keep you healthy. They're even working on a way to create synthetic pheromones based on a sample, so hopefully, if I don't get enough stored up for you, they'll be able to do that if the time comes."

She breaks her eyes away from me and looks at the paper, not saying a word. I can barely breathe as I watch her read it. Will she be happy that I did this? Will knowing that she has another option now make her change her mind about me?

"Doesn't it hurt?"

That's not what I expected her to ask when she found out.

"It's not great. There's a machine that squeezes my knot to collect... the fluid." She wrinkles her nose in disgust. Yeah, the whole thing sounds gross in a medical context. "And they take extractions from my armpits, too."

"Three times a week?"

"It's the maximum amount. I'd go every day if I could. I want to make sure you never have to feel pressured to stay with me. Ivan said he's going to start donating, too. That way, if anything ever happens to us, you won't go through what Calvin did."

A startled sob escapes her, but she tries to smother it with her hand.

She's not fast enough.

I gather her in my arms and pin her to my chest while burying my face in her neck. I can't make sense of what I'm feeling from her in our bond right now. "I'm sorry I hid this from you. I didn't want you to know because I worried you'd think I was just doing it to win you over."

"This is the nicest thing anyone has ever done for me."

I'm not sure what reaction I expected from her. I wasn't sure when to tell her, because I don't like the idea of making her think about her pack dying, but I feel a weight has lifted off of me now that she knows.

When her tears don't seem to slow, I sweep her up in my arms and carry her out of the clinic. I try not to jostle her as I place her in the passenger seat and pull her seatbelt over her lap. It's not until I turn the car on and click my buckle into place that she sniffles away her tears enough to talk.

"I was so worried when I realized you were keeping something from me. Don't be mad at Marlie for telling me where you were."

"She warned me not to keep it a secret from you. I should have listened to her. I never wanted you to go through this kind of stress, and she knew this would happen. She's a good friend. One of her brothers works in a lab at the storage facility, so when I mentioned what I was doing to her, she hooked me up with him."

Ariana turns toward me with her arms wrapped tightly around her body. "And you did this because of Calvin?"

"For you." I hit the blinker and turn into the parking lot of a superstore so I can look at her while we have this conversation. "Calvin's death destroyed you. I hated that you lived in fear every day. I knew that when you met me, all you could think about was what happened to him, and if I could do something about it, I needed to. You faced your fears going onto *Expected*, and I didn't want that to be in vain. I want you to have a safety net. If something happens to me, or you come to your senses and realize that

I am not good enough for you, I needed to make sure that you would be okay."

She reaches across the console and grabs my hands. "I love you, Derrick. So fucking much. You gave me my life back."

I brush some of her hair behind her ear before cupping her cheek. "I'd give you anything, honey."

When she leans forward and presses her lips to mine, all of the tension I was holding onto drains out of me. "I don't need anything. Just my pack."

Chapter Forty-Four

"I WISH you had felt comfortable telling us. I hate knowing that you've been holding onto this."

"I was just so angry at him, Mom. And then at myself for being mad at him. He couldn't help dying."

I curl up in my nest, cradling the phone against my shoulder. I told the guys I wanted to be alone so I could call my parents and tell them about Calvin's last request and the letter before the show airs. It took me ages to get up the nerve to press the call button, but now that I've told them everything, my heart feels lighter.

Calvin was my brother, but he was their son. They deserve to know how he felt at the end and why I acted the way I did.

"I'm sorry I waited so long to tell you."

Dad coos at me like he did when I was small. *"You don't need to apologize. None of us were our best then. We should never have let you shut yourself in the way you did. Our grief isn't an excuse for not helping you with yours."*

"We love you so much, Ari." My Papa's gruff voice soothes

my frayed edges. He's always had that effect on me. *"I'm sorry if we ever made you feel like you couldn't come to us."*

"It wasn't anything you did. I felt so guilty."

"You do not need to feel guilty. He never should have put that on you. It was an impossible thing to ask of you." Guilt twists inside my chest as my mom comforts me. I hate that I've missed out on so much time with her. I struggled to be around her after Calvin died, and that wasn't fair.

"So." Pops's teasing tone is a departure from the somber nature of the conversation. *"Marlie called us."*

My back stiffens. I hadn't planned to have the 'I have a pack now' conversation. I was going to tell them next week. Maybe two weeks.

"She did?" My voice is tight. "About what?"

"She said you were on a TV show." Father always sounds stern, even when we're having a casual conversation. *"Why didn't you tell us?"*

"Uh. Well." I feel a bit like a scolded child. "Do you have time?"

An hour later, I curl up in the nest, pulling one of the blankets that smells like Grant around me and burrowing deep. The conversation ended well, and they're so excited to meet the guys, but having to admit how Sax was, in fact, lying on the internet like they warned me he was as a teenager, and cautioning them against watching the show because of the things they'd see, I'm exhausted.

A pleasant weight meets my back, and Ivan's rich scent wraps around me.

"You okay, sweetie?"

I roll over and nuzzle into his chest. When he holds me against him like this, all the tension drains out of me. "Just tired, really. My parents are excited to meet you guys."

"You told them about us? You made sure that I'm the favorite, right?"

I laugh and scratch his beard. He leans into me like a cat. "How could I make sure of that?"

"Telling them how handsome I am. How well I take care of you. How I'm not the one who decided to lie to you. That kind of thing."

"You're going to throw Derrick under the bus, aren't you?"

He hums and looks anywhere but at me. "I would never do such a thing to my packmate, but if I did, it'd be okay, because all is fair in love and war." He pushes me onto my back and hovers above me. "Though Grant will be a tough one to beat."

His weight above me, so close to my heat finishing, leaves me panting. How am I going to live a normal life when everything these guys do has me slick and desperate? I wrap my leg around his thigh and try to pull him against me, but he doesn't budge.

"Why, Omega. Are you trying to take advantage of me?"

"Is it working?"

He dips and ghosts his lips across mine. "Oh yeah. But I wanted to talk to you first. It's kind of important."

I drop my leg and prop myself up on my elbows. Anxiety twists my gut. "What's going on?"

"It's nothing bad!" He can tell by the look on my face that I don't believe him. He drops beside me and rolls onto his back, looking at the string lights decorating my nest.

"What's going on?"

"Nothing is going on. I told you, it's nothing bad." My Alpha weaves our fingers together and pulls my hand to his mouth. "My grandmother wants to meet you. On my Pa's side. She knows we're bonded, but there is an exchange of rings that happens in my family. The oldest person in the family is the one who puts them on us, and she's eager to be the one to do it."

It takes a minute for his words to hit me. "Ivan. Are you proposing?"

"It's an engagement, but we don't have to get married. We're bonded. That's bigger than marriage. But Nene wants you to have her ring, and she's so excited..." His words trail off, and if he didn't have a beard, I'm sure his cheeks would be bright red. "It's not a big deal."

"I'd love to, Ivan."

His eyes light up, and he rolls onto his side, resting his face on his fist. "Yeah?"

"Yeah."

When I press my lips to his, my Alpha melts into me. Ivan is soft in all the right places. He's comfortable and cozy, and I always feel safe in his arms. But one part of him is certainly *not* soft. I palm his cock, and he grinds into my hand.

"This is not why I came in here, you know?"

I wiggle my body down his and grab the waistband of his sweats. "Are you going to tell me to stop?"

"Absolutely not."

I pull his shorts down and take him into my mouth, the weight of his head on my tongue causing arousal to pool between my legs. My Alpha weaves his fingers through my hair and holds me still. When I look at him through my lashes, he rubs the apple of my cheek with one hand.

"You look beautiful when you suck my dick, Omega." A wicked smile stretches his face, and I clench my thighs. "But I want you to sit on my face while you do it."

He doesn't have to ask me twice.

I scramble to get my pants off and perch above him. He grabs my hips with one hand and slams me onto his tongue while his other pushes on my back to get me to lean down and taste him again.

Focusing on his cock is nearly impossible when he sucks my clit between his lips and slides two fingers inside me. I grip his base, squeezing his knot as I swallow around him. Every time my throat flexes around his length, he moans into my pussy.

His beard is scratchy between my thighs, contrasting the warmth of his tongue in the most delicious way. It's not long before I shatter on his tongue. Once I do, he doesn't hold back, grabbing my head and fucking up into my mouth.

After we're both spent and panting, wrapped in each other's arms, a throat clears behind us.

I look behind me to see Grant, his cock tenting his loose shorts, watching us. "Uh. Dinner is ready."

Ivan stands and crosses, naked, to our Beta. He grabs the front of Grant's shirt and pulls him into a passionate kiss that gets my pulse rising again. When our Alpha pulls away with a nip to Grant's lower lip, he chuckles.

"I had dessert first."

Chapter Forty-Five

VEGAS IS gorgeous through the wide windows of the penthouse suite. Sure, it's a little gaudy, but I don't mind it. It's not somewhere I'd come frequently, because I'm not a gambler, but the shows we've seen have been amazing. I've watched a few of the fountain shows out of the windows of our penthouse room at Hedonistic Heat.

God, I hope these windows are tinted.

Ivan ruts into me from behind, my breasts flattened on the glass as I brace myself against it.

"You're always so fucking desperate for our cocks," he growls through gritted teeth. "Wouldn't leave us alone."

"I'm sorry, Alpha." My whimper is needy and high-pitched.

My men love our free use agreement.

So do I.

"Don't let her come." Derrick directs my Alpha from the couch, where he's stretched out, legs spread wide, and his arms resting loosely on the back. Grant kneels in front of him, taking our Alpha's cock down his throat.

"You don't think she's earned it?" It doesn't sound like

Chapter Forty-Five

he cares one way or the other. I think he loves working with my other Alpha to drive me higher and higher before he gets to push me over the ledge.

Grant makes a choking sound, and when I seek out his reflection in the glass, I see Derrick holding our Beta's face flush against his pelvis. Just the sight of the two of them together has me clenching and dripping slick around Ivan's cock.

My Alpha wraps an arm around my knee and lifts it, opening me to him even more. The stretch of the position and his knot bumping against my entrance has me wailing.

Despite my begging, he won't knot me here. Not when we have tickets for tonight's Cirque de Mordu performance.

Derrick ruins one more orgasm for me before he says I'm allowed to come. He's already filled Grant's mouth and is now roughly jerking our Beta off as they watch the two of us. My Alpha reaches around my hips and flicks at my sensitive, desperate clit, and I fall, fall, fall. It feels like the pleasure goes on forever, and by the time I come down, he's pumped his release into me and is lowering my leg.

We were very lucky, after my first heat together, that I didn't get pregnant. None of us was thinking about birth control at the time. The doctor said I didn't ovulate because it was off-schedule. Even though we are in Vegas, we're not rolling the dice again. I got on the birth control shot as soon as I could.

My heat ended a few days ago, so we had time before and after it to enjoy the city. The network didn't spare any expense when they set up the trip. We've been eating and living like kings, attending the hottest shows. It's been six months since we left the *Expected* house, and we leave for the reunion show tomorrow.

It's been awkward, trying not to be noticed, but in

Vegas, people are more focused on themselves than on those around them. We've disguised ourselves as we walk around with hats and glasses. I don't think it really works, but it's at least plausible deniability.

I'm looking forward to the reunion show. There will be a live audience asking questions, and based on everything I saw online, it's been a popular season. Reading the posts as the show aired has been a blast. We get together as a pack, watch the episodes, and then spend a little too much time online looking at audience reactions.

They've been positive, for the most part. Sure, there are always asshole on the internet, but most have been surprisingly kind, all things considered.

The network did not shy away from showing our intimate moments, either. I'm surprised some of it was allowed. It got pretty risque, especially after I bonded Ivan and Grant. I'm not as embarrassed about it as I was at the time. Watching our love story unfold over the past four weeks has been amazing.

Someone wrote a think piece about how our season was a study on grief and healing. Psychologists weighed in on the way I handled everything, which was obviously not healthy, but the main focus was on how the guys honored my grief over Calvin.

That has maybe been the most unexpected thing about this experience. My brother's makeup tutorial videos are trending again. It was a bit jarring the first time I scrolled past one, but now it makes me smile when I do.

He's living on, not just in my memory, but in other people's.

"Let's get cleaned up." Ivan taps me lightly on the butt. "We don't want to be late."

"Do you guys have your hats and sunglasses?" Grant tucks his brilliant hair under a hat and puts on his massive aviator glasses before flipping up the hood of his sweater. We look like celebrities trying to hide out from the paparazzi, but we haven't been recognized.

Yet.

CIRQUE DE MORDU is not a regular circus. It's high-flying, death-defying acts, and darkly seductive.

It was amazing.

The network set us up with a private box where we watched the acts put themself in danger over and over again.

The Twisted Twins on the trapeze had me clenching Grant's hand so tight he almost lost circulation. They're flying around with no nets under them! What happens if they fall? There was a duo, Quick Cut and Maestro, that started with knife throwing and ended with the Alpha swallowing a sword while hanging from the ceiling by hooks driven through his skin. I've never seen anything like it.

The whole show was dangerous, thrilling, and captivating, and I am so excited that the network arranged for us to meet some of the performers afterward.

By the time the show is over, and security leads us to the backstage area, several performers and the ringmaster are hanging out in a green room waiting for us.

A dark-haired man covered in tattoos bounces to us. He's wearing a pair of track pants but no shirt, his lithe, muscular torso on display. "Hello! I'm Dario, one of the Twisted Twins. It's nice to meet you." When he bows deeply, the other half of his act, his twin with bleached-blond hair, peeks over his shoulder and gives us a half wave.

I peel off my hat, sweater, and glasses. The network wouldn't have set this up if they needed us to remain anonymous. There's no way they could expect us to, and there are so many people in this hot and stuffy room. My pack follows my lead, and Ivan collects all of the loose articles before piling them up on an empty chair.

"Hi, Dario, I'm Ariana."

A man with shaggy hair and sleepy eyes straightens against the wall. "Oh shit." It's barely more than a breath, and then he's out of the door.

"Don't mind him." The ringmaster, a giant man with hands the size of dinner plates and dark, wavy hair, steps up and greets us. He's changed out of his performance outfit into more casual jeans and a plain t-shirt. "I'm Jude. We knew we were meeting some television personalities, but forgive me for not recognizing you."

"That's because you don't watch *Knot What You Expected* with us." The quieter twin speaks for the first time. "They're this season's pack."

I didn't consider that they'd watch the show. They don't seem like the target audience for reality television. At least the last episode has already aired, and the reunion airs tomorrow, so seeing us as a group doesn't spoil anything. This is the first time I've been noticed for being on the show, and I don't know how to handle it.

It's hard to look any of them in the eye when I know they watched me have phone sex.

The door bangs open, and the shaggy-haired man comes back, dragging an Omega with dark hair behind him.

"See! I told you!"

She pats him on the chest with a smitten smile. "So I

Chapter Forty-Five

see, Quinton. Forgive my rude Alpha, he forgot his manners. I'm Alex. We've been watching your season, so he got a little excited to bring me to meet you."

The other Omega takes a step toward me, reaching her hands out and hovering them over mine, giving me a chance to decide if I wanted to let her touch me. I turn them over and clasp hers.

Alex is one of those people who looks smart, even though smart doesn't have a specific look. She's probably ten years older than me, if I had to guess, and she's wearing a pair of athletic leggings and a plain top. I doubt she was expecting to meet anyone tonight, and yet she looks adorable and put together.

"I was diagnosed with Foresaken Omega Syndrome a few years ago. My case was milder, brought on by years of heavy suppressant use, so it wasn't as bad as Calvin had it, but it was scary. You're so fucking strong, Ariana. I know you probably don't think you are, but what you went through was something no one should have to endure. I sobbed through most of your episodes. FOS is a miserable illness, and I'm lucky my Alphas were here to help me through it."

"Oh." This moment of connection with another Omega, one who understands my fears, isn't something I've ever had before. "Thank you. Going on the show was difficult, but my anxiety has gotten a lot better since the show wrapped."

The man who dragged her in here moves to her side to jump into our conversation. He's thin, with a pointed chin and heavy eyelids. An Alpha, but not muscular like most are. I'm pretty sure he was the one hanging from the ceiling by his flesh. I kind of want to see what his back looks like right now.

"She's a doctor. Been doing some research into FOS

since the first episode." He's preening like a proud peacock. Is that how my Alphas look when they talk about me?

My boys finally find their voices, as Grant steps forward and slings an arm around my waist. "Really?"

She waves his sentence away. "It's no big deal. It got me thinking, is all. What Calvin went through shouldn't have happened. There has to be something more that can be done than hoping donor pheromones work."

A Beta twirling a knife sits on the floor, leaning against the wall. That must be Maestro. "Don't let her downplay it. She's been obsessing over it. She's even made several calls to specialists."

"Specialists?" That gets Derrick's attention. "What have they said?"

The other Omega waggles her hand. "Not much. The funding is so limited. The show has shone a light on it, though, and it's possible that, with enough community support, things could change."

"What if you two traded contact info?" Ivan reaches into my purse and pulls out my phone. "Maybe we can help somehow. We're about to have a massive platform. We might as well use it."

Alex doesn't hesitate to take my phone from his hand and plug in her number. "I'd like that. I think we could do a lot of good together." After she hands me my phone back, she plants her hands on her hips. "Enough shop talk. How did you like the show?"

Derrick steps forward, looking like a million bucks in his tight trousers and a button-up shirt that brings out the stormy grey color of his eyes, and extends his hand to the quiet twin. "You were incredible on the tightrope. I've never seen anything like it. I'm Derrick."

The Alpha ducks his head, avoiding eye contact, but

Chapter Forty-Five

tentatively reaches out and shakes Derrick's hand. "I know. I watch the show. Dexter."

Dario swings his arm over his brother's shoulders. "Don't let his lack of enthusiasm fool you. It's his guilty pleasure. He's seen every episo-oof." He bends over after catching an elbow from Dexter in the gut. "Rude. I'm your own flesh and blood!"

Jude releases a long-suffering sigh and rubs between his eyes. "Knock it off, you two."

Quinton steps around everyone and approaches Grant. "I'm scent matched to a Beta, too." He waves his hand at Maestro. "That's Matteo. Don't meet a lot of Betas with scent matched Alphas, and I've never heard of two matching the same one. Pretty cool, honestly."

My Beta, dressed in a pair of flowing trousers and a low-cut silk shirt, looks gorgeous as he angles his body toward the other Alpha. "Yeah, we're pretty lucky. A lot of people don't believe us, though."

The circus Alpha bobs his head as Grant talks. "Yeah, I've seen that on the internet. Why would you lie about something like that? Stupid."

"Was any of it fake?" Dexter's voice is kind of flat, and he's not smiling at me, but he doesn't seem unfriendly. I would wager that he's shy when not on stage with his brother, because he's wearing a baggy black shirt that he almost disappears into.

"Nope. No script. We watched it as it aired to see how they edited it. They got a little creative to make things seem more tense or stressful than they were, but the rest of it was right. They didn't encourage any fake storylines or anything."

Why did I say that?

I should've claimed some of the sex stuff was faked for the cameras to save me some dignity.

"Nice. Cool that you guys met on an *Unexplainable and Bizarre* forum. I loved that show, too." His eyes have grown brighter with every word, especially when his Omega slides to his side and rests her head on his shoulder. "But I agree with Ariana. There's no way it's fake."

Derrick groans and throws his head back. "Not you, too! I can't believe how many of you are gullible enough to believe that."

After a few minutes of arguing about the possibility of paranormal activity, we drift into natural conversation groups. Dexter and Quinton bombard me with questions about the show and the filming process. They really are super fans and had a lot to say about Bridgette and Bradley.

I overhear Dario asking Grant for tips on becoming a model. My Beta has gotten several messages inviting him to collaborate with brands since the show started airing, so hopefully, he can quit his day job soon and model full-time. His almost androgynous beauty is in high demand, and there are more fan edits featuring him than for any of the rest of us. Even the network has been using him the most in ads. I can't blame them. My Beta is a stunner.

My goofy Alpha looks right at home with Matteo and Quinton. His dark hair is falling into his eyes, and I struggle to look away from the V of exposed skin on his chest and the curls of dark hair. He looks amazing in a luxe maroon tee and tailored denim. I have to intervene when Ivan asks how to get started with sword swallowing.

No way am I going to let him attempt that.

Jude and Derrick are deep in conversation, and I catch them looking over at Alex and me several times. It's incredible to see Derrick look small compared to the other Alpha.

We talked long past the end of our meet-and-greet time. They were all down-to-earth and fun, not at all what

Chapter Forty-Five

I expected from popular, high-end entertainers. Since the Cirque appeared on the strip a few years ago, it's been sold out for nearly a year in advance. It's almost impossible to get tickets.

The whole night felt like hanging out with old friends, and it was the perfect way to end our trip. By the time we're walking out of the theatre where the circus is, we have to head right back to Headonistic Heat since we have an early flight.

As we're getting ready for bed, I pull Derrick to the side.

"Did you have fun? You and Jude talked a long time."

"I'm glad I got to meet him. He gave me some tips on what he did when Alex got FOS. Apparently, he was the one who donated pheromones for her treatment. It was nice to talk to someone who's been there. Of course, we spent most of the time bragging about how wonderful our Omegas are."

He sweeps me up in his arms and tosses me onto the bed. Grant and Ivan are already stretched out, the latter of whom started snoring as soon as his head hit the pillow.

"Get some sleep, sweetie. Tomorrow is going to be interesting."

Knot What You Expected

REUNION SHOW

BRADLEY: WELCOME, AMERICA, TO THE *KNOT WHAT YOU EXPECTED* REUNION SHOW!

BRIDGETTE: WE HAVE LOVED SEEING YOUR REACTIONS TO THIS SEASON. IT WAS SOMETHING ELSE, WASN'T IT?

BRADLEY: FROM THE SURPRISE OF A LIFETIME TO AN EMOTIONAL BONDING, THIS SEASON HAD US ALL ON THE EDGE OF OUR SEATS.

BRIDGTTE: LET'S TAKE A LOOK BACK ON SOME OF OUR FAVORITE MOMENTS OF THE SEASON.

Chapter Forty-Six

THE CROWD IS loud for being small. There are maybe only a hundred people in a semi-circle around the raised stage where Bridgette and Bradley stand, introducing the show and playing a recap of the season.

Grant fusses with his outfit, making sure his wide-sleeved shirt billows over the thick belt just perfectly. He's wearing clothes from an up-and-coming designer and has struggled with nerves from the moment he got dressed.

"What if I sit weird and it lies awkwardly and people think the designer is terrible?"

I grab his shaking hands and squeeze them. "Stop worrying. People will be talking about your outfit for weeks. The designer is going to get so much free publicity over it. Bridgette is going to ask you who made it, so you can give him a shout-out. You look incredible."

"Yeah, like a sexy swashbuckler." Ivan claps our Beta on the back and swoops down to kiss his cheek. "I have no doubt you will spawn another round of thirst trap videos centered entirely around the outfit."

Designers who want to work with Grant dressed us all

Chapter Forty-Six

tonight, but his outfit is the most "out there". Ivan is wearing a well-tailored black shirt that clings to his thick arms and a pair of grey trousers with an interesting pattern sewn down the sides.

My peach trousers are so wide-legged they look almost like a skirt, and my white top is form-fitting with a sweetheart neckline but a back held together only by gold chains. Normally, I'd never wear anything like this, but when the guys saw me and nearly tackled me to the ground to rip it off, it boosted my confidence.

Derrick stands off to the side, flexing his hands. He's nervous. Most of the negative reception to the show has been pointed at him, which we expected. He knew going into the experience that he wouldn't be the fan favorite, and he's afraid of the questions the audience will ask tonight. He wears a patterned Oxford like armor, but his eyes are worried behind his gold, wire-framed glasses.

"It's going to be fine, Alpha." I weave our fingers together.

"They love to have a little drama at these reunions. I'm the drama. Asking questions to bait me, to degrade me. That's what's going to give them that."

"I won't let them. Just squeeze my knee if you want me to answer instead of you."

He doesn't have a chance to agree before Bradley is crooning from the stage, "Welcome, Pack Sax!"

We chose to adopt the moniker for our official pack name. It felt right when I thought about it. My pack was always Sax. So we made it official.

The stage lights are blinding until we get settled on the navy velvet couch, and my eyes adjust. I sit between Ivan and Derrick, with Grant on Derrick's other side, angled slightly toward where Bridgette and Bradley perch on a matching loveseat, but mostly facing the audience.

Bridgette looks incredible in a tight ivory dress as she reaches out and grabs my hand. "Ariana. Happiness looks good on you."

"Thanks, Bridgette. I am happy."

Her husband leans back and crosses his legs. "And you guys. America loves you."

Grant comes alive under the studio lights, his prior nerves forgotten. He cocks his head with a flirty smile. "What's not to love?"

Bradley laughs at his quip. "I think what everyone wants to know is how everything has been since you left the show? Give us the scoop!"

"Everything has been great. The guys moved in with me, and we're getting used to being a pack and everything that comes with it." I drop my hand to Derrick's knee, giving him a reassuring squeeze. "It's been really wonderful getting to explore our dynamic without cameras on us."

Bridgette's eyes brighten. "Does that mean you bonded with Derrick?"

Ivan wraps his arm behind me and squeezes the other Alpha's shoulder. "Oh, that didn't take too long."

"Oh?" Bridgette looks like an excited child. "Do tell! When did it happen?"

Derrick blushes and pulls his shirt collar aside to show the silvery scar of my bonding mark. "On the plane home."

The audience's gasps and cheers at my eagerness have me blushing. "There was no reason to wait. I love Derrick, and I didn't want to have a pack without him. We grew so close those last few days over the phone, and it felt right. Natural."

"Do you want to talk about *that* phone call, Ariana?" Bradley's suggestive tone clues me in to exactly what call he's talking about.

My cheeks are on fire. "Not really. How about a question from the audience?"

The Beta man throws his head back with a laugh, right along with the audience. "Fine, fine. Let's take our first question."

Bridgette grabs a card from beside her on the couch. "This one comes to us online, from user 'maybe.beta.baby'. They want to know, 'How did Derrick and Ivan react to the story Ariana told Grant about Calvin?'" Bridgette turns toward the audience. "This is, of course, in reference to the emotional moment between Ariana and Grant, where she talked about her last moments with her brother. I know that was a hard conversation to have, and it has sparked a lot of debate online about the need for laws allowing death with dignity."

That conversation with Grant has been used on social media as a jumping-off point for others to tell their stories. Even some people with terminal illnesses have weighed in, advocating for more states to pass legislation allowing death with dignity. Of course, plenty of people don't agree with it, but that's no surprise.

Ivan pulls me tight against his side. "She told us about it not long after we left the house. It's a story filled with grief that America has already heard and discussed countless times. I don't think anything else needs to be said on it."

"It's a shitty question to ask, especially right out of the gate." Derrick sits up a little straighter. "It's like saying, 'Hey, Ariana, good to see you. Want to talk about your darkest memory?' Let's move on, please."

"Fair, fair." Bradley holds his hands up, not forcing the issue. "Let's go to the live audience."

A crew member hands a microphone to a cute woman with dark curly hair and rich, deep skin. Her simple red dress falls to her thighs. She looks terrified. "Hi, I'm Becca. My question is for Grant and Ivan. What was it like to meet Ariana as yourself for the first time?"

She sits down with an embarrassed swiftness and ducks her head.

"It was amazing and terrifying. When we first talked, and I realized that I was in love with someone who had no idea who I was, my heart broke a little." Grant crosses one leg over his knee and plays with the string at his shirt collar. "It felt like I had studied for a test, and when I sat down, it was on an entirely different subject. I wasn't expecting her to fall into my arms right out the gate, but the fact that there was no recognition at all weighed heavier than I expected it to."

"I felt a bit like a stalker." The crowd laughs at Ivan's interjection. "She's terrified of Alphas, and here I am popping up in front of her like, 'Hi, I love you, and I know you don't like cantaloupe.' I'm honestly not sure why we thought the show would be a good idea."

"There are still some things that I'll say, and I'll forget that they already know it. It's hard to keep it straight."

Ivan bumps his shoulder against me with a playful smile. "We humor her and pretend like it's the first time we've heard it."

Bradley and Bridgette gesture for another audience member to ask a question. The man takes the microphone and directs his question to Derrick.

"I wasn't exactly rooting for you through the season, and when it was over, I still didn't feel like you'd earned her forgiveness. Do you think you have?"

Derrick looks like a deer in the headlights. My normally confident, charming Alpha knew this was coming, but he's freezing up in front of the camera. He's so concerned that people will take their frustration at him out on me for choosing to bond him.

I don't give him a chance to answer.

"I think he has, which is all that matters, right? I know there are a lot of people out there who say they could never, but you don't really know that. You won't unless you live it. But Derrick didn't assume I would forgive him. In fact, he was convinced I wouldn't, and he took steps to protect me if I didn't want to be with him."

Bradley's eyebrows would hit his forehead if he didn't use so much Botox. "And what steps did you take, Derrick?"

Grant places a reassuring hand on our Alpha's bicep. "Tell them."

"After I left the house, I began working with a clinic to donate and store my pheromones. I wanted to create a stockpile for Ariana, so she didn't have to worry about FOS if she didn't want to be with me."

"Oh my God." Bridgette's voice is breathy with emotion, and she clutches her chest. "That is so moving. How did you react when you found out, Ariana?"

"I, uh." I stumble over my words. Ivan hands me a bottle of water that was resting on the table beside him, and I take a greedy gulp. "No one wants to think about something happening to the people they love, but for years, it was all I thought about. Death terrified me, and I locked myself away so I didn't risk it. When I found out Derrick had been going through pheromone extraction to make sure that, even if the worst happened to him, I wouldn't meet the same fate as my brother, I felt like he had faced death for me. Like he bought me more time. I hope I never have to use them, because I made all three of them promise I could die first, but knowing that he wanted a way to take care of me, even after he's gone?" He pulls my hand to his mouth and places a sweet, reassuring kiss on the back of it.

"Knowing that he did that for me just reminded me of why I fell in love with Sax in the first place. It gave me a new lease on life."

We get peppered with questions from the raunchy to the strange for the next hour. One guy wanted to know Grant's skincare routine, and another asked Ivan if he ever considered voice acting.

"We have time for just a few more, so let's check the live feed." Bridgette accepts a piece of paper from a crew member and reads it outloud. "Okay, this one is from Wilson, a Beta from Wyoming. He wants to know what was in the letter from Calvin."

I was waiting for that question. I've been practicing what I'm going to say, how much I'm comfortable sharing.

Derrick speaks before I can even open my mouth. "Next question."

Bradley, quite used to Derrick refusing to answer questions at this point, rolls with the punches. "I know everyone wants to know about the final challenge. Ariana, when you spoke directly to America in your room, our viewers said they felt like they were your friend in that moment. Tell me the truth. Are you pissed at us for giving you that challenge?"

"I mean. Kind of?" Nervous laughter from the audience wasn't the reaction Bradley was expecting based on his expression. I'm not sure why, considering it was the most controversial thing that happened this season. They've gotten a lot of flak for even asking it of me.

"Look, it turned out well for us. I knew that I loved my pack, even then. The whole thing was confusing, the lies were overwhelming, but buried under all of that was true love. And it's not just because we're scent matches. We had years of a foundation before that. But I worry other people would have felt so pressured that they may not have thought through their decision. I needed that kick in the pants, but it was a risky gamble on your part."

"About the scent matching. How has your anxiety been since the show concluded? Your biggest fear came true. Are you still stuck in your house?"

Bradley's question rubs me the wrong way. I know that the level of anxiety I had was abnormal, but the way he phrased it felt like it came from a place of judgment, not understanding.

"Anxiety doesn't go away overnight. It's not always logical, either. Of course, I know what I was hiding from has happened, but that doesn't remove a decade of fear. But I'm here, aren't I? I don't love being out in public, especially by myself. When my pack is with me, it's a lot easier. I do spend a lot of time worrying that Derrick won't make it back from work, that Ivan will get sick, or that Grant will get kidnapped, but I know those are irrational fears."

"I've started taking self-defense classes. Just in case someone decides to kidnap a grown man." Grant delivers the line with such a straight face that the audience bursts into laughter. It's a welcome distraction from putting my anxiety on display.

"Anyway, I'm healing. I have a wonderful support system."

Bridgette scoots onto the edge of the loveseat and reaches for me like she did when I first sat down. "Was it worth it? All of the fear, the hurt from their lies, the show?"

My guys crowd me, squeezing in so close that I may as well be straddling Ivan and Derrick's laps.

"Yeah, it was. It may not have been what I expected, but it was what I needed."

Epilogue

TWO YEARS LATER

GRANT'S HIPS dimple under my grip, and his whimpering groan has me panting and slick.

"Fuck, Omega." His voice is strangled and muffled as he buries his face in the sheets of my nest.

Sweat rolls down my spine as I thrust into him.

The guys make this look so easy. The first time I fucked Grant with a strap-on, I did not make it very long on top. He ended up shoving me to my back and riding me while I jerked him off. The o-ring around the base of the toy vibrates, and the pressure of his weight and movement hit my clit just right as he chased his pleasure on the toy. We fell apart together, and when the Alphas got home and found us sprawled naked together, they were pissed they missed the show.

They're missing this one, too.

I angle my hips like Derrick taught me until I'm stroking into Grant in a way that has him begging. I love that sound and know exactly what he's asking for.

His dick is heavy and leaking when I reach around him to grip it in my fist. He fucks himself on me, alternating between pushing back on the fake cock and thrusting into my hand. When he comes with a sweet and pathetic moan and collapses onto the plush surface, I follow him right down.

My beautiful Beta is spent, but I'm not worried about being left wanting. Ivan and Derrick leer at me from the doorway of the nest. They've been standing there for a few minutes, watching us together and biding their time. I smelled the burst of their pheromones when they walked in and saw what we were doing, and now that Grant is taken care of, they've set their sights on me.

Derrick's gaze is predatory as he stalks closer, pulling his shirt off as he moves.

Ivan looks giddy, bouncing as he crosses to me. "You two started the party without us." It's a playful chastising from him, but I still fix my face in a pout.

"I'm sorry, Alpha. I just felt so needy."

Twin predatory growls answer, and they're both on top of me in seconds. Ivan works on getting the strap off of me while Derrick grabs my hair and exposes my neck.

"Are you saying you're not a well-taken care of Omega? That your Alphas aren't good to you?"

As soon as the harness is off my hips, Ivan dives between my legs and licks up the slick mess left behind. Derrick tightens his grip on my hair and grabs my chin, making sure I am locked in his storm colored eyes.

"Ivan, don't let her come. Our girl needs to be taught a lesson."

MARLIE'S pretty voice sings about broken hearts for the fifteenth time as I work on getting the clip cut down to the perfect twenty-second sound bite. She didn't know I was recording at her open mic last week.

That I have been recording her for weeks.

It's taken me a few years, but I finally know how I'm going to get Marlie back for signing me up for *Knot What You Expected*. Even though it worked out wonderfully for me, I can't let her get away with her meddling.

She's been lulled into a false sense of safety by this point. I bet she's forgotten that I swore I'd get her back one day.

"Still working on the application?" Ivan braces himself in my doorway, arms crossed over his chest.

"I'm almost done. I've already got the letter written already. I just need to get the video right."

With the Band is the newest concept show from the producers of *Knot What You Expected*. Five massive names in the music industry will build a band from individual submissions, who will compete for a recording contract. Every submission must be from a single person. No preformed bands or duos will be accepted. Each coach has to choose a vocalist, guitarist, bassist, and drummer. They're all given a fifth 'wildcard' spot to round out the band.

Marlie is a triple threat. She has the voice of an angel, can play guitar, and her theatre background means she can dance, too. They'd be fools not to put her as the lead of a band.

My Alpha crosses the room and leans over my shoulder as I press play again. "It looks like the clips played at the beginning of a true crime special. 'Susan lit up the room' type shit. And then we find out her Alpha murdered her."

I smack him on the chest with the back of my hand. "It does not!"

I did my best to find a mix of clips to make the submission video well-rounded. Ivan rests his ass on my desk as I finish up and attach it to the submission email. Marlie did such a spectacular job writing my application letter for *Expected*, so I have spent weeks making sure hers is top-notch.

She needs this.

She's been down lately because she still hasn't met her pack. She could use the distraction. I hate seeing how she's losing some of her spark every time she comes back from a social empty-handed.

Ivan peeks over my shoulder at the email. "It looks good, sweetie. They'd be a fool not to accept her. It's missing one big thing, though."

I run my eyes over the words again, but I don't think I left anything out. I've talked about her passion, her background, and her skills. I went personal, talking about her teaching career and touching on her relationship with her parents and brothers. I even managed to convince them to give me some childhood videos of Marlie dancing and singing to put in her audition tape.

They'd be fools if they didn't accept her.

"What am I missing?"

He taps the "cc" line of the email. "You didn't include Bradley and Bridgette in the email."

IVAN HANDS me a glass of wine before throwing himself onto the couch next to me.

"What are we watching tonight?"

I click through the streaming offerings, wrinkling my nose at the options on offer. "Nothing sounds good."

"Can we watch that campy horror movie?" Grant leans around the kitchen wall with a dish rag in his hands. "Where they're having a sleepover, and then someone dies, so they start turning on one another?"

"No, we watched that two weeks ago." Derrick flops onto the floor at my feet. I throw my legs over his shoulders and wiggle my toes. I don't have to ask, he knows what I want and starts massaging my soles.

Ivan throws out the next suggestion. "What about the one where the NPC of a game is the main character?"

Grant finishes up in the kitchen and squeezes between Ivan and the arm of the couch. "Eh. A stand-up special?"

Derrick makes a dismissive noise. Our tastes in comedy are so different that it's hard to find one we all like. Whenever we end up watching a special, it's a given that at least two of us spend most of it with our faces in our phones.

Sometimes, I forget that it was less than three years ago that I learned the truth about Sax. Things just work with the four of us, and sometimes it feels like we've been together forever with how in sync we are.

In the aftermath of the show, we all received a lot more attention than we were used to. Grant was able to quit his job as a pharmaceutical sales rep and focus on modeling. He's done several print campaigns and has even been on a few billboards. He was invited last week to model for a famous underwear line, and I'm going to fly to New York with him for the photoshoot. His social media has blown up, and he's constantly getting hit up for brand deals.

Ivan got a promotion from a very expensive pencil pusher at a cell phone company to the *lead* pencil pusher at the same company. That didn't have anything to do with the show, but he's convinced that the only reason they looked at his application for the role was that they recognized his name.

I never cared much about my job as an accountant, so when I was contacted by a charity focused on fundraising for Foresaken Omega Syndrome research and asked to join the organization, I jumped at it. It has been so good for my soul to know that every day I am working toward ensuring that what happened to Calvin never happens again. We have a long way to go, because they still don't know how to create synthetic pheromones, but it feels like every day we learn something new about the disease.

Derrick was brought on as a partner at a PT Practice, and he's starting to be a bit pickier about the clients he takes on, so his hours are getting better.

We make sure to spend every Saturday night together as a pack, whether it's playing board games, watching movies, or going on a date, it doesn't matter. Unless Grant is traveling for shoots, then it gets shifted a day or two.

"Well, that's three no's, you all know what that means." I exit the service we're on, switch to one of the other four we have, and pull up the search. "Time for another rewatch of *Unexplainable and Bizarre!*"

"Actually, that sounds good. It's been a while since we've gotten in a fight. Let me go get a snack first." Derrick shoves my feet away and heads to the kitchen. "Anyone need another drink?"

"Oh my God!"

Derrick comes running back into the room at my exclamation. "What?"

I point at the screen. "It has a red banner! It says coming soon!"

"No fucking way." My Alpha leans over the back of the couch, squinting behind his glasses.

"Why would I lie about something like this?" I click into our favorite show and page over until I find a trailer for the new season.

"Oh, apparently it got picked up last year." Ivan grins over the top of his phone. I knew it was put on streaming services shortly after our season aired because of all the chatter, but I didn't expect this. "So many people were streaming it that it was greenlit for a new season. You two single-handedly brought back your favorite television show."

Grant snags Ivan's phone to read it for himself. "Then why weren't they asked to host it? God, how cool would that have been?"

I press play on the trailer, which mostly features spooky music and a deep-voiced narrator talking over establishing shots of different locations. It's nothing revolutionary, but I'm on the edge of my seat.

"Join me, Remington Burke, along with my Omega cohost, Emmett Montgomery, as we travel around the world and investigate the Unexplainable and Bizarre.*"*

"Who's Remington Burke?" Derrick asks once the trailer is done.

Ivan grabs my glass of wine and takes a sip, like he doesn't have his own drink. "He's an Alpha comedian. He's one of the big ones on social media."

I snatch it back. "Why would they invite a comedian to host?"

Grant looks up from his phone. "I wonder if he doesn't believe in the paranormal? I looked up Emmett Montgomery, and he's a well-known paranormal investigator. They may be setting him up to be the butt of Remmington's jokes."

"If that's true, I'm going to be pissed. Putting an Omega in a position to be made fun of by an Alpha for

Epilogue

what, ratings?" I accept the bowl of popcorn that Derrick hands me and shove a handful in my mouth.

"I think we've learned there are a lot of things they'll do for ratings." My Alpha's eyes sparkle behind his glasses. "I seem to remember that a certain show challenged an Omega to bond with two strangers."

Never once in the two and a half years since I bonded with the guys have I regretted it. They annoy the shit out of me sometimes, but I'd be worried if they didn't. Being in a pack with the three of them just makes sense.

"And their ratings haven't been as high since."

Acknowledgments

I love you, Carlos. Thanks for not catfishing me on OkCupid in 2013.

Thank you to my amazing Beta and Omega readers - Brit, Britt, Ariel, Cat, and Mica. I am SO appreciative of your feedback and encouragement as I got this book out in the world for everyone!

About the Author

Holly Monroe reluctantly lives in Florida and writes fantasy, Omegaverse, and paranormal romance books you can disappear in with characters worthy of obsessing over. She's never met a character she couldn't traumatize, but she always gives them their happily-ever-after.

Visit her online at www.authorhollymonroe.com or through social media, @authorhollymonroe.

Sign up for her newsletter for updates, sneak peeks, ARC opportunities, bonus content, and more!

Also by Holly Monroe

The Shadowweaver Trilogy

The Last Winter

The First Fall

The Eternal Equinox

Lunarcrest City Omegaverse

Knot All is Perfect

Knot All is Forgiven

Knot All is Crystal

Knot All is Whole

Trapped on the Tightrope Duet

One for the Money

Two for the Show

The Copper Hill Omegaverse

Heat for the Holidays

Reality TV Omegas

Knot What you Expected

Not-So-Grimm Retellings

Just Crumbs

The Rift Wars

Reformed

www.ingramcontent.com/pod-product-compliance
Lightning Source LLC
LaVergne TN
LVHW040132080526
838202LV00042B/2877